THE CREOLE CHASE

Also by Cap Daniels

The Chase Fulton Novels Series
Book One: *The Opening Chase*
Book Two: *The Broken Chase*
Book Three: *The Stronger Chase*
Book Four: *The Unending Chase*
Book Five: *The Distant Chase*
Book Six: *The Entangled Chase*
Book Seven: *The Devil's Chase*
Book Eight: *The Angel's Chase*
Book Nine: *The Forgotten Chase*
Book Ten: *The Emerald Chase*
Book Eleven: *The Polar Chase*
Book Twelve: *The Burning Chase*
Book Thirteen: *The Poison Chase*
Book Fourteen: *The Bitter Chase*
Book Fifteen: *The Blind Chase*
Book Sixteen: *The Smuggler's Chase*
Book Seventeen: *The Hollow Chase*
Book Eighteen: *The Sunken Chase*
Book Nineteen: *The Darker Chase*
Book Twenty: *The Abandoned Chase*
Book Twenty-One: *The Gambler's Chase*
Book Twenty-Two: *The Arctic Chase*
Book Twenty-Three: *The Diamond Chase*
Book Twenty-Four: *The Phantom Chase*
Book Twenty-Five: *The Crimson Chase*
Book Twenty-Six: *The Silent Chase*
Book Twenty-Seven: *The Shepherd's Chase*
Book Twenty-Eight: *The Scorpion's Chase*
Book Twenty-Nine: *The Creole Chase*
Book Thirty: *The Calling Chase*

THE CREOLE CHASE

CHASE FULTON NOVEL #29

CAP DANIELS

ANCHOR WATCH
PUBLISHING
** USA **

The Creole Chase
Chase Fulton Novel #29
Cap Daniels

This is a work of fiction. Names, characters, places, historical events, and incidents are the product of the author's imagination or have been used fictitiously. Although many locations such as marinas, airports, hotels, restaurants, etc. used in this work actually exist, they are used fictitiously and may have been relocated, exaggerated, or otherwise modified by creative license for the purpose of this work. Although many characters are based on personalities, physical attributes, skills, or intellect of actual individuals, all the characters in this work are products of the author's imagination.

Published by:

** USA **

13 Digit ISBN: 978-1-951021-65-8
Library of Congress Control Number: 2024951687

Cover Design: German Creative

Printed in the United States of America

The Creole Chase

CAP DANIELS

Chapter 1
Man's Work

Autumn 2013

"Why does dey calls you Gator, huh?"

The tough-as-nails young covert operative sat near the bow of the pirogue, a look of utter disbelief blended with a splash of fear on his bearded face. He turned to me as I tried to balance myself in the tiny boat beside his.

After getting my laughter under control, I said, "He wants to know why we call you Gator."

The man sitting in the rear of Gator's boat cocked his head, revealing a weathered face in testament to a life spent under the scorching sun on the bayous of South Louisiana. Most of his left hand was missing, and a jagged scar ran from his chin across his cheek and past the spot where his ear had once been. He raised the front of his filthy hat and stared at me through one eye as dark as the water in which we sat and another that was blue and milky and couldn't tell light from dark. "Tell me one more 'gain what your name is, you."

"I'm Chase Fulton."

The old man roared with laughter and drove the only index finger he had left through the air at me. The appendage curved in more directions than any human finger should ever do, and his reaction was just as crooked. "Whoo! Dat der be some mo' kinda gettin'-after-it kinda name. I gar-ohn-tee dat. Chase... Oh, my. Das one o' dem der names o' action. Is dat boy der gonna tells to me why e'rbody be callin' him Gator?"

The look on Gator's face grew even wilder as he silently pleaded for my help.

I said, "Tell him why we call you Gator."

He seemed to gather himself and said, "Well, my real name is Clint Barrow, and I'm from Kansas—"

The old man interrupted. "Kansas? Ain't never heards o' no such place. Where dat be?"

"It's in the Midwest," Gator said.

The Cajun pulled off his hat, wadded it into a ball, and said, "Midwest... Does dat be over somewheres 'round Baton Rouge?"

Gator froze, and the old man burst into laughter and shook the pirogue like a carnival ride. "I'm just foolin' ya, boy. I knows where Kansas be, and they fo' sho don't gots no gators up der."

Gator shook his head. "No, sir. There are no gators in Kansas. That's partially how I got the nickname. When I moved to Georgia with Chase and those guys, I saw my first alligator on the bank of the river. He wasn't very big. Maybe four feet. Anyway, I remembered watching Steve Irwin on *Crocodile Hunter*. Remember that show?"

The man stretched his hat and pulled it back onto his head. "I seed a show one time up in N'awlins, but weren't no gators in it, no, sir. Was some of dem Bourbon Street dancin' girls a whirlin' 'round and actin' crazy. I seen that show but ain't ne'er seen no crocodile-huntin' show, me."

Gator jerked his head toward me for an interpretation, but it was time for him to figure it out for himself.

He finally said, "Yeah, well, anyway. I jumped on the alligator because I thought it would be funny and give me a chance to prove to those guys that I wasn't afraid."

The Cajun raised what was left of his hand. "You best be 'fraid. Trust me on dat, you."

"Yeah, I learned. That little alligator was a lot stronger than me, and he carried me into the river on his back. Any thought I had of proving how tough and brave I was went out the window. I was terrified, and I scampered out of the muddy water faster than I thought I could move. Ever since then, everybody calls me Gator."

Watching a Cajun laugh is a show like none other, and the man in the boat brought down the house. The four visible teeth in his mouth were on full display until he broke into a fit of coughing, and I wondered if we were on the verge of attempting CPR in a tiny canoe on a blackwater bayou a thousand miles from everywhere.

Fortunately for us, and the old man, he survived the episode. When he finally caught his breath, he pulled a hand-rolled cigarette from his pocket, stuck it in his mouth, and struck a wooden match on the side of the pirogue. As the aromatic smoke rose above his head in a white plume, he said, "Dat sho' nuff be one fine story, I do declare, me. So, let's us go gets us one. What you say, you?"

I could see the wheels turning in Gator's head, but he couldn't put it together. The French-accented Cajun dialect is one of the most beautiful and melodic of all the American colloquial languages. Although I couldn't read, speak, or even fully understand it, I'd grown fascinated with its beauty from the moment I met Cajun Kenny LePine, the son of the four-toothed man in the boat beside mine. Kenny owned the only heavy earth moving company in Camden County, Georgia. I made my home in that county, in the small town of St. Marys, on a gorgeous piece of property that had once been a pecan plantation called Bonaventure. The property was handed down through my mother's family until it finally fell to me.

Bonaventure became not only home for my team of covert operatives, but also a world-class private tactical training facility to keep us at the top of our game. When an arsonist reduced my family's ancestral home to ashes, Cajun Kenny LePine cleaned up the mess and dug the foundation for the house we then rebuilt. From that moment, I found—or made up—reasons to spend time with Kenny. Hearing him talk was only one of the many benefits of being in his presence. He possessed wisdom and common sense of the highest caliber, and I never failed to learn and laugh every time we were together.

His courtship and resulting marriage with a magnificent woman who was, in every way, beyond description, made my life better every time I saw the two of them together. His bride Earline, affectionately known as Earl by everyone who loved her, was the reason Gator and I were in a pair of tiny boats on that murky body of water, near a one-horse town I couldn't pronounce, somewhere southwest of New Orleans.

Kenny LePine's father was the four-toothed Cajun paddling Gator around, and if anyone asked his name, his answer was always "Keef Lap I Too," which I assumed was his way of saying Kenny LePine, also.

Keeping my pirogue as close to his as possible gave me some unreasonable belief that I wouldn't capsize my popsicle stick of a boat and that I wouldn't be devoured by a swarm of hungry alligators.

"So, Mr. LePine, why did you need to talk to us?"

He lowered his chin and closed his one good eye. "You not ready to leave ol' Keef already so soon is you, huh?"

"No, sir. I'm having the time of my life, but I'm starting to feel like we're taking advantage of your hospitality. Earline told us you needed somebody to help you with a problem you couldn't take care of yourself. So, if we can help, all you have to do is ask."

He opened his eye. "That Earline better not o' said no such thing. It ain't that I can't do it me-selfs. It just be bettah if somebody else be da one who done it 'cause the way I'd done be dunning it might put ol' Keef back in da big house, don'tcha know."

The look on Gator's face said his head almost exploded, and mine wasn't far behind.

I said, "We're happy to help any way we can because you're way too pretty for prison."

He burst into another fit of laughter, laced with coughing, that ended in his crooked finger pointing into a clump of what we call "marsh grass" in coastal Georgia, but I have no idea what they call it in the bayou.

He said, "Der he go. Dat be a biggun, him. Get ready, boys. We's gonna have our handses full wiff dis one, we."

He paddled furiously until his pirogue slid against a length of nylon rope stretched taut. He grabbed the rope with his hand and a half and hauled it in as if his life depended on it.

"Get that gun o' yous ready, boy. We 'bout to fine out if you is Gator or you is ain't."

Gator clearly understood that one, and he lifted the single-shot.22 from between his feet. Mr. LePine gave one final, mighty heave on the well-worn piece of rope, and an alligator's head the size of a refrigerator popped out of the black water and thrashed with a violence I'd never seen. The pirogue turned into a bucking bronco, and Gator slammed the tiny rifle against his shoulder.

"Choot 'im in da brain, boy. Choot 'im!"

I'd watched Gator shoot a target the size of a cantaloupe at a thousand yards, so hitting an alligator two feet away should've been a cakewalk. But the sniper missed.

Mr. LePine shoved his crippled hand toward Gator. "Here, boy! Take dis here rope an' don' let go, no."

Gator dug his heels into the bottom of the boat, grabbed the rope, and leaned back. Almost before he'd let go, Mr. LePine drew something from somewhere and drove it through the top of the alligator's head until the thrashing ceased.

The dead alligator floated beside the boat, and Mr. LePine tucked away his tool. "I do hopes yous job ain't chootin', boy, 'cause you done misseded from that close. Is you any good at knittin' or tendin' to babies? 'Cause I ain't sho' you's cut out for no man's work, you."

Gator relaxed and stared in wide-eyed wonder at the senior LePine. "Did you just kill an alligator with a knife?"

Mr. LePine drew the weapon again. "Nobody be a fool big enough to try killins a gator wiff a knife. What's wrong wiff you, boy? Dis don' be no knife. Dis here be a spike that my daddy done made a hundred years ago. Dis be all he had to give down to me when he pass on to dat big ol' bayou up in Heaven, him."

We tied the gator to the pirogue and paddled to what qualified as dry land in South Louisiana. It took all three of us to heft the monster into the bed of Mr. LePine's ancient pickup truck.

Two hours later, the alligator was cleaned, and we had fifty pounds of gator meat—most of it from his tail.

I made two more attempts to get Mr. LePine to tell us what problem he needed us to solve, but he skillfully dodged the question. As the sun went down somewhere over Texas, Gator and I found ourselves in the backyard of someone whose name seemed to be Teton, but I couldn't be certain. We were far from alone, but we appeared to be the only humans on Earth who spoke English.

Gator tapped the neck of his beer bottle to mine. "What planet are we on?"

I took a sip and did my best Cajun accent. "Me don' know, me, but dem skrimps sho' nuff be fine eatin', dem."

He rolled his eyes. "I wonder how far I'd have to walk to find somebody I can understand."

I laughed. "You might find somebody in New Orleans, but probably not on Bourbon Street."

He asked, "Is he ever going to tell us what he needs us to do?"

"I get the feeling that timing is everything down here. We're their guests, and it would appear there's some sort of protocol involving feeding us before asking us for anything."

Before Gator had time to respond, a sound pierced the night air like nothing I'd ever heard. We spun to see a striking woman surrounded by five men under a collection of torches. Each of the men had an instrument. There was an accordion, a fiddle, a harmonica, a snare drum, and a washboard, and what resonated from those instruments was the most melodic sound I had ever heard. The gathered crowd paired off and danced as if the world were coming to an end at daybreak.

A woman who could've been eighteen, or perhaps forty, danced toward our table, took Gator by the hand, and dragged him toward what apparently qualified as a dance floor in the bayou. Nobody took my hand and dragged me anywhere, or perhaps Kenneth LePine II was dragging me into a scenario I probably couldn't understand, but one I felt obligated to take for a spin.

It was challenging to define when one song stopped and the next began. The zydeco rhythm seemed to beat in time with the hearts of the people around me. In the short time I'd spent with them, it was obvious that their lives were physically demanding, but when the music played, so did they. Escaping the reality of their arduous daily grind brought their souls alive, but behind the dark eyes of men like Kenny LePine's father lay an ancient beast not unlike the gators that patrolled and reigned supreme in the stifling depths of the bayou. Whatever those obsidian eyes were going to ask of me would be a task unlike anything I'd ever undertaken, but I believed it would be a mission I couldn't turn down, no matter how sharp the teeth of our adversary.

The woman who abducted Gator delivered him back to his seat across from me, and she planted herself beside him, astride the bench. His breath was coming hard, and sweat rolled from his hairline.

The woman picked up a boiled crawfish from his plate and wiggled it through the air toward his face. "Why ain't you eatin' no mudbugs, you?"

He seemed to understand the words flowing from the lips of the beautiful young woman at his side, even though he spent the afternoon demanding that I interpret Mr. LePine's patois.

He put on a sheepish smile. "I don't really know how to eat them."

"Oh, dat's simple. Get you one in 'tween you big thumb and da next finger, like dis." She held up the crawfish and separated its tail from its head, then she squeezed the meat from his tail and savored the taste of the spicey, sweet meat.

Gator followed suit and said, "Hey, that's not bad."

She giggled. "You think dat ain't bad, just wait 'til you suck da head, you." She held the crawfish's head between her fingers and sucked the contents from the shell, then chased it with a swig of Gator's beer. "Now you."

He recoiled. "I don't know. That's not really..."

The woman sat his beer back on the table and took his face in her hands. She planted a long, passionate Cajun kiss on him and said, "Now, if you want more o' that kind o' lovin', yous best be suckin' dat mudbug head."

Gator was rewarded for obedience to his Cajun queen, and she soon had him eating out of her hands.

She dabbed at the corner of his mouth with a well-used napkin. "What do you do, Boogaloo?"

Gator cocked his head. "Boogaloo? What does that mean?"

She cackled. "That's you, Boogaloo. Dat's what we coonasses call folks who is way offs down here in da bayou where you don't belong, no."

His confusion seemed to triple. "Coonasses?"

The woman's laughter continued until she finally said, "You don't know nothing, does you, Boogaloo? Dat's me, a coonass. Just like e'ry-body else 'cept you and him boogaloos."

Suddenly, I was lumped into the boogaloo category with Gator, and although I didn't understand it, I was okay with it.

Gator didn't seem to share my acceptance of the moniker. "Wait a minute," he said. "You call yourself a coonass, and everybody who's not from here is a boogaloo?"

"Not e'rybody. There's another mess o' folks from N'awlins who be Creoles."

"Ah, the plot thickens," Gator said. "So, Cajuns are coonasses?"

She kissed the tip of his nose. "You catchin' on, you."

Gator shoved the plate of mudbug leftovers away. "Come on. You don't really talk like that, do you?"

She leaned close and whispered, "I can speak your language just as well as you, but honey, you're in the bayou, and down here, there's only one language, and it sure ain't English."

"I knew it!" he said. "It's all an act."

"It's no act, Sugar Britches. It's what we are down here. Are you going to answer my question?"

"I don't even remember your question," he said.

"What do you do?"

"For work?"

"Yes, for work."

He pointed to me. "I work for him."

She leaned forward and directed her attention across the table. "Your employee over here doesn't seem to know what he does for a living. Would you mind telling me?"

I wiped my mouth and took another swallow. "When people get themselves in situations they can't get out of, we do what we can to help."

"Lawyers?" she asked.

It was our turn to laugh. "No, we're definitely not lawyers. You might even say we're the opposite of lawyers. If we do our job right, whatever we're dealing with never ends up in court."

She took a moment and stared between the two of us. "Ah, so that's why you're here. You're going to find out what's going on with the dead bodies, aren't you?"

Chapter 2
Dead in the Morning

The beautiful woman leapt to her feet. "Come on, Pretty Boy. We ain't through dancin'."

Gator threw up both hands. "Oh, yes, we are. At least for now. You don't get to drop a bombshell like that and just dance away. What bodies are you talking about?"

She waved a dismissive hand. "There'll be time for that tomorrow. Tonight, we're having a party."

I sat, silently trying to imagine how I would've reacted back when I was young, naïve, and impatient like Gator. Watching him deal with the surprises that inevitably fill the lives of covert operators like us was like watching old game tape of how I used to play.

He patted the bench. "Sit back down, and tell me what bodies you're talking about."

She reached for his hand and pulled it against her body. She straightened his index finger and made a fist with the rest of his fingers. Then, she waved Gator's pointed finger around the yard.

"What are you doing?" he asked.

She said, "Making you point at all the boys I'm gonna dance with if you don't get off your cute little tush and take me for a spin."

My protégé looked at me as if begging for help, and I shooed him away with the back of my hand. "Take your cute little tush, and go dance with that pretty girl. Whoever the bodies are, they'll still be dead in the morning."

I peeled a few boiled shrimp and deposited the shells on Gator's mudbug plate. Thinking back over the life I'd lived, I was never less than astonished at how the son of missionaries from Georgia ended up in the situations and places in which I'd been. While watching two dozen people dance, laugh, and sing somewhere in a swamp they called a bayou, under a brilliant moon that would be full in forty-eight hours, I thanked God for the first time in my life that I wasn't a major league ballplayer.

"What be goin' on in dat head o' yours, you?"

I spun to see Mr. LePine claiming the bench across the table from me. "I was just being thankful for the fact that life never turns out the way we expect."

He raised a bottle. "Ain't that da troof? When I's a comin' up, I figured me to be one of dem rich mens wiff fine tings and shiny cars, but all I gots is dis right here, me."

I watched the dancers and listened to the band's melody as the warm, humid air brushed against my face. "I don't know, Mr. LePine. From where I'm sitting, you look like the richest man in the world."

He smiled, exposing the few teeth he had. "You'd be right 'bout dat, you. I see Cecilia done gots her hooks in dat boy o' yours. He best be careful or dat girl'l break his big ol' heart, she will."

"Cecilia?" I asked.

He pointed toward Gator and the Cajun girl. "Yes, sir. Dat be Cecilia Lachaussee. She be my great-niece, I guess she be. Dat girl dun runt off up to LSU and gots her one of dem fancy paper degrees. She don't want nobody to know 'bout it, dough. I bets she don't even tell you she can speaks your English, do she?"

"It's slipped out," I said, "but that's not all she let slip."

He set his beer on the table and tapped a finger in time with the music. "What she said, her?"

"She said there are dead bodies."

"She don't always knows when to keeps her educated mouf shuts, her."

"Is that why we're here?" I asked.

He spat between his bare feet. "You be here so I can looks in your eyes and shake your hand. Ain't no two other tings on dis Earf dat says more 'bout a man den his lookin' in your eyes and shakin' your hand."

I stood, extended my hand, and never broke eye contact.

He looked up at me and then back down at the bench. "We done did dat, Chase. Ole Kennef done knows what kinda man you is. Me believe maybe dey done gived the wrong name to da wrong man. Maybe you is the Gator for reals, 'cause you is da kind o' man what chomps down on sompin' and don't never lets it go—just like dem big ol' hungry gators out in da bayou."

I did my best Cajun accent. "Tells ol' Chase 'bout dem bodies, you."

He cackled until I thought another tooth might fall out. When he opened his mouth again, he spoke in the clearest voice I'd heard until that moment. "I can speak English, too, but I have to think about it awfully hard."

"Stop stalling," I said. "Let's hear about the bodies."

He watched the moon staring back at him for a long moment. "It prolly ain't none of my business, but I make my livin' out der in dem bayous."

"You catch alligators for a living?"

He shook his head. "No, I just hunt dem gators for to eat and 'cause it's fun. I sell a few, but I'm in the loggin' trade."

"The logging trade?" I asked. "I didn't know there was a logging industry down here."

He said, "It prolly ain't the kind of loggin' trade you be tinking 'bout. Dem good logs—dem ones what have been under da water for long as you been on dis Earf—dem is the ones I make a livin' on."

It wasn't his accent that confused me at that moment. "I'm not following. How do you make a living with trees that are underwater?"

He made a fist and tapped it to his mouth several times. "Do you know how to breathe tru one of dem scuba tings?"

"Yes, sir. I'm a diver, but I've not seen any water down here that I was excited to get into."

"Tomorrow's da day, Chase. How 'bout dat Gator boy? Do he know how?"

"Yes, sir. He's an excellent diver."

"Good. Den, tomorrow, we goin' divin'."

He reclaimed his beer and stood. "Get youself some sleep. We be goin' 'fore dat ol' sun make it hot out der."

Gator staggered away from the horde of dancers and planted himself back on the bench.

"You look like you had quite the workout. Where's your new girlfriend?"

He wiped his brow. "She said she had to work early in the morning, so she handed me off to a pair of her friends. You've got to get me out of here. These girls are going to kill me."

"What a way to go," I said. "Did you learn anything about the bodies?"

He swallowed half a beer. "No. Every time I brought it up, she danced around the subject...literally."

"I got the same treatment from Mr. LePine, but he's taking us diving in the morning 'fore dat ol' sun make it hot out der."

He shook his head. "Please don't ever do that again. Where are we going diving?"

I shrugged. "I have no idea, but we're apparently going early."

* * *

The shower in the camper Mr. LePine provided for us was apparently built for horse jockeys. I banged my elbows, knees, and head on every surface, but I managed to get mostly clean before crawling into the bed that was at least a foot shorter than me.

Sleep came, but it was brief. Mr. Lepine woke us at 4:30 the next morning by banging on the camper and yelling something neither of us understood. We rolled out of our racks and stumbled our way to the truck. He threw a pair of brown paper bags toward us, and we managed to catch them. Upon opening them, we discovered sandwiches of meat and eggs.

"You bellies gonna need dat, boys. Eat up."

We obeyed and scarfed down the sandwiches while drinking the strongest coffee on the planet out of paper cups.

"Thank you for breakfast," Gator said. "What was it?"

"Dat der be nutria and eggs."

Gator leaned toward me and whispered, "What's nutria?"

"Trust me. You don't want to know."

We rode for almost an hour as the morning sky lightened to the east.

After we pulled into a parking area at a boat launch, Gator asked, "Did we forget the boat?"

Mr. LePine motioned toward the dock, where a strange-looking machine rested, bobbing on the water. "Dats my boat and driver right der. Let's go, boys. You don't wanna keep her waitin'. She charges by da hour."

We climbed from the truck and followed the old Cajun to the dock. The boat was empty except for piles of chain, line, lift bags, and scuba gear. We climbed aboard, and Mr. Lepine pressed the starter switches. The machine roared to life and sounded a little like the Merlin under the cowling of the P-51 Mustang back in our hangar at Bonaventure.

"Those things sound like monsters," I said.

He grinned. "Just wait, you. You ain't never seen nothin' like dis here. You best hold on to you's toes."

"I've never feared losing my toes on a boat, but I'll take your advice. Where's the captain you mentioned?"

He pointed toward the tree line. "Der she come. She prolly been peein' on a stump."

When the captain arrived on the dock, she smiled down at her dance partner from the previous night. "Good to see I didn't wear you out last night, Boogaloo."

Gator offered a hand, and Cecilia took it and jumped aboard. My partner enjoyed watching her walk to the cockpit a little more than he should have, but I couldn't blame him. As beautiful as she was dancing under the moon eight hours earlier, there's something undeniably sexy about a woman at the controls of a boat.

I cast off the lines, and she shoved the throttles forward. The bow of the metal boat leapt into the air, blocking our view, but only for seconds. As the hull planed on top of the water, the bow sank, and we settled onto the surface at what had to be fifty knots.

Mr. LePine turned his hat backward and yelled, "I told you! Where dem toes at now, huh?"

We raced across the body of water that was only slightly less murky than the bayou on the previous day's gator-hunting adventure. As the sun broke over the horizon, I admired the endlessly flat terrain dotted by tree lines in every direction.

"We gotta get us one of these," Gator yelled.

I leaned close to his ear. "Are you talking about the boat or the captain?"

He didn't hesitate. "Both."

Cecilia eased the throttles back, and the boat settled into the water. She brought the sonar online and slowly trolled a course parallel to the gently sloping bank fifty yards away. She and Mr. LePine stared at the small screen as we progressed to the northeast with the boat barely moving across the water.

Kenneth said, "There they go! Right there!"

Cecilia tossed a buoy overboard with a spring-loaded reel and lead weight attached to the base. When the contraption hit the water, the weight sank to the bottom while the spring kept tension on the thin line. We continued moving slowly forward until the sonar screen changed dramatically, and Cecilia tossed a second buoy overboard.

We anchored in thirteen feet of water about ten feet off the line between the two buoys, and she shut down the engines.

"Uncle Ken tells me you're both divers."

We nodded, and Gator said, "We're both combat diver qualified from the Army's school in Key West."

She nodded, but Gator's attempt to impress her crashed and burned.

She cocked her head. "They got gators at that school?"

My Gator shook his head.

After we donned our dive gear, still unimpressed, Cecilia asked, "How about the four Fs? Did they teach you those at the Army school?" Gator sighed, and she said, "We're going to find 'em, flag 'em, free 'em, and float 'em. That's the four Fs. The visibility is less than zero down there, so everything will be by feel. Which one of you wants to go first?"

Gator looked at me with something akin to terror in his eyes, and I volunteered. Cecilia and I stepped over the stern and sank into the black water. She held my hand, and I wondered just how much Gator would enjoy that part of the adventure. She led me to the bottom, and we swam toward the first buoy. When we arrived, she guided my hand to a log that must've been four feet in diameter. She tacked a piece of surveyor's flagging to the end, and we swam the length of the log. She repeated the process of flagging the distant end of the log and drew a pair of small, folding shovels from our gear before demonstrating the technique of freeing the log from the muddy bottom with the blade of the shovel. We worked on opposite sides of the log until we reached the end where we'd begun.

Next, she drew a massive lift bag from her gear and rigged the line around the log, and then we rigged four more lift bags along the length of the log. After tugging on the rigging to ensure it was secure, Cecilia inflated each of the bags to half capacity. With that done, we surfaced, and Mr. LePine tossed a jumbled collection of chain and straps at us. We caught the mess, and the weight of the rigging pulled me beneath the water. I inflated my buoyancy compensator and returned to the surface.

She said, "We're going to rig this about two feet from each end of the log."

I nodded my understanding, and Mr. LePine extended a massive steel structure over the back of the boat with a cable extending from the end of the boom. Cecilia connected the cable to the cradle, and we headed back for the bottom.

With the cradle connected, we began the slow process of filling each lift bag with air until the log separated from the muddy bottom and began its slow rise. After double-checking the rigging, we surfaced again, and she gave the thumbs-up.

Mr. LePine cranked the engines and backed the stern of the boat almost directly above the log. The homemade crane brought the cable taut and slowly lifted the log from the bottom. When it broke the surface, he stopped the crane, leaving the log resting with the top half of its diameter above the water. He handed a wire brush to Cecilia, and she scrubbed the surface of the log in one spot for several minutes. When she backed away, Mr. Lepine produced a nozzle that must've been attached to a pressure washer somewhere in the boat. In seconds, the exposed wood shined almost white in the early morning sun.

"Dat's a goodun der, girl. How many mores?"

She said, "Maybe a dozen. It's going to be a long day."

We swam away from the boat, and the crane's work began again. It took it several minutes, but the log was finally resting on the gunwales of the boat and hanging over each side. When it was securely chained to the craft, Cecilia said, "Okay, Pretty Boy. It's time. Let's see if you learn as well as your boss."

Gator stepped over the transom and descended beneath the surface, hand-in-hand with Cecilia.

"I reckon dat boy be sweet on my gran'-niece, don't you?"

"Who wouldn't be?" I asked.

He rubbed a hand across the log. "Ain't she somethin'?"

I shrugged. "I don't know anything about timber. To me, it just looks like a huge, muddy log."

I'd come to love Kenneth LePine's laughter. The whole world should get to laugh like that a dozen times a day. Although I didn't envy the physical demands of his life, I began to envy him living in that uncomplicated world. He didn't have a cell phone, a watch, or any need for dental floss.

After the second successful lift of the day, Gator and Cecilia climbed back aboard, and she studied the two logs carefully.

"Are they cypress?" Gator asked.

I was impressed.

Cecilia still was not. "No, they're Nyssa aquatica, the water tupelo, but cypress wasn't a bad guess. Some people call them black gum tupelo. That's not technically correct, though. These have probably been down there for seventy-five years or more."

Gator shook like a dog shedding water. "How do you know so much about logs?"

She said, "I may not have graduated from that fancy Army diving school of yours, but I do have a master's degree in agronomy from LSU."

Gator chuckled. "You're just full of surprises, aren't you?"

She plucked a glob of mud from his hair. "Don't worry, Pretty Boy. Sooner or later, you'll do something to impress me."

Once Gator was fully trained on the underwater operation, the three of us found, flagged, freed, and floated sixteen logs that day. The boat was only capable of carrying four at a time, so we made several trips to the timber yard, where the logs were measured and graded. Each visit to the yard landed a thicker wad of cash in Mr. LePine's hand, and when the day was finally over, he threw an arm around me and said, "I guess it be time to tell y'all 'bout dem dead bodies."

Chapter 3
Ma Chérie

We spent the hour-long drive back to the camper in near silence. I didn't like the feeling of being put through a two-day job interview by Kenneth LePine II and Cecilia Lachaussee, but I had stepped outside the world in which my team and I were well-respected—and even feared—tactical professionals capable of handling almost any situation anywhere on the globe. I was learning that in the world that revolved around the bayou, everything had its own pace, and outsiders—boogaloos like us—were regarded with extreme caution and even distrusted...possibly for good reason.

When we pulled into the tiny speck of dry land beside the LePines' three-room shelter that would never qualify as a house anywhere else in the country, Kenneth said, "Build a fire. I'll be back in a minute, me."

A collection of cypress logs stood on end around a rock-lined pit that had clearly been the site of far too many fires to count. Gator gathered wood while I lit a few pieces of kindling. By the time Kenneth came back, we had a respectable fire popping and cracking. We each claimed a stump, and the old Cajun handed me a stack of small scraps of paper. The moon was still a day away from being full, but it cast enough light to barely see the sketches on the slips of paper.

Kenneth pulled a stick from the fire and held it beside the papers. "Dem be hard to sees by only da light of dat ol' moon."

I drew the small light from my pocket and illuminated the sketches.

Kenny tossed the burning stick back onto the fire. "Ain't dat handy?"

I carefully studied each sketch before handing it off to Gator. The detail was incredible and macabre.

I said, "Mr. LePine, who made these drawings?"

He sat upright. "Me did. Ain't gots no camera, me."

"You drew all of these?"

"Dat's right."

Gator shuddered at the sight of each drawing and quickly handed them back to me.

"Did you find these bodies somewhere?" I asked.

The old man slowly shook his head. "No, dey founds me, dey did."

"They found you?"

"That's right. When ol' Keef first saw them floatin' on da bayou, I didn't thinks dey was real, me. Dey was pale and all swole up, dem. And I says to myself, I says dem can't be real, no. Why not da gators be eatin 'em if dey real?"

"And you think these body parts came to you?"

He nodded. "Me knows it don't make no sense to yous, but I was in da war and folks be dyin' all 'round. When dey left dey bodies, dey spirits came to me 'fore dey went on to Heaven. I knowed dey goin' to Heaven 'cause we done been tru hell in dat jungle."

"Vietnam?" I asked.

He nodded slowly. "Dat musta been a tousand years ago, but sometimes, it was just yesterday inside me old head."

As the firelight danced in his one dark eye that could've been obsidian, I could almost see the Southeast Asian jungle rippling in the glassy sheen.

"How long were you over there?"

He held up his good hand and spread his fingers.

"Five months?"

He shook his head. "Five tours. Me goes the first time as a private soldier and comes home from the last tour a first-class sergeant, me. I hads two good eyes back den, and ol' Keef sees more death than any man ought to in all of his life, yeah."

I suddenly wished we were still at the previous night's party eating crawfish and listening to zydeco music, but reality had consumed the fantasy of laughter and dancing.

I pulled up my pants leg and exposed the state-of-the art prosthetic extending from my knee into my boot.

Kenneth leaned toward me and ran his fingertips across the piece of medical wizardry. He whispered, "You too young to been in da war, you."

"For those of us who volunteer to fight it, the war never ends, Mr. LePine."

He looked into the heavens as a billion stars flickered beyond the dancing specks of floating embers from our fire. "Dat be da truest ting any man ever said. We was fightin' when that Boy King David flung dat rock at da big ol' giant, and we'll be fightin' when da good Lord come back for dat final battle at Armageddon, Him."

I sat in silent awe of the wisdom inside the man most people would disregard as crazy. The more I listened, the more I wanted to study his sketches. The gruesome detail called to me as if the same spirits that visited Kenneth in the sweltering jungle were now clawing at my soul and beseeching me to free them from whatever torture was consuming them second by second and eon by eon.

"Where did you see them?" I asked.

"Out on dat same bayou where we killed dat gator yesterday. It was yesterday, right?"

"Yes, sir. It was yesterday. When did you see them?"

He motioned toward the scraps of paper. "It's on da back."

I flipped over the papers and found odd-looking, simple sketches of a round object with arced slices removed from the orb. "What does this mean?"

He pointed toward the moon, and I suddenly understood. "You don't know what day it is, do you, Mr. LePine?"

His bony shoulders rose and fell. "What dat matter, huh? A day is a day, just like another day. It don't matter whats you call it, no. Men who tinks dey know better than e'rybody else write dem calendars, but le Bon Dieu put dat big ol' moon up der for a fine calendar what don't never have to be wrote down, no."

The absurdity of his concept of time fascinated me, and the more I tried to shoot holes in his theory, the more I came to believe he was right. "Who else saw these body parts?"

"Don't know, me. I hopes don't nobody sees 'em."

"So, you're the only person who saw them, is that right?"

He shrugged again. "I done tolds you I don't knows who saw dem 'fore me, but nobody sees 'em after me. Dat's for sure."

"What do you mean?"

"'Cause I burned 'em up when I founds 'em, I did."

"You burned the remains? Why would you do that?"

"Dey had evil on 'em. Even da gators know it. Dey won't eat 'em."

Gator finally spoke up. "Did you call the police?"

Kenneth stared into the fire for a long moment. "Kenny didn't tell you 'bout his ol' pappy, do he?"

"What do you mean?" Gator asked.

Kenneth said, "When ol' me was young likes you, a boogaloo puts his hands on Kenny's mama, and I see it wiff dese two eyes o' mines when I had two good 'uns, and I cuts him tree ways."

Gator furrowed his brow. "Tree ways? What does that mean?"

Kenneth said, "You knows. One way, two ways, tree ways."

"Oh, three ways."

"Das right. Tree ways—long, wide, and deep. He don't touch ma chérie never 'gain, him."

"Did you kill him?" Gator asked.

The old man shook his head. "No. He kills him own self when he tinks is fine to put hands on my Veronique. I just helped him along a little."

Gator grimaced. "So, you think because you've been to prison, the police won't help you."

"What da parish sheriff gonna do when I says to him ol' Keef gots a gris-gris on me dat be callin' spirits to me, and dey bring what left of dem mortal bodies too, huh?"

Gator suddenly looked as if his brain was turning to mud, so I said, "Let me make sure I understand what's going on. You found some body parts out on the bayou that the alligators didn't eat, so you picked them up and burned them because they were somehow cursed. Is that right?"

Kenneth nodded, and I continued. "And you didn't call the parish sheriff because you think he won't believe you. Am I still on the right track?"

"Dat be 'bout right."

"So, what is it you want us to do?"

He looked back at me with the look of a disappointed father on his weathered face. "What you mean? Kenny's pretty wife, Earline, done told me you da best in all da world at finding out what's going on when can't nobody else know."

I held up the sketches. "May I keep these?"

Kenneth said, "Only if you's gonna helps me figure out who dem parts belongs to."

I glanced at Gator and then back at Kenneth. "I'll tell you what. Let me keep these for twenty-four hours. We'll talk to some people, and I'll let you know tomorrow night if we can help."

"Dat's fair 'nuff, but no sheriff, no."

"We won't tell the sheriff. You have my word."

Mr. LePine stood and turned to go, but he paused long enough to say, "Me knows how crazy all dis sounds to you, but you hear me when I tells you dat somebody be out der *fait du mal*, and he be draggin' ol' Keef right into his mess."

Gator and I sat alone by the fire, and I had a thousand questions burning holes in my head.

Finally, Gator said, "What on Earth was that?"

"I'm not sure. What did you think of his story?"

He glanced over his shoulder at the shack barely standing behind us. "I think he's crazy. That's what I think. He lives by himself out here in...God knows where we are, and he believes the spirits of dead people come to him before they go to Heaven. You're the psychologist, but that sounds like the textbook definition of crazy to me."

"What about the drawings?" I asked.

"Okay, he can draw severed body parts. I'll give him that. But that doesn't mean he's actually seen them out there on the bayou. It could be flashbacks from Vietnam or something."

"You could be right," I said, "but I'm not ready to walk away yet. Earl believed him enough to send us out here to meet and talk to him."

He huffed. "No disrespect, but she's at least as crazy as he is. You've got to admit that."

I chuckled. "Maybe Earl isn't the poster girl for psychological stability, but she wouldn't send us all the way down here for nothing. Maybe she's just trying to get you hooked up with Cecilia."

He almost blushed. "If that's what this is, I'm all about it. And thank you, Earl!"

We watched the fire flicker and burn out. On the way inside the camper, Gator asked, "What does *fait du mal* mean anyway?"

I said, "Who knows? Maybe you should ask your girlfriend."

"Maybe I will."

I gave him a playful shove. "Get some sleep, and we'll start fresh in the morning."

"Start on what?"

"I don't know, but if there are body parts floating around in the bayou, there's no way Mr. LePine is the only one who's seen them. I say we poke around a little and see if we can get a bite. Maybe you're right and the old man is crazy, but when was the last time our cup wasn't running over with crazy?"

I lay in bed after another subcompact shower and stared at Mr. LePine's drawings. After half an hour of studying every detail, I decided that photographs would've been less graphic.

My watch said it was almost eleven o'clock. That meant it was only nine in L.A. and not too late to make a call.

My wife, Penny, had been Hollywood's golden child for a little over three years. She'd written thirty screenplays, including four that had become Oscar-winning movies. I made an extremely comfortable living traveling the world and pinning bad guys to the wall, but the bacon I brought home barely paid the taxes on what Tinseltown paid her.

"Hey there, my little bayou boy. How's it going down there?"

"It's getting weird," I said.

She laughed. "When was the last time things didn't get weird for you?"

"Touché, but this one is really weird. Gator and I are the only two people who speak English. There are trees that have been underwater for a hundred years. We've eaten stuff we can't pronounce. And to top it all off, I think Gator's in love with a cute little Cajun girl."

She giggled. "He's young. He'll get over it. Have you figured out what you're supposed to be doing yet?"

"It's starting to trickle out, but that's even stranger than everything else that goes on down here. For some reason, Kenny's father thinks the spirits of dead people come to him on their way to Heaven."

Her laughter came but trailed off. "Uh...okay. That is weird."

"Believe it or not, that's not the weirdest thing. Apparently, there are human body parts floating around in the bayou and the gators won't eat them because—get this—there's some kind of evil on them."

Penny said, "If I wrote a screenplay of your life, every producer in California would write me off and ship me back to Georgia. Nobody would believe this stuff."

"I live it, and I don't believe it."

"So, what's your next move?"

"I want my next move to be onto *Aegis* with you so we can sail off into the sunset and finally take our honeymoon."

She said, "We live on the East Coast, sweetheart. That makes it impossible for us to sail off into the sunset."

"My head hurts. I'm going to bed. I'll call you tomorrow."

"Don't get tangled up with any spirits or dead bodies. I love you."

Sleep was the one thing I wanted more than anything else at that moment, but it wasn't in the cards. The second I closed my eyes, someone yanked open the door of the camper, and I leapt to my one remaining foot with my pistol in hand.

Chapter 4
Dungeons and Dragons

I had practiced the delicate balancing act hundreds of times. Standing on one foot with the remaining half of my right leg dangling eighteen inches above the ground was easy enough...when I wasn't in a gun-fight. When hunks of supersonic lead are zipping through the air in both directions, the demands of the one-foot dance grew exponentially. Using the rack that almost qualified as a bed became essential as I braced to repel whoever was clearly raiding our tiny camper.

My protégé proved he'd been paying attention over the previous year when every member of my team pounded wisdom into his skull. I was surprised he didn't have the adage tattooed somewhere on his body.

The only purpose of a pistol is to fight your way to your rifle.

When his even number of feet hit the deck, instead of raising his Glock as I had done, he shouldered his M4 and thumbed the switch to flood the intruder's pupils with the most powerful weapon-mounted light in existence.

The assault worked, and the attempted breaching of our trailer was thwarted without firing a single round. The wall of unimaginable light accomplished more than merely stopping the intruder; it caused her to belt out a string of Cajun obscenities no one could understand. Gator instantly dowsed his light when Cecilia threw her arm over her face to block what must've looked like the surface of the sun.

"What are you doing?" she demanded.

Gator lowered his rifle. "Trying to get some sleep. Have you ever heard of knocking?"

Still squinting, she said, "Sorry, I forgot you were in here."

"You forgot we were in here?"

"Yeah, I live a half hour away, and I had a few beers, so I was going to crash here for the night. I do it all the time."

My bright young operator didn't need my help negotiating the sleepover, so I holstered my pistol and slithered back under the sheet.

Gator grabbed his poncho liner and a spare pillow. "Come on. You take the bed. I'll take the floor."

She giggled. "What's the matter? Afraid I'll take advantage of you?"

I'm not sure which one of them got to be the big spoon, but the distraction was exactly what I needed to get my mind off the floating body parts. I was asleep in minutes with absolutely no interest in knowing what was happening five feet away in Gator's bunk.

The smell of coffee drew me from the best night's sleep I'd had in weeks. Cecilia handed a cup toward me while I attached my prosthetic.

When the foot was securely in place, I accepted the steaming cup and took my first taste. "Thank you. It's good."

"I'm glad you like it. It's chicory."

"I don't know what that means."

"It's a plant," she said. "The binomial nomenclature is Cichorium intybus. They roast the root and then grind it into the same texture as coffee. Chicory is cheap and plentiful around here. Coffee is not."

She motioned toward my cup. "That's a fifty-fifty blend."

I took another sip. "Nice."

Gator came from the mini shower dripping and trying to wrangle enough space inside the camper to dry himself while still feigning modesty.

Cecilia peeked around the towel. "Good morning, Snuggle Bunny. Want some coffee?"

"Don't do that," he said.

"Don't do what? Are you not a coffee drinker?"

"No, I like coffee just fine, but please don't give Chase any more pet names to torture me with."

She leaned close and whispered, "Chase is sleeping alone, and you're not. Now, who do you really think is being tortured around here?"

Changing the subject suddenly became a necessity, but I was going to keep Snuggle Bunny tucked away in the back of my mind for a rainy day. "Aren't you logging today?"

She shook her head. "Not today. Uncle Kenneth made enough yesterday to keep him in cheap whiskey and Marlboros for a while."

"So, he only pulls logs when he runs out of money?"

"That's right."

Gator pulled a T-shirt over his head, and Cecilia watched, obviously enjoying the show.

She glanced at me. "Why don't your abs look like that?"

I poked Gator in the ribs. "Because strength and stamina are more important than aesthetics to me."

She turned back to her Snuggle Bunny. "Please tell me you don't have stamina issues."

He planted himself on the edge of his bunk. "The only issue I have is with this conversation right now. My stamina is just fine."

She shrugged. "We'll see."

I redoubled my effort to change the subject. "Normally, I wouldn't pry into your business, but as of last night, prying became my job. Why is it that Kenneth gets all the money for the timber, but you seem to do all the work?"

"He pays me," she said. "Just not in front of anybody."

"Who owns the boat?"

"Technically, I do, but let's not bring that up in front of Uncle Kenneth."

"So, he thinks it's his?"

She deflated. "It's a long story, but the brief version goes like this. He likes to gamble. Okay, that's an understatement. He loves to gamble."

"What's his game?" I asked.

"D and D."

I recoiled. "Dungeons and Dragons?"

She laughed. "Dominos and dice."

"That makes a lot more sense."

She continued. "He was shooting dice with Lil' Tuck and Tito a couple of years ago and having a really bad night. His luck started to turn, but he was out of cash. He put up the boat against a three-thousand-dollar spot and lost."

"Ouch."

"Exactly," she said. "Especially considering that without that boat, he has no way to make a living."

"Does that mean you reclaimed the boat from the Tik-Tok twins?"

She chuckled. "If I were you, I wouldn't call Tito and Lil' Tuck the Tik-Tok twins, but that's up to you. Yes, I bought the boat from them at a price significantly higher than the three grand they spotted on the dice game, but I never mentioned it to Uncle Kenneth. We just kept pulling logs like nothing ever happened."

When I was a newly minted operator, Clark Johnson took me under his wing and taught me exponentially more than I learned at The Ranch. In the never-ending world of covert operations, everyone remains a student until the day they either take a bullet in the skull or finally walk away from the game. My world had come full circle, and it was my turn to teach Gator everything Clark taught me. Part of that training included giving the new kid time to ask the right questions, and in that moment, somewhere south of normalcy, class was in session, and my student was about to get a gold star by his name.

He said, "Wait a minute. You work for your uncle as a diver and boat captain, right?"

I shrank into the background and watched him work.

He sat with a look of anticipation on his face until Cecilia said, "That's right."

"And he pays you enough to have bought back his boat?"

She looked away, and I waited for Gator to pounce. If he didn't, I would, but he didn't disappoint.

"You drive a really nice truck with commercial plates. Your uncle isn't your only source of income, is he?"

"No. The truck isn't mine. It belongs to an oil exploration company. I do some contract work for them."

Keep pouncing, young Gator.

He did.

"Oil exploration? Why does an oil exploration company need an agronomist?"

She wouldn't make eye contact, and I could almost see the wheels turning inside her head. I was pretty sure Gator saw the same, and he made a brilliant move. "Never mind. I'm sorry. We jumped off in a direction that's none of our business."

She looked relieved. "I guess dat mean ol' Uncle Kenneth done tol' you bouts dem body parts."

"Where did that come from?" Gator asked.

She waved a hand. "Sorry. That happens sometimes when I forget the rest of the world doesn't speak patois."

Gator smiled, proving Cecilia's trap worked. "It's okay. I like it, even though I don't understand it."

"You're sweet, Kansas. So, what did Uncle Kenneth tell you about the body parts?"

I handed the drawings to Gator, and he passed them to Cecilia.

"Well, he showed us these and told us he burned them."

She flipped through the sketches. "He's a really good artist, but these aren't easy to look at." She handed the stack back to Gator. "Are you going to help him figure out where they're coming from?"

Gator turned to me, and I took the handoff. "We don't know yet. This isn't the kind of thing we usually deal with. I told your uncle that we'd ask some questions and let him know if we thought we could help."

She said, "He *did* tell you not to contact the authorities, though, right?"

Gator clamped his hand over his mouth and leapt to his feet. In an instant, he was through the door and outside the camper.

Cecilia watched him go. "What was that all about?"

I shrugged. "I guess something didn't sit well in his stomach. He's not used to eating like we have in the past two days. You can look at him and tell he's pretty careful about what he puts in his body."

She smiled. "Oh, yeah. That's obvious. Maybe I should check on him."

"That's probably not a great idea. He doesn't like attention when he's not feeling well. He'll be back in when he gets rid of whatever his body's rejecting."

She peered around the partially closed door. "If you say so."

While waiting for Gator to make his return, I said, "You must have a theory on the body parts. I mean, you're a well-educated woman with roots in this community. Who's better qualified to explain it than you?"

"How should I know? It's creepy, but there's all sorts of creepy stuff that happens out here. It's not like we're in the French Quarter. There's a lot that can't be explained in the bayou."

I said, "I noticed you had a St. Christopher's medal on the boat. Is that yours or Kenneth's?"

"Why do you ask?"

"Just curious," I said. "Your uncle mentioned something about spirits of the dead, so naturally, I wondered about his faith. If he's Roman Catholic, what he said wouldn't make much sense."

The camper rocked as Gator climbed back aboard, wiping his mouth. "Sorry about that. I'm not used to all this spicy food. I need to get back on my diet."

She hooked a finger beneath the hem of his T-shirt and pulled it up far enough to expose the abs he worked so hard to maintain. "Yeah, don't let us mess up what you've got going on there."

Gator pulled the shirt away from her and brushed off the compliment. He squeezed his way into the head and brushed his teeth again.

When he returned, I said, "We were just talking about Kenneth being Roman Catholic."

Cecilia took the bait. "He was baptized Catholic, but he's not been to mass in years. In fact, I don't ever remember him going except for weddings, funerals, or baptisms. The medal is mine, by the way."

"So, do you attend mass regularly?" I asked.

"Not really, but I'm sure you know about St. Christopher saving people from drowning. That's why I keep the medal on the boat."

"I get it. Tell me about the spirits your uncle was talking about."

She scoffed. "Oh, it's silly. It's a bunch of that voodoo garbage from New Orleans."

She suddenly had Gator's attention. "Voodoo? Are you serious?"

She shrugged. "To a lot of people, it's very real. In New Orleans voodoo traditions, most of the practitioners believe in the same God you and I do, but they think He doesn't get involved in our daily lives very much. They believe He leaves that up to the spirits, and practitioners of that type of voodoo believe they can commune with the spirits through all kinds of crazy rituals like dancing, music, incantations, and even snakes."

"And that's what your uncle believes?" Gator asked.

"Who knows? I love him, but he's not exactly the kind of man you'd say has all of his mental faculties. He's a little bit out there sometimes."

Gator turned to me as if I were supposed to rescue him. Instead of pulling him out of the fire, I waved both hands in front of his face, rolled my eyeballs back in my head, and said, "Boogedy boogedy boo."

He slapped my hands from the air. "Cut it out. That's not funny. You don't play with that kind of stuff."

Cecilia and I laughed, but Gator did not. "I'm serious, man. That stuff is weird. Chicken bones and blood and stuff...I'm out."

She stood, kissed him on the forehead, and dropped a set of well-worn rosary beads in his hand. "I've got to be going, but don't worry, Boogaloo, this will keep those bloody chicken bones and evil spirits away until I get back."

When Cecilia closed the door behind her, I said, "Nice show, Boogaloo. You almost had me convinced."

"Convinced of what?"

"That you're afraid of voodoo."

"That was no performance, Chase. There's *some* stuff you just don't play with. Ask Singer. He'll tell you."

Singer was the deadliest sniper I ever met, but he was so much more than that. He earned the moniker Southern Baptist sniper because of his devotion to his faith and his tendency to hum old Southern Baptist hymns while sniping. I loved the dichotomy that was my friend and teammate.

"You don't think Singer's afraid of the chicken bones, do you?"

He said, "It's not the bones. It's the evil. You know it's real, and Singer would kill me if he caught me carrying rosary beads."

"You hang on to those," I said. "Singer would never disapprove of anything that made you think of God. He'd want to make sure you didn't believe the beads were somehow protecting you. Just like the chicken bones, those beads only have the power that you allow them to have."

He tossed the beads on top of his backpack propped against the wall, and I asked, "Is your stomach all right?"

He rubbed his abs and tossed his phone to me. "Oh, yeah. I'm fine."

I checked his phone and found a pair of photographs. The first was a close-up shot of the lettering on the door of Cecilia's truck, and the second was a picture of her license plate.

"Nicely done," I said. "We'll have Skipper run both, and we'll find out just exactly why Flambeau Exploration needs an agronomist from LSU."

Chapter 5
Demand a Prenup

During my college years, I spent far more of my waking hours at the home of Coach Bobby Woodley than in the athletes' dorm at UGA. On the list of reasons I loved being in my coach's home, Laura Woodley's lasagna ranked number one, but only slightly behind my favorite meal was their daughter, Elizabeth. She was bratty and loud, but she always seemed to be happy. She danced, hopped, and skipped everywhere she went, so, naturally, I called the teenager I saw as my little sister, Skipper, and the name stuck. Back then, it would've been impossible to convince me that I'd become anything other than a professional baseball player and that Skipper would be anything but that giggling girl everybody adored. The old adage says, "Man plans, God laughs." A dancing career and pro ball weren't in the cards for Skipper and me, but fate, the universe, or the hand of God tied the two of us together, each dependent on the other and sharing a bond even stronger than genetics. I grew to become the leader of an elite team of operators who were willing and capable of facing any foe, and Skipper became one of the finest intelligence analysts in the game. I'd found myself surrounded, outnumbered, outgunned, and running out of ammo all over the world, but Skipper's calm, confident voice in my ear never failed to make me believe anything was possible, and so far, she'd never steered me wrong.

For almost a decade, Skipper's lair had been the operation center on the third floor of our house at Bonaventure. From inside the op center, she had the power of a supercomputer at her fingertips, as well as an array of communication technology second to none. During an operation anywhere in the world, I could contact Skipper and the op center by using any of the thousand methods I had in my environment. Anything stronger than a smoke signal would find its way back to the analyst's ears. As efficient as our operation was when Skipper was locked away behind the heavy doors of her cave, establishing comms with her from deep within the bayous of South Louisiana was a challenge.

I tried the cell phone, but it looked like some of Kenneth's spirits were conspiring to block the transmission. Gator drew the satellite phone from his pack and tossed it to me. I snatched it from the air and scrolled through the contact list until Skipper's name filled the screen. I'll never understand technology, but the signal from the sat-phone must've been faster than the spirits.

Skipper answered on the fourth ring, but the roar of the wind made her almost impossible to hear. "Hey, Chase! You should be here with us. This place is amazing."

"Are you in a wind tunnel?"

"What?"

I yelled into the phone. "What are you doing? I can barely hear you."

I think she said, "Hang on a minute. I can't hear you." A few seconds later, the roar disappeared, and she said, "Can you hear me now?"

"Much better. How about me?"

She said, "Chase, you've got to come down here. This place is awesome. We spent most of the morning exploring a cave with pictographs, and we're racing dune buggies now. I was winning until you called."

"It sounds like you're having quite the vacation. I'm a little envious."

"Oh, it's great," she said. "I really needed this."

Seven months before that moment in time, Skipper's husband,

Tony Johnson, was murdered by a sniper who was bent on killing every member of my team before finally putting a round in me as his coup de gras. We ended the gunman's reign of terror, but not before he'd killed three people I cared about and brutally wounded my dear friend and teammate, Stone W. Hunter.

As any young woman would, Skipper spent a great many hours in tears over the loss of the man she loved, but hearing the laughter and joy back in her voice made me feel as though she may have turned a corner and was ready to live again.

She was vacationing on the island of Bonaire with the unlikeliest partner. Anya Burinkova, a former Russian SVR assassin, had once been the woman I thought I loved, but circumstances far beyond my control ended that relationship...or at least the romantic element of it. The Russian defected to the U.S. and worked alongside my team and me on more missions than I can remember. Needless to say, my wife, Penny, wasn't Anya's biggest fan, but the Russian's insistence on whisking Skipper away for an all-girls Caribbean adventure even made Penny smile.

I said, "I'm sorry to interrupt your vacation, but we need a little analyst support. It's pretty basic stuff, so I can have Ginger or Celeste handle it if you'd prefer to keep playing."

She said, "Yeah, about that... Celeste is with me, and Ginger is, well, let's just say she's unavailable at the moment. I guess that means you're stuck with me. So what can I do for you?"

"Gator and I are still in Louisiana, and we need the goods on a company called Flambeau Exploration. They're apparently an oil and natural gas exploration company, but that's all I know."

"What do you want to know?"

"Everything."

"Oh, one of those," she said. "Is it time sensitive?"

"Isn't everything?"

"Okay. Give me a couple of hours, and I'll get back to you with whatever I can find. Is there anything else?"

"Yeah. I'll send you a license plate from one of Flambeau's trucks, and I'd like for you to start a deep dive on a woman named Cecilia Lachaussee. I think Gator's in love, and we need to know if he should demand a prenup."

"Good for Gator," she said. "Please tell me she's cute, 'cause he's yummy."

"He's listening on speaker."

She laughed. "Good. He knows he's hot. It's no secret. Text me the spelling of the chick's name, and I'll see what I can find. Oh, and if I can't find a picture of her, you'll have to send me one. Celeste, Anya, and I have to approve before this goes too far."

Gator said, "You're making me blush, Skipper. Cecilia's not as beautiful as you, but she can certainly dance."

"Hey, I can dance."

I said, "This is getting out of hand. Let's focus. I'll send you what we have. Get back to me as soon as you can, and tell Anya I said *spasibo*."

Her tone turned stern. "That doesn't mean anything dirty in Russian, does it?"

"Thanks, Skipper. Talk soon."

I tossed the phone back to Gator, and he said, "That means thank you, right?"

I chuckled. "Your Russian is better than your Cajun."

He tucked the sat-phone away. "What now, boss?"

I stood. "Let's take a stroll around the neighborhood."

"No thanks," he said. "I've seen the neighbors. They're ten feet long with a mouthful of teeth and a brain the size of a pea."

"Are you talking about Mongo?" I asked.

"Not hardly. Nobody's dumb enough to talk about Mongo like that."

We stepped from the camper and into the morning sun and air so humid it felt like a blanket wrapping around us. We walked a quarter mile to our beached amphibious Cessna Caravan. The plane was tied in three directions to prevent her from taking a leisurely stroll of her own if the bayou water ever decided to flow anywhere.

I tossed the keys to my partner. "You take the big-boy seat. I call shotgun."

He stopped in his tracks. "I can't fly that thing."

"Sure you can. You just don't know it yet."

We pumped the pontoons dry and performed the preflight inspection before untying and climbing inside. I walked Gator through the engine-start checklist, and soon, the Pratt & Whitney PT6 was whistling one of my favorite songs. There's something so elegant about the sound of a turbine engine taking her first breath in the morning.

"Okay, Hotshot. Put the water rudders down and back us out of here."

He looked at me as if I'd just told him to fly to the moon. "I don't know how to do either of those things."

I showed him the water rudder control. "These have to be down for taxiing. Otherwise, we can't steer very well, especially going backward."

He lowered the lever. "I'm still not sure about this whole going backward part."

"It's simple. Just pull the prop control over the detent and all the way to the aft stop. That'll cause the blades of the propeller to move to a negative angle and push us backward. Don't try it on the ground, but it works great in the water."

After a bit of a wrestling match, he finally had the Caravan pointed into the wind with plenty of open water in front of us.

"All right, Lindbergh. Pull the yoke into your lap and slowly advance the throttle. Just like in the One-Eighty-Two, steer with your feet. When the nose comes up, look around the cowling to make sure we're not going to hit a pirogue or a gator. Both of those have the right-of-way."

He followed my instructions, and just as described, the nose climbed upward several degrees and blocked our line of sight. He leaned left, and I kept my toes on the pedals and fingertips on the yoke, just in case.

"Keep that yoke in your lap until the nose comes up a second time. When that happens, gently ease the back pressure and let her pick up some speed."

As the pontoons came out of the water and onto plane, the nose fell and slowly rose again. I helped with the yoke as our speed quickly increased.

I called out, "Airspeed alive and building. Make us go straight with your feet."

As we accelerated across the black water, I could see the tension in his hands.

"Just relax and glance at the airspeed. As we pass seventy knots, apply just enough pressure to fly us off the water."

He gripped the yoke as if he were planning to rip it from the console, and I said, "Relax. This is supposed to be fun. There's your seventy knots, so give it just enough back pressure to fly."

He did, and our pontoons left the water.

"Now it's a normal climb. Take us to five hundred feet, and let's see if we can find that gator hole of yours."

Once we were an airplane and not a boat, Gator was right at home. He reduced the power, set the propeller RPM, and settled into a beautiful cruise at five hundred feet above the bayou. He said, "You know, in its own way, it's kind of pretty from up here. Who knew five hundred feet could make such a difference?"

"Life is all about perspective," I said. "And I can prove it."

He turned to me. "I'm probably going to regret this, but how can you prove it?"

He took the bait.

"What did the snail say when he was riding on the turtle's shell?"

"I'm sorry I asked," he said.

I laughed. "He said, 'Slow down, you maniac!'"

He shook his head. "Is this going to happen to me when I get old?

Will I start laughing at my own corny jokes and spouting what I believe are words of wisdom?"

I slapped him on the shoulder. "Only if you're lucky, kid. Only if you're lucky."

We toured the seemingly endless bayou at a hundred and ten knots, but every speck of water looked exactly like every other spot until Gator pointed through the windshield. "Is that it?"

I took the controls and rolled us onto our right side so I could examine the slough. "I believe you're right. You have the controls. Take us down there."

He reclaimed the controls and began a descent.

I asked, "How low can we legally fly? Just in case the FAA is watching..."

He never faltered. "Five hundred feet AGL, except over open water or sparsely populated areas. In those areas, we can't fly closer than five hundred feet to any person, vessel, vehicle, or structure unless we're maneuvering to take off or land."

"You've been studying. I'm impressed. Now, try not to hit those trees."

He banked around and followed the winding bayou until it led us back to Kenneth's shack.

I said, "Let's see where it goes the other way."

We climbed above the trees and followed the waterway until it intersected a wider body of water that turned south. I watched the world below open up into the massive Gulf of Mexico.

I said, "That's a handy little waterway to the Gulf."

"That's what I was thinking," he said. "That would make a nice escape route for somebody who wanted to drop off a few body parts and head for open water."

I studied the route and the maze of bayous intersecting what appeared to be a nearly straight shot to the Gulf. "Take a look out there. There must be a few hundred sloughs and offshoots that would be better for hiding body parts."

Gator leaned forward and surveyed the wetlands below. "You're right. It's a long way to Kenneth's bayou. Whoever's dumping the body parts must have some affinity for Kenneth's corner of the world, or they're dumping parts in several locations and we only know about one."

Chapter 6
What a Pair

For a moment, the sight of the Gulf left me daydreaming about sailing across blue water with Penny, to some destination I can't spell, and leaving the world behind. When I pulled myself from the dream, I said, "Take us home."

Gator spun his head toward me as if I'd asked him to jump off a cliff. "Seriously?"

"Yes, seriously. I have faith in you."

He shrugged. "If you say so."

Fifteen seconds later, I recognized the breakdown in our communication. Gator programmed the GPS to take us directly back to St. Marys and began a climb to eleven thousand five hundred feet.

Before he armed the autopilot, I said, "Not *that* home. I meant the camper. Besides, you can't leave without your little Creole princess."

His shoulders fell. "She's Cajun, not Creole, and that camper is *not* our home."

"It's our temporary home, but I've got a better idea. Instead of heading back, let's drop into that airport about thirty miles north. I can't remember the name of it, but maybe they've got a rental car."

He reprogrammed the GPS. "It's Terrebonne Parish, and I think the town is Houma, but who knows how they pronounce either one of those names?"

"Hand-fly it," I said. "You need to get used to the feel. The autopilot is an excellent tool, but I want to see you make the airplane behave."

He thumbed the autopilot disconnect on the yoke and settled into our short northbound hop. "Tell me the approach numbers."

I said, "Let's do one-oh-five in the downwind, ninety-five on the base, eighty-five on final, and cross the fence at seventy-five. Don't get slow. That's a turbine out there, not a recip, so you won't have power on demand. It'll take a couple of seconds for the turbine to spool up before it delivers the extra power you need. Just manage your speed, and remember, you've got four wheels instead of three. Touch down on the mains, but don't hold the nose off like you do in the One-Eighty-Two. It'll feel pretty flat."

"Got it," he said, and he flew a beautiful pattern.

We turned final, and I asked, "What's your airspeed?"

"Seventy-six."

"What should it be?"

"Uh...eighty-five?"

"Is that a question?"

He lowered the nose and added a little power. "No, it's not a question. It definitely should be eighty-five."

"Feel that delay?"

His eyes widened, and he pushed the throttle even farther. I laid my hand on top of his and reduced the throttle slightly. "Don't get carried away. Just be patient."

He squirmed in his seat. "This feels a lot different than the Skylane."

"It is a lot different, but the same principles still apply. Pitch for speed and power for descent rate."

I extended my legs and let my toes rest on the rudder pedals, but after his little battle with the throttle, he came back nicely and greased the landing.

"Nicely done. Now, take us to the FBO. It looks like they've got a few rental cars over there."

We taxied to the apron and worked through the shutdown checklist together.

"How's that feel?" I asked.

He grunted. "To be honest, it felt like landing a school bus."

I laughed. "That's a pretty good way to describe it. Come on... Let's get your feet back on the ground and see if we can find any body parts floating around."

We got lucky and scored a 4-wheel-drive pickup truck from the young lady at the counter who couldn't keep her eyes off my partner.

I tossed him the keys and climbed inside. "You've sure got something these Cajun girls like."

He stuck the key into the ignition. "What can I say? All the girls love the Gator."

"All right, Love Gator. Let's see if you can get us lost. If there are body parts floating, Kenneth LePine can't be the only one who's seen them."

"So, that's our plan?" he asked. "We're just going to drive around asking people if they've seen any arms and legs floating by?"

"Do you have a better idea?"

He nodded. "Yeah, I do. I've got the same idea the rest of the civilized world would have. We call the sheriff, then pack up and go home."

I laid a hand on his shoulder. "Kenny LePine and Earline back in St. Marys are my *friends*, and that's not a word I throw around. They asked me to look into what was going on down here. When a friend asks for a favor, the only thing that trumps that request is family and God. Kenny and Earl are practically family, and I don't think God has any objection to us doing whatever we can to help."

He said, "I didn't mean we shouldn't..."

"I know what you meant, and you're right. This isn't our typical mission, but what if Singer came to you and asked for a favor? What would you do?"

He swallowed hard. "I'd do whatever he wanted because he—and the rest of you guys—are the closest thing I'll ever have to a family ever again."

I motioned through the windshield. "Keep driving. I'll tell you when to turn."

He nodded and made himself comfortable behind the wheel.

I took a long breath to steady myself for what was about to come out of my mouth. "You were a good football player, huh?"

The look in his eyes said he was reliving the glory days of not so long ago. "Yeah, I was pretty good."

I scoffed. "I watched some tape. You were better than pretty good. You set the all-time NCAA Division-One record for most interceptions by a safety in a single season."

He nodded, and I admired what I perceived as humility until he said, "That's not a bad stat, but the one I'm really proud of is most pick-sixes by not only a free safety, but by any player in D-One history. And I did it in less than three full seasons. I was going to stack some serious paper when the draft rolled around, but after what happened to my family, suddenly, everything called a 'game' felt useless."

We sat in silence as the sand-covered road hummed beneath us. "I guess you can't really understand what it's like to see your whole family murdered. It screwed me up, and I was done."

It took another deep breath for me to say, "I think I know how you feel. I was barely a teenager when my parents and sister were murdered by some leftist guerrillas in Panama."

He hit the brakes and slid the truck to a stop. "What? Are you serious?"

I didn't bother checking the mirror. Instead, I nodded. "Yep. I didn't see it happen, but I know how it feels. I was just a kid, though. You were an adult."

"Wait a minute," he said. "What were your parents and sister doing in Panama?"

"They were missionaries and aid workers, as far as anybody knew, but there was a lot more to them than just spreading the Gospel and passing out antibiotics. They worked for the State Department or something like that. Some people called them spies, but based on what I've learned from people who knew them best, they were communist-killing, badass freedom fighters operating under the cover of missionaries."

Gator sat in stunned silence for a long moment. "So, this is like a family tradition for you."

"I wouldn't go that far. I played a little baseball in school, and like you, I wasn't bad. I never intercepted any passes and ran them back for a touchdown, but I still hold the D-One record for gunning down the most runners attempting to steal."

"No way!"

I said, "They named a whole section after me at Foley Field in Athens."

"You played at Georgia?"

"Yep."

"If you were that good, why aren't you in the majors right now?"

I held up my scarred right wrist and hand. "A little trainwreck at home plate in ninety-six relegated me to the ranks of the has-beens. Some folks who knew and worked with my parents recruited me into this, and here we are, a couple of old ballers blocking a one-lane dirt road somewhere in Terrebonne Parish, Louisiana."

He shook his head and pressed the accelerator. "What a pair we make."

We drove for several miles without a word until I said, "Turn left when you can, and let's head south."

He made the turn, and we followed the even rougher road toward the Gulf.

I pointed to a shack on the edge of what qualified as a road in that part of the world. "Pull in there."

The area beside the structure that wasn't swamp held a dozen pickup trucks and perhaps half that many people standing beneath a lean-to with smoke pouring from a concrete block pit.

We stepped from our rented truck and ambled toward the scene.

Gator whispered, "Please tell me you won't try to speak Cajun with these guys."

"Watch and learn, Grasshopper."

One of the men gathered around the pit, looked up, and spat a long stream of tobacco juice onto the dusty ground. "*Comment ça va?*"

I shrugged. "*Laissez les bon temps rouler.*"

That got a hearty chuckle, and the man said, "Go on inside, you. I bring in da chicken when it done, me."

We turned for the open door of the shack, and Gator continued whispering. "What was that?"

"I think I said 'Let the good times roll,' but I'm not sure."

He shook his head. "You're going to get us killed."

I gave him a wink. "Not before lunch."

I had no expectation of a hostess inside the door, but I also didn't expect to see the small place packed with people. Most of them sounded a lot like the guys outside by the fire pit, but a few sounded more like Gator and me.

A woman stomped by, wiping her hands on a dirty towel. "You two eatin'?"

"Yes, ma'am."

She gestured toward the corner. "It'll be ready soon."

We planted ourselves at the only empty table, and Gator asked, "Have you seen a menu?"

Before I could answer, two Styrofoam cups of water and two bottled beers landed on our table.

My partner watched the lady come, deposit the drinks, and vanish. "Okay...that's different." He never stopped scanning the crowd, and he drummed his fingertips against the well-worn table.

"Relax," I said. "We're just having lunch."

"I'm way out of my element here."

"Is it the people?"

He leaned back and scanned the room again as if memorizing every face. "You're doing that Dr. Freud thing, aren't you?"

I laughed. "I have no idea what you're talking about, but Freud was wrong about everything."

He sighed. "It's not really the people that freak me out. It's the fact that it's impossible to predict what's going to happen next. When we're downrange, I expect people to shoot at me, and I know exactly what to do when that happens. Down here, though, I've got no idea what's going on. It's like the rules of the rest of the world don't apply here."

"Keep talking," I said.

He pulled himself closer to the table. "I mean, think about it. What language do they speak?"

Before giving me a chance to answer, he threw up his hands. "Nobody knows. It's not a real language. They suck the brains out of crawfish heads, for Pete's sake. Alligators eat everything made out of meat except for severed body parts. What's that about?"

He grew louder with every word, so I stepped in. "Let's not have this conversation quite so loud. I'd like to make it through lunch without starting a fight in this place."

"Sorry," he said. "I'm just letting it all out. And the voodoo... My God, voodoo? Really?"

In the middle of his rant, the same young lady who'd delivered our drinks appeared again and plopped two paper plates in front of us. Each had a mound of white rice several inches thick with half of a grilled chicken resting on top. As we sat admiring the feast before us, a second lady appeared with two enormous bowls of something and slid them onto the table. She drew a handful of silverware from her back pocket and dropped it between us. "If you need more, just yell out." She vanished, leaving us in utter disbelief at the amount of food on our table.

Gator said, "Mongo's going to love this place." A few seconds later, he wiped his mouth. "Forget all that stuff I said earlier. I'm never leaving. This is the best chicken I've ever had."

We ate for half an hour, but it would've been impossible to prove it by what remained on our plates. The contents of the bowls proved to be gumbo, and I wanted fifty gallons of it to go.

Gator's beard was dripping with gumbo and chicken grease, but I never remember seeing him happier...unless Cecilia was involved.

"It looks like you're enjoying yourself," I said.

He leaned back and exhaled a long breath. "I love everything about this place."

Before I could remind him how out of his element he'd been only minutes before, someone threw a table through the air, landing it upside down on a second table.

Gator spun in his chair and reached for his pistol, but I got a hand on his arm before he could draw. "Don't. It's not our fight. There's a door ten feet behind me and a pair of windows fifteen feet to your left."

The table wasn't the only thing that became airborne. A massive man plucked a much younger man from his chair and threw him over his head and onto the metal counter near the front door. The victim expelled every drop of air in his lungs at the instant of impact and gasped as he worked to refill his chest.

The giant drew a knife that would be considered a machete in most circles and swung it like a broadsword toward his target. With air finally back in his lungs, the younger man rolled from the countertop and yanked a cast-iron skillet from a hook. The makeshift shield provided just enough protection to ward off the wildly swinging blade.

The fight continued through the front door and onto the sandy ground. A lucky swing of the skillet knocked the knife from the bigger man's hand and sent it skittering beneath our truck.

Clear of the front door, Gator and I stepped between a pair of trucks, putting a few thousand pounds of steel between us and the fighters.

The smaller man was much faster than his attacker, and he dived into the cab of a truck I assumed was his, but the escape was far from over. The engine roared to life, and sand and gravel exploded from the rear tires, but Mongo's twin brother was still on a rampage. He hoisted a concrete block in each hand and hurled them toward the fleeing truck. The first hit the windshield directly in front of the terrified driver, and the second found its way through the open driver's side window. The block struck the man's head and shoulders and sent blood spraying all over the interior of the truck.

The enormous man thrust both massive arms through the window and grabbed the man behind the wheel as the truck continued rolling toward the bayou. With a powerful twist of his body, he yanked the smaller man through the window and onto the road just as the front wheels of the truck left solid ground.

No one seemed concerned about the truck sinking in the black water. Everyone's attention was focused on the battle royale in the middle of the dirt street. Blood continued flowing from the younger man's head, but he wasn't unconscious. The rate at which the crimson flow was leaving his head said his eyes wouldn't be open much longer, and if Goliath had his way, it was likely the young man would never open those eyes again.

Either of us could've ended the fight with the press of a trigger, but we were outsiders, and picking sides in a fight we didn't understand had great potential to end badly for us, no matter how well armed we were.

The big man straddled his victim and raised a sledgehammer fist above his head. The coming blow would surely render the man unconscious and deliver more than a few fractures to his face.

"We've got to do something," Gator said. "He's going to kill that guy."

From my vantage point, I could see something Gator could not. A second truck threw sand into the air behind it as it accelerated toward the melee. In the bed of the truck stood a man in cutoff jeans and no shirt, swinging a lasso over his head. With the precision of a professional rodeo cowboy, he floated the lariat through the air and around the monster's torso. The instant the rope came taut, the Cajun cowboy released it from his hands, and I saw for the first time that the other end of the rope was tied to the trailer hitch of the truck.

The beast of a man who was an instant away from ending the young man's life suddenly left the ground and landed on his back as he was dragged across the roadway at what must've been twenty miles per hour.

Chapter 7
Call Me Doctor

Pivotal moments in life, and especially in tactical operations, fall in place at our feet like beautifully wrapped packages from Heaven, and the one in front of me was adorned with an enormous red bow.

I grabbed Gator's arm. "Get the kit from the truck and call me Doctor."

Clark Johnson taught me more than anyone else by dragging me into situations no one really wanted to encounter, and it had become my turn to pass that wisdom and knowledge on to the next generation. Gator and I were more alike than anyone could imagine, but his bank of experience was just as empty as mine had been fifteen years before.

By the time I slid to a stop on one knee beside the bloody, convulsing body in the middle of the road, my assessment of the scene was well underway. His chest was rising and falling, and that was a good sign, but his feet were pointed sharply downward. The neurological symptoms would come into play several steps down the checklist, but the immediate concerns were ensuring airway, breathing, and circulation. The rise and fall of his chest took care of the first two, and a pair of fingers on the man's wrist, coupled with the blood flowing from his head, covered circulation.

Gator dropped the med kit beside me. "What do you need, Doctor?"

At the sound of the revered title, the circled crowd subconsciously took a step backward to give me room to work. Although I'd never be a medical doctor, I had enough battlefield medical training to likely keep the young man alive long enough to put him into the hands of the help he truly required.

I extended a hand. "C-collar."

Gator placed the device in my palm, and I carefully situated it around the victim's neck and secured the Velcro strap. With his neck and spine protected, I said, "Large-bore IV."

Gator pulled an IV bag of saline from the kit and laid a catheter and needle in my hand. As I felt for a vein, Gator applied layers of dressing to the head wounds caused by the flying cinderblock. Once the catheter was in place, I connected the bag of fluid and pointed toward the cleanest man in the gathered crowd. "You! Come here."

He lunged forward, and I stuck the bag in his hand. "Hold this and keep it above your belt, but don't squeeze it."

He took the bag. "Whatever you say, Doctor. Is he alive?"

I ignored the question, mostly for dramatic effect. The man wasn't going to die from his wounds, but his condition was serious enough to require a good trauma team in a good hospital, and from what I saw, no such facility existed in Terrebonne Parish.

With the ABCs done, it was time for triage. I pulled open one eyelid at a time and studied the pupils. What I saw wasn't good. They were dilated to at least twice the size they should've been, and they showed no reaction to my penlight. His convulsions slowed until he finally lay still on his back, but his feet were still pointed downward at an extremely unnatural position.

Convinced he was stable enough to transport, I looked up. "I need something I can use as a backboard. Anything that's six feet long and flat will work."

A man appeared with a table from inside the restaurant. "How 'bout dis here?"

I patted the ground beside the victim. "Perfect. Rip off the legs and lay it down here."

With Gator's help, I strapped the unconscious man onto the table and loaded him into the bed of our rented truck. I closed the tailgate and climbed into the truck bed. "Does anybody know this guy well?"

A small man in a grimy Chevron Oil hat leaned around the people in front of him. "Yeah, I know him. He's my brother."

"Get in," I said.

Gator leaned over the sidewall of the truck. "Where are we going?"

"Get us to the airport, double-quick."

He leapt behind the wheel, and in seconds, we were making well over sixty miles per hour and leaving a cloud of dust in our wake.

"What's your name?" I asked the man.

"Billy. Is he gonna be all right?"

"Nice to meet you, Billy. I'm Chase. If we can get him to the hospital in New Orleans fast enough, he should survive."

"New Orleans?" Billy almost yelled. "That's over an hour."

"Don't worry. We'll get him there in no time. What's your brother's name?"

"Cory."

"Last name?"

He said, "Campbell. Cory Campbell. He just turned twenty-one."

I wrote his name and age on the pad from the med kit. "Does he have any medical conditions?"

"Yeah, his head is busted open!"

"We're managing his injuries. I need to know if he has any preexisting conditions."

He shook his head. "No, he's twenty-one. He ain't got no medical conditions."

"How about an address?" I asked.

He gave me the information, and I added it to the notes.

"Do you have any idea what the fight was about?"

He looked away as the wind in the bed of the truck threatened to yank his hat from his head.

I spoke louder. "What was the fight about?"

"Why does that matter?"

"The police are going to ask, so I'd like to be able to tell them what happened."

"He got his ass beat for messing with the wrong guy's daughter. That's what happened. I told him to leave that girl alone, but he's stubborn as a stump."

I ran through another status check on Cory and then asked, "So, it was a fight over a girl?"

Billy said, "Yeah. Me and Cory work the Chevron Genesis rig offshore, and there's a Cajun girl in the office named Sammi. She's trouble, but she's sure-nuff something to look at. All the guys... Aww, never mind. Anyway, the guy who did this to my brother, he's Sammi's daddy."

"Does he work the rig, too?"

"He did before he got hurt, but he's on disability now."

"Disability?" I asked. "He didn't look disabled to me."

"You should've seen him before the accident."

I had ignored my patient long enough, so I connected a second bag of fluid when the first one ran dry, and I double-checked his vitals. "He's going to be all right, Billy. I'm sure he has a concussion, but hopefully not a TBI."

He cocked his head and studied his unconscious brother. "TBI?"

"Yes, a traumatic brain injury. He's showing some signs, but the doctors should be able to rule that out after some tests at the hospital."

"Doctors?" he said. "But you're his doctor."

I shook my head. "I'm not that kind of doctor. Cory will be under the care of a neurosurgeon when we get him to the hospital."

"He'll have to have surgery?"

"We're getting ahead of ourselves. Right now, we need to focus on keeping him stable and getting him to the hospital as quickly as possible."

He said, "Chevron has a bunch of helicopters. Maybe we could get one of them."

Gator pulled us through the gate and onto the parking apron at the airport, and I pointed toward the Caravan. "We've got that."

Billy grinned, and we carried Cory from the bed of the truck and up the ladder into the cabin of the plane.

Gator took a knee beside me on the floor. "I've got him from here."

I parked Billy in a seat, and he buckled his belt. "Are you a doctor, too?"

Gator shook his head, but instead of sticking around to hear his answer, I hopped into the left seat and spun up the turbine. I leveled off at twenty-five hundred feet, headed straight for downtown New Orleans.

Leaning into the aisle, I asked, "Is everything all right back there?"

Gator said, "He's convulsing again, but not too bad."

"Keep him on the backboard, and don't let him hurt himself. I need you to get East Jefferson ER on the phone and give them Cory's info. Tell them we'll land in the canal in less than fifteen minutes."

Gator looked up. "The canal?"

"Yeah, there's a big canal right beside the ER."

He stared at me with a look of disbelief, so I snapped my fingers. "Make the call."

He yanked his phone from his pocket, and I turned my attention back to flying the airplane.

My curiosity drew my eyes back into the cabin, where Gator knelt with his phone pressed to the side of his face. I couldn't hear the conversation, but I could imagine what the nurse on the other end of the line was about to say.

Gator covered the phone with a hand and yelled, "They say you can't land in the canal. They want us to land at the airport, and they'll have an ambulance meet us there."

"Tell them to get a gurney and a team of orderlies to the canal. We'll splash down in less than five minutes."

Gator might've been the new guy, but given the choice between picking a fight with me six feet away or a nurse on the phone, he'd go to war with the nurse every time.

The Louis Armstrong International Airport Class B airspace began at six hundred feet above Lake Pontchartrain, so I maneuvered the Caravan beneath the floor of the airspace to avoid an uncomfortable conversation with air traffic control. Thankfully, the wind was out of the south, so my approach over the lake would end in a nice, slow splashdown in the canal that was never intended to be used by a seaplane piloted by a covert operator with a concussion victim lying in the passenger compartment.

I flew over the canal gate at the north end of the waterway at less than a hundred feet and stared down a long, straight stretch of canal that was only slightly wider than the Caravan's wingspan. Precision flying in a low, lumbering, bulky airplane was akin to one of the Flying Wallendas walking a tightrope a thousand feet above the Earth. Clipping a wingtip on a light pole, fence, or the embankment on either side would spell disaster. Just like the Wallendas, there was no room for error and no safety net.

The wind on the nose stabilized the approach and lowered our groundspeed, but the lower I descended, the less consistent that wind was. The buildings of downtown caused the breeze to swirl and dance, leaving me doing a dance of my own with both feet on the rudder pedals, one hand on the yoke, and one on the throttle. The touchdown wasn't graceful, but it was perfectly positioned. The floats slid across the surface until I pulled the power to idle and flattened the propeller. We drifted to a stop, pointing south, with the hospital off our right wingtip. If the engineers at Cessna had chosen to put a passenger compartment door on the starboard side of the 208, my maneuvering would've been complete, but in their infinite wisdom, they left out that particular door. Their oversight meant I had to make a 180-degree turn in the canal to position the port side of the plane against the bank of the canal on the hospital side.

I lowered the water rudders and directed us toward the eastern bank as far as we could go without running aground. The wind from the south would do its best to weathervane the Caravan, keeping her tail pointed northward, but I had no choice but to force the plane into the turn. It took a lot of power and all the right rudder the plane possessed, but I finally completed the maneuver and brushed the portside pontoon against the bank of the canal.

Four orderlies descended the bank, dragging a backboard down the slope. As I stepped from the cockpit and climbed down the ladder, two of the orderlies climbed the stern ladder and made their way into the cabin. Digging my heels into the grassy embankment, I held the shoreline tightly to keep the Caravan from drifting away.

Gator followed the orderlies down the stairs, helping them carry Cory Campbell strapped to the broken tabletop. As they stepped from the pontoon and onto the slope, my partner gave me a thumbs-up, and I said, "I'll meet you in the ER ASAP."

He glanced between me and the Caravan. "Are you leaving the plane here?"

I curled a finger, summoning him to leave Cory with the orderlies. He followed my command and joined me on the bank.

I said, "We can't leave her here. I'll take it to Lakefront Airport about a mile east and grab a cab. I want you to stay with Billy, and don't let him out of your sight. He's our best shot at figuring out what's going on in that bayou, and he owes us a favor."

Chapter 8

Bring in the Cavalry

I expected to see half a dozen New Orleans police cruisers waiting for me on the ramp at Lakefront Airport, but the only reception party in sight was a lineman in a yellow reflective vest waving me to a parking spot. He guided me to a stop, and I shut down the turbine.

"Good afternoon," he said, glancing at his watch. "Will you be overnight?"

"Good afternoon. I'll only be here a couple of hours, but if you could top her off, I'd appreciate it."

I slipped him a folded bill, and he pocketed it without looking. There's no rule stating a pilot should tip a lineman, but experience taught me a few bucks went a long way when I needed a favor on a parking ramp.

He called for the fuel truck over his handheld radio, and I headed through the electric double glass doors and into the FBO. The bright-eyed attendant behind the counter said, "Hello, sir. Welcome to Lakefront. Do you require any service?"

I motioned back through the doors. "He's topping off the tanks. I'll only be here a couple of hours, but I'll need a taxi if you could order one."

She said, "I'll be happy to, but if you'd prefer, you're welcome to use the courtesy car. If you're only going to be here for two hours, that's fine."

I handed over my driver's license and signed the logbook for the courtesy car. She made a copy, and I slid my license back into my wallet. "Do you need a credit card?"

She typed a few characters and studied the computer monitor. "No, sir. You have a card on file. We can bill that one for the fuel, and of course, there's no charge for the car."

I took the keys and found the sedan parked exactly where she said it would be. Airport courtesy cars are notoriously clunkers, but that one didn't fit the mold. It was relatively new, and everything seemed to work.

A five-minute drive put me in the ER parking lot, and I hustled inside. Gator and Billy were nowhere in sight, so I stepped to the information counter. "Excuse me, but I'm looking for Cory Campbell. We delivered him by airplane a few minutes ago."

"Are you the pilot?" she asked, and I felt the hammer falling.

"Yes, ma'am. I thought since Cory was critical, landing in the canal was our best bet for getting him into your hands as quickly as possible."

"Well, I've been here almost thirty years, and that's the first time I've ever seen anything like it. Give me just a minute, and I'll find Mr. Campbell for you."

She hunted and pecked her way around the keyboard until she pushed her glasses up the bridge of her nose and said, "It looks like he's in radiology right now, but you can find his brother in curtain seven. Just go straight through those doors and follow the hall around to the left. The curtains are numbered."

"Thank you, ma'am. I'm glad I could deliver a little excitement, but I don't think I'll try it again."

She grinned, and I followed her instructions. She was right. Cory and his hospital bed were missing from behind curtain seven, but Gator and Billy sat in a pair of the most uncomfortable-looking chairs I'd ever seen.

Gator jumped to his feet. "Here, you can have my chair."

I waved a hand. "That's all right. I'd rather stand. How's Cory?"

Gator said, "He's stable but definitely concussed. They just took him for an MRI. They called in the neurosurgeon just in case they have to open him up."

Billy said, "What do you think, Doctor?"

"I told you before that I'm not that kind of doctor, but he's in good hands here. If he were my brother, this is exactly where I'd bring him."

Billy said, "I can't tell you how much it means that you'd go to all that trouble for somebody you don't even know. Maybe it's none of my business, but I'd love to know what a couple of doctors with an airplane were doing messing around Bayou Cane."

Gator's youth floated to the surface. "He's the doctor. I'm just a dude."

Billy said, "Still, what made you guys show up all the way down here?"

I took the floor. "Before we get into that, is there anybody you should call? Does Cory have a wife? Maybe your mother? Anybody?"

He shook his head. "No, it's just me and him. We worked the rigs together in Oklahoma for a couple of years before signing on with the offshore company. The money's a lot better offshore, but we're gone a lot."

I nodded. "I get it. Do you guys live in Bayou Cane?"

"We don't really live nowhere. When we're not on the rig, we live in our RV. It ain't much, but we don't need nothing fancy. We're socking away money so we don't have to work ourselves to death for the rest of our lives."

"I don't know much about oil rigs. What do you do out there?"

A gurney rattled down the hallway, and Billy glanced through the curtain. "That wasn't him. I'm a driller, and Cory's an assistant driller. He's learning fast, so he'll make driller... Well, I guess it depends on how this goes."

"As I said, he's in very good hands here, and if it turns out that they need to get him to UAB or Mayo, they'll make that happen."

Billy studied the white tile floor. "I already told you I really appreciate what you did for Cory, but I still can't figure out what you guys are doing down here."

I wrestled with the decision. Revealing too much might draw more attention than we wanted, but not taking advantage of Billy's local knowledge could be a wasted asset. "We're looking into a situation a little farther southwest. Have you ever heard of a company called Flambeau Exploration?"

Billy huffed. "Yeah. Everybody knows those guys. They're everywhere, but the name of the company is a little deceiving. Nobody named Flambeau owns the operation, and they're not just an exploration company."

"Keep talking."

He repositioned himself in the torture device of a chair. "Most of the time, exploration companies hire a bunch of geologists, and they study every bit of data they can find about possible new sites to drill. After they isolate a particular region, they send out more geologists and engineers to perform test drills in search of ground that's likely to produce a few million barrels of oil. If they find what they're looking for, they sell the information to drilling companies like Chevron or BP. You know, the companies that can afford to buy or lease a site and put up a rig."

I made mental notes as he spoke. "And you said Flambeau is different. How so?"

"They're real tight-lipped about it, so nobody outside the company knows for sure, but rumor has it they like to buy up what's called 'first right of refusal' on oil and mineral rights, and sometimes land, too."

"I'm familiar with the term," I said. "It means the owner can't sell to anyone else without giving Flambeau the first shot, right?"

"Yeah, I guess that's how it works. I hear some of the engineers and geologists talking about them sometimes. They don't have the best reputation in the business, but they're a big player with a ton of money to spend."

It was time to push my luck a little further. "All right. Maybe you can explain this to us. We saw the carcass of a wild pig while we were doing a little exploring last week."

He cocked his head. "Exploring where?"

I said, "We were in a boat. I think they call it a pirogue down here."

"In the bayou?"

I nodded, and he said, "It weren't no pig. Gators would've gobbled it up."

"I'm pretty sure it was a pig. It hadn't been dead long. It was still in good shape, and there were no signs of any gators chewing on it."

He continued shaking his head. "No, that can't be right. Even if it had only been dead a few minutes, the gators would've got to it."

Gator eyed me as if asking how far I was going to take the conversation, so I showed him. "Let's assume I'm right, and it was a pig. Is there anything out there in the bayou that would keep a gator from eating it?"

He chuckled. "A bigger gator, maybe, but those things are eating machines, man. They've got a brain the size of your thumb and only think about two things—eating and...well, you can guess the other one."

"So, there's nothing that you know of that would keep a gator from eating any kind of meat left in the bayou, right?"

He made a show of shaking his head. "Absolutely not. I mean, I've heard of people falling out of boats and half a dozen gators hitting them at the same time. I don't know what you saw, but it weren't no pig."

Before I could press further, someone pulled back the curtain and stepped into the space. A woman in a lab coat and glasses perched on her nose asked, "Mr. Campbell?"

Billy stood. "Yes, ma'am."

She extended her hand and shook his. "Mr. Campbell, I'm Doctor Carmichael, the on-duty radiologist. Your brother's condition is significantly more serious than the doctors initially believed. There is hemorrhaging, and blood and fluid are building up inside his skull. That's likely why he's still unconscious. He's being prepped for surgery to relieve the pressure inside of his skull. If you'll come with me, I'll take you to the surgical waiting area."

Billy turned to me as if begging for answers, so I took a step closer to him. "Go with Dr. Carmichael. They'll take excellent care of Cory."

I handed him my cell phone. "Send yourself a text from my phone so you'll have my number. My name's Chase, and he's...believe it or not, Gator."

He showed no reaction as he manipulated the screen and handed it back. "Thanks. I guess you guys have to go, but can I call you if I've got questions about what's going on with Cory?"

"Call anytime you'd like, but the doctors here will spend as much time as you need to make you understand what's happening."

He extended his hand. "All right. Thanks again for what you did. It sounds like you may have saved Cory's life by getting him here so fast."

Dr. Carmichael said, "Wait a minute. Are you the guys who brought Mr. Campbell here in the seaplane?"

I said, "That was us."

"Then you definitely saved Mr. Campbell's life. He wouldn't have survived another hour without surgery."

Billy stared up at me, but he couldn't seem to put the words together, so I let him off the hook. "Keep us posted, will you? I look forward to meeting Cory when he walks out of here."

At that moment, Billy Campbell did the last thing I expected him to do. He grabbed my shirt with both hands, yanked me toward him, and hugged me as if we were long-lost family. Uncertain what to do or say, I returned the hug.

He wiped his face on my shirt as if trying to dry the tears before I saw them come. "Thank you, man. Cory's all I got left. For real...thank you."

Back in the borrowed airport courtesy car, Gator said, "Okay. Let's start with the pig story. What was that about?"

I made the turn into the Lakefront Airport. "Kenneth is either lying about the body parts, or there's something nobody can explain going on out there."

He said, "Come on. Billy's from Oklahoma. What does he know about gators?"

"He knows how small their brains are."

Gator shook his head. "That dude is as crazy as everybody else down here, and there's some trauma in that bloodline of his."

"I'd agree with that," I said. "I don't know what happened to his folks, but he sure loves his brother."

"What about Flambeau Exploration?"

I tapped the steering wheel, buying time while I came up with an answer. "This thing may have just gotten a lot bigger than we thought. It's time to bring in the cavalry."

Chapter 9
Show Me the Bones

Gator ran the checklist from the left seat while I watched from the right. He never missed an item, and the Pratt and Whitney PT6 turbine whistled to life. The enormous propeller followed and spun up to speed in seconds as the engine converted jet fuel into jet noise. My feet hovered over the rudder pedals just in case our junior pilot needed a gentle correction, but my concerns were wasted. He flew the airplane as precisely as I would've as we climbed out over Lake Pontchartrain and made our turn to the southwest.

The concentration on his face soon gave way to aeronautical euphoria. "I could get used to power like this."

"Just wait 'til you strap on the P-Fifty-One. That's real power."

He chuckled. "I'm a long way from ready for the Mustang."

"You're closer than you think. When this is over, we'll get you finished up in the One-Eighty-Two and move on to bigger and better things. It'll be nice to have another pilot on board."

He let the idea of learning to fly our fleet of magic carpets wash over him for a moment, but he didn't dwell on the idea. It pleased me to see him refocus and ask, "Are you bringing in the whole team?"

"I'm not sure yet. What are you thinking?"

He scoffed. "What difference does it make what I think?"

"You're second-in-command."

He chuckled. "That's because there are only two of us."

"Still, I want your opinion."

He scanned the panel, ensuring everything was in order while his brain converted his thoughts into words. "I think we need to see the bones. If all of this is in that old man's imagination, there's no reason to spend the money to fly the rest of the team in. Maybe he's just going senile, and all that voodoo stuff is starting to feel real to him. If that's the case, there's nothing we can do to help him."

"What if he's telling the truth?"

Gator scratched his beard. "If he's telling the truth and Flambeau Exploration is somehow involved, that's a matter for the police and not a bunch of steely-eyed knuckle-draggers."

"Steely-eyed?"

He shrugged. "I don't know. It just sounded cool in my head."

"Steely-eyed...I like it."

Gator's landing at Houma wasn't perfect, but all of the big pieces stayed on the airplane, and any landing is a good landing if you can use the airplane again.

Gator drove our rented truck back to Kenneth LePine's camper, but I beat him there by almost an hour. When he pulled up, he ambled across the sandy ground and joined Kenneth and me under the shade of a lean-to beside an outbuilding that looked even worse than the old man's so-called house.

"Where you been, you? We's been looking all 'round for you."

Gator grinned and took a seat on an overturned bucket. "I've been doing a little sightseeing and trying to avoid rush hour."

Kenneth cackled. "You is sho'nuff a mess, boy. Your big brother here tells me you's learnin' to fly that big ol' airplane. Do that be the truth?"

He tossed a pebble at my boot. "My brother is a pretty good teacher."

Kenneth said, "Dat ain't all he be tellin' me, no. He say you wanna see dem bones o' dem parts I done burnt up, me."

Gator scratched a circle in the sand with a small stick. "Yes, sir. I'd like to take a look. Are they close by?"

Kenneth stared at Gator for a long moment until my partner finally made eye contact. "Don't you know a man look another man in the eye when he accuse him o' lying, you?"

On the football field, the all-American free safety from K-State could read a quarterback's eyes from twenty yards away, but on his new battlefield, that perception wasn't quite as astute. It was time to watch my protégé grow.

He sat up straight. "I'm not accusing you of lying, sir. I need to know how the bodies were dismembered, and the bones will tell that story."

Kenneth stared through the man who was fifty years his junior as if daring him to look away. "E'rybody know you don't burn bones together. Nobody need that gris-gris on himself, him. I show you dem bones, but you don't put them back together, no. You hear?"

Gator leaned in. "What do you mean?"

Kenneth spat between his bare feet and turned to me. "This kid o' yours sho'nuff got some learnin' to do, him."

I followed Gator's lead and leaned in. "Teach us both."

He threw up his hands. "This ol' body ain't nothin' buts a box for a spirit. Once that box get torn up and thrown apart, it can't never be brought back together, no, 'cause den dat box be wide open for wanderin' spirits who be lookin' for themselves a body for to be inside. Once dem bones is aparts, dey got to stay aparts, and dey ain't no way 'round that. You hear me?"

Gator's eyes said he was ready to write the old man off as a bona fide head case, but he held it together and said, "I guess I learned something today. Don't worry, Mr. LePine. I won't even touch the bones, let alone put them back together."

Kenneth leapt to his feet, shoved Gator off his bucket, and roared with laughter. When he finally stopped, he pointed down at my partner lying on his back. "Ol' Keef just be messin' with you. Dem bones is just bones, boy. Get on up out dat dirt, and I show you where dey be."

I pulled my partner to his feet, and he dusted himself off. He watched Kenneth walk away and said, "That guy's either completely insane or the smartest person on Earth."

I whispered, "I'm leaning toward option number two. Now, come on. Let's go see dem bones, we."

He shook his head. "I thought we agreed you weren't going to do that anymore."

"No, *you* agreed that I wasn't going to do that anymore. *I* made no such agreement."

When Kenneth returned from inside his shack, he led us around the structure and pulled a heavy canvas tarp from atop a contraption neither of us had noticed before that moment. When the tarp was fully removed, a gleaming, flat-bottom airboat with an enormous propeller appeared. He pulled three headsets from a locker beneath a seat and tossed one to each of us.

Before we slipped them on, Gator asked, "Have you ever done this before?"

I said, "What? Hunting burnt bones from dismembered bodies in a bayou? Sure... I've done it too many times to count."

He gave me a shove and covered his ears.

Kenneth fired up the engine, cast off the lines, and hit the throttle. The boat accelerated across the black water doing at least fifty knots. There's never been a carnival ride invented that's more thrilling than the adventure Kenneth LePine took us on that day. We soared through waist-high grass and passages of water barely wide enough to accommodate the beam of the half boat, half flying machine beneath us.

Ten minutes into the joyride, Gator turned, pointed toward the driver's seat, and then back to himself. Kenneth got the message and reduced the throttle until we were drifting across the bayou as slowly as the boat could move.

"Sure! Get up here. Ol' Keef'll shows you how."

Gator climbed into the seat, took the controls in his hands, and we were soon racing across the swamp at breakneck speed. His turns weren't as smooth as Kenneth's, but the young operator obviously had the feel for the machine. Every time I looked back, Gator's grin grew wider, and the engine grew a little louder. I can't deny that I wanted to try my hand at flying the boat, but I wasn't going to steal my partner's thunder.

Kenneth directed with his hands until we came to a slough with a muddy beach at the end. He directed Gator in the beaching technique, and soon, we were resting on somewhat solid ground with the engine silent. We climbed over the bow and mucked our way through the slop until we came to an area that was surprisingly dry. There was even a patch of normal-looking grass. In the center of the grassy area stood a collection of rocks forming a circle. Each stone was stained black from countless fires through the years.

"What is this place?" Gator asked.

Kenneth said, "We calls it the camp. It be da only high ground in da whole parish. This be where all dem young folk come to get dey lovin'. It look to ol' Keef like maybe Cecilia be wantin' to bring you out here, maybe. What you tink of dat, you?"

"She's a nice girl," Gator said. "I wouldn't—"

"She not no girl no more, boy. She a growed woman who need her a man who ain't no coonass. She don't gots no business wasting her life down here in da bayou, her. She need her a good man to takes her outta here. You hears me?"

"How about the bones?" Gator said.

Kenneth shook a finger at him. "You not foolin' ol' Keef. I knows what you thinking inside dat head o' yous."

To my surprise, the old man stepped across the rocks and into the blackened ash of the fire pit. He dug with his hands like a dog excavating a well-hidden, favorite bone. As it turned out, that is exactly what he was doing. A few minutes later, his efforts produced half a dozen charred bones, and he laid them on the grass beside the rocks.

"Der dey be."

"Is that all of them?" Gator asked.

"Dat's all dey is here. I gots me one more place. I can show dat one to you, too."

I knelt beside Gator, and we examined the bones carefully.

Gator touched the tip of one of the bones with his pen. "This looks like a femur."

"It sure does," I said, "but that's not the interesting part."

He rolled the other bones with his pen until we'd seen each one from every angle. Then, he glanced at Kenneth fifty feet away and back at me. "They're not damaged. There's no tool marks and no breaks."

I whistled. "Hey, Mr. LePine. Come here for a minute if you don't mind."

"I don't want to see dem things," he called back.

I stood and closed the distance between us. "I understand. You don't have to look at them again, but I'd like to ask a couple of questions if you wouldn't mind."

He nodded without a word, and I asked, "Did you say there was flesh on those bones before you burned them?"

"Dat's right."

"And you said the gators hadn't eaten any of the flesh, right?"

He said, "They might have ate da part I didn't find, but weren't no teeth marks on dem."

"This is a gruesome question, but did all of the body parts look like they came from the same body?"

He bowed his head. "No, weren't the same person. It was at least five or four different peoples maybe. It ain't right dat dey peoples don't know what happen to dem. Dey prolly worried sick thinking 'bout where dey be at all dis time, dem."

I said, "Why wouldn't the alligators eat the flesh, Mr. LePine?"

He waved a hand around. "How many gators you see 'round here, huh?"

"I figure we scared them off with the airboat."

"Gators ain't 'fraid o' no airboat. Dey ain't smart enough to be 'fraid."

"Then why don't we see any?" I asked.

He dug at the grass with a bare toe. "You wouldn't believe me if I tolds you."

"Try me."

"It be a rougarou. Dat be da onliest thing a gator be 'fraid of."

Chapter 10
That Can't Be Real

"A rougarou?" I asked.

Kenneth LePine nodded. "Dat's da only thing it could be."

"I'm afraid you have me at quite the disadvantage, so you'll need to explain that one to me."

He stared back at me as if I didn't understand sunlight. "You knows the rougarou don't eat nothin' but da heads, hands, and hearts."

"Hold on a minute," I said. "Gator has to hear this."

Kenneth laughed. "Dat boy don't know nothin' 'bout da world, but surely he know 'bout dem rougarou."

"Let's find out."

We reconvened around the makeshift firepit, and I said, "We solved the mystery. It was the rougarou."

Kenneth and I waited for the reaction, and we weren't disappointed.

Gator threw up his hands and said, "Is that supposed to mean something to me?"

Kenneth said, "You know, da rougarou. It lives in da bayou, and even da gators—like you—are afraid of it."

Gator blinked several times in rapid succession. "Is this a real thing?"

Kenneth nodded enthusiastically. "Look 'round. You don't see no gators, does you?"

"No, but that doesn't mean there's a monster out here. What did you call it? A roo-ga-roo?"

"That's right...rougarou. It eats da heads so it knows e'rething dat brain be thinking. It eats dem hands so it knows all da skill dem hands had. And it eats dem hearts so it can live forever. It don't eat nothin' else. That's why der don't be nothin' 'cept legs and arms for ol' Keef to find out here. It rips dem off and throws 'em in the bayou. Once dey get dat rougarou smell on dem, ain't nothin' gonna eat 'em."

Gator hopped to his feet. "Okay, that's enough. You guys are messing with me again, and I'm over it."

The three of us stared at each other in silence until Gator finally said, "You're serious, aren't you? You really think there's a monster out here ripping arms and legs off people and eating the rest of them."

Kenneth glared up at him. "You believe der be a God up in Heaven, don't you?"

Gator nodded. "Of course."

"And you knows dey be peoples who don't believe God is real. You know dis, right?"

"Sure," Gator said. "Atheists."

Kenneth softened his tone. "Do dem folks who don't believe in Him make God not exist?"

"Well, no. That's ridiculous."

Kenneth laid a hand on his shoulder. "Just 'cause you believe something don't be real don't mean it ain't."

Gator squeezed both eyes closed and shook his head. "I want to drive the airboat some more."

Kenneth said, "I gots to put dem bones back if you's through lookin' at 'em."

Gator took a step toward me. "What do you think? Should we keep the bones?"

"Do you want to get caught with bones from a dead body? I'd love to hear you talk your way out of that one. If we need those bones, we know where they are."

He palmed his forehead. "I've got so much to learn."

Gator took us for another high-speed adventure through the bayou aboard his new favorite toy, and I could clearly see an airboat in his future.

Back at Kenneth's humble abode, I was surprised to see a Ford dually pickup truck parked beside the camper. Gator helped tie up the airboat while I investigated the new arrival, and to my delight, my suspicion was confirmed.

Earline came waddling down the makeshift steps with both arms waving. "There you are, Stud Muffin. I was startin' to get worried about you. How are you liking the Cajun life?"

I checked across my shoulder before saying, "I'll be honest. It's a little strange, but the food is amazing."

We threw our arms around each other and hugged until Kenneth and Gator rounded the shack. The old man let out a long, high-pitched sound that I couldn't identify, and he followed it up with, "If it ain't my daughter-in-law. How dat girl be, her?"

Earl pulled away and wrapped her arms around the old Cajun. "How you doin', Crawdaddy?"

Kenneth peered around her as if examining her truck. "You didn't bring dat boy o' mine with you, did you?"

Earl huffed. "No, he ain't with me."

"Good," he said. "He don't belong here no more, him."

Earl brushed hair away from Kenneth's face. "Don't say that, Daddy. It ain't right."

"It be e'rething dat is right. Dat boy made him own decidings, and now he gots to sleep in da nest he made."

Earl cocked her head. "That's my nest now, too, you know."

"I don't holds nothin' 'gainst you for dat nest. Ol' Keef loves you, him do for sure."

"You love Kenny, too. Admit it, you old coot."

He huffed and turned on a bare foot. "You done et, or is you hungry?"

"I'm always hungry, Pops. You know that. But I need to talk to Chase first. Is that all right with you?"

He kept walking. "I'll put on a fire. You come on in when you done."

We climbed into the camper and planted ourselves wherever we could find a spot.

I said, "Sorry about the cramped quarters, but it's all we've got."

Earl laughed. "I lived on a boat for twenty years, Baby Boy. What you talking 'bout, cramped quarters? This is luxury living."

I said, "You're a long way from home, Earl. What are you doing way down here?"

"I told you I needed to talk to you."

I held up my phone. "Don't you have one of these?"

She slapped my hand out of the air. "You know I do, but this kind of talking has more to do with the way you look than the way you sound."

"I'm intrigued. Let's hear it."

She cleared her throat. "Did he tell you about the bones?"

"He did. He even took us to see some of them."

"What do you think?" she asked.

"They're definitely bones."

"Are you going to do it?"

"Do what?" I asked.

"Find out who put 'em out there."

I repositioned on the edge of my bunk. "That's not the kind of thing we do."

She sighed. "Yeah, I know, but it's me asking, and I don't ask for much."

"You've never asked for anything," I said. "Kenneth won't let us call the sheriff, and without Tony and Hunter, criminal investigation isn't in our bag of tricks."

"Haven't you learned anything since you've been down here, Baby Boy?"

"What do you mean?"

"The law ain't how they do things in the bayou, and I guess Kenneth told you about..."

"Going to prison?" I asked.

"Yeah, that. If the sheriff gets involved, he ain't gonna look no farther than right over there in that run-down house, and my daddy-in-law will be headed right back to Angola."

"What's Angola?" Gator asked.

"It's the Louisiana state prison farm. They named it after the plantation that used to stand on the property, and from what I hear, conditions haven't changed a whole lot since those days."

Gator chewed his bottom lip for a moment and then said, "I hate to be that guy, but if we get caught working a murder investigation and not reporting the murders, aren't we on the hook for charges of some kind? I know what we do overseas, but here in the States, if we know multiple murders have been committed and we don't tell somebody, we may end up in Angola with ol' Keef."

I said, "You know how this works. Nobody is obligated to work any mission we're handed, or any mission we pick up, so if I decide we're doing this, you're free to back out and nobody will hold it against you."

He drummed his fingertips against his knees. "I'm the new guy, so I don't have the bankroll you guys have yet. If we get busted, I can't afford a good attorney, and—"

"Stop right there," I said. "If you're working a mission at my direction and operating within the rules of engagement I define, your legal fees are my responsibility."

"What about the Board?" he asked.

My team and I worked for a quasi-governmental organization we knew only as the Board. When missions of national concern came to us, those missions were assigned by the Board, and we reported directly to them on those missions.

"This one is personal," I said. "The Board has nothing to do with anything we do on our own. As a professional courtesy, I notify them before embarking on a freelance gig, but I don't ask them for anything when we're on our own."

He seemed to let the reality of our world sink in. "But what about the equipment?"

"We own it all," I said. "We get reimbursed for expenses on authorized operations as well as drawing our contractual fees, but if we sever ties with the Board, we'll keep all the hardware."

His mouth fell open. "Including the ship?"

The Research Vessel *Lori Danielle* was nothing short of a ship of war masquerading as an oceanographic research platform. Her hundred-person crew was paid from my coffers, but I drew a significant stipend from the Board for her operation, staffing, and maintenance. Between missions, we occasionally took on humanitarian projects, but that happened outside the purview of the Board.

I held out a hand and waggled it. "That's a little murky. I treat the LD like she's ours, but I doubt I'd have the freedom to sell it on the open market if I chose to do so."

He nodded and made small circles in the air with his fingertip. "So, are we doing this?"

I glanced at Earl, and she said, "I've never asked you for anything, Baby Boy, and I promise it'll never happen again, but I need this one. Kenny and his daddy need this one."

"What's the story there?" I asked. "What happened between those two?"

She made a clicking sound for several seconds. "To be honest, I don't know. I know Kenny's side of the story, but his daddy won't talk about it. Apparently, Kenny decided to leave the bayou and make his fortune on his own, and his father told him if he left, he wouldn't get a penny or a piece of land from him when he died."

I scowled. "A penny or a piece of land? Everything Kenneth owns can't be worth more than a few thousand dollars."

Earl shrugged. "I don't know. That's all Kenny's ever told me, and he's done pretty well for himself. He's got four or five million dollars' worth of earthmoving equipment, a lot of trucks, thirty employees, and a bunch of land in Georgia. I don't poke my nose into his business, but it looks to me like everything southwest of New Orleans ain't worth what my lovin' man's got back home."

She paused, stared at the ceiling for a moment, and said, "That's why this is so important to me. I know Kenneth would be proud if he knew how well his son has done, but they've not talked in decades. And if he goes back to prison, there's no chance they'll ever say another word to each other. If you do this for me, I just might be able to get those two stubborn asses in the same room together again before the old man dies."

As the weight of the situation settled on my shoulders, I glanced at Gator, who appeared to be hanging on every word out of Earl's mouth. He was in. I had no doubt. But he and I couldn't pull it off without the rest of the team.

I looked into Earl's weathered, tired eyes. "We're headed back to St. Marys."

She deflated and grimaced as if my words had driven a stake through her enormous heart, so I laid a hand on hers. "We're going home to get the rest of the team, old girl. After all you've done for me, there's no way I could ever say no to you."

Chapter 11
All Your Fault

Gator needed very little direction in turning our eight-thousand-pound pontoon boat into a graceful flying machine, and we climbed out over the vast expanse of the Louisiana bayou. From five hundred feet, it would be easy to believe the whole world was nothing but endless swamp, with fingers of semi-dry land winding through its interior, making way for mankind to infiltrate the timeless firmament. But from a thousand feet, the green and blue of the Gulf developed on the horizon, turning wasteland into the promise of a world beyond black water—a world of color and fragrant breezes whispering their siren call of distant paradise. Turning for home, the skyline of New Orleans formed like apparitions dancing in the distant haze and crying out to the souls of men—souls both godly and pagan—enticing them into the Quarter, where sinner and saint toil side by side, each peddling their own spiritual escape from the madness of modernity.

When we leveled off in cruise flight with the shoreline stretching out beneath us, I said, "You don't have to hand-fly the whole route. Set the autopilot and relax."

The two-and-a-half-hour flight back to St. Marys gave us more than ample time to reflect on what we'd seen, heard, and felt in a world so distant from ours.

"Do you have a theory yet?"

Gator scanned the panel. "Yeah, but you're not going to like it."

My eyes followed his across the instrumentation, not because I didn't trust his scan, but because I didn't trust his inexperience behind jet-fuel-burning turbines. Everything was in the green, and the propeller pulled us through space and time exactly as it had been designed and built to do.

"I don't have to like it for it to be true. Let's hear it."

He said, "I think the old man is crazy. Maybe he's doing it in some kind of voodoo trance brought on by smoking too much whatever and rattling chicken bones, but I think he's killing people and dragging their bodies out to that island so he can burn them. Who knows? Maybe it's some kind of ritual thing. Maybe he does it—like I said—in a trance, and when he comes out of it, he finds these body parts and has no memory of where they came from. I wouldn't say this to Earl, but maybe the old man belongs in Angola."

I sat in silence as the hum of the engine lulled me toward a nap.

Gator said, "See? I told you that you wouldn't like it."

"It's not that I don't like it. It's just that I hope you're wrong."

"Let's hear *your* theory," he said.

"Mine's the same as yours."

* * *

Overconfidence is the only thing more dangerous than lack of confidence, and I was guilty.

Gator flew the traffic pattern at our private airport adjacent to Kings Bay Naval Submarine Base in St. Marys, Georgia, and I was more interested in watching a massive ballistic missile sub motor up the channel behind Cumberland Island than monitoring my student's performance in the left seat. By the time the sub was out of sight and my brain was back in the cockpit, Gator had the Caravan so slow that any aft movement of the yoke would've stalled the wings and destroyed a two-million-dollar airplane and her occupants. My reaction was quick, but not quick enough. My left hand shoved the throttle ahead at the same instant my right eased the yoke forward just enough to keep us flying while the turbine spun up.

The airspeed continued falling, and the Earth kept climbing. I wasn't certain we were going to make the runway. In fact, I wasn't certain we were going to survive.

Finally, the turbine howled and produced the power to save us and the airplane from pranging into the trees. The airspeed increased, and I slowly raised the nose. Soon, we were climbing away from the airport and turning left.

Gator sat with his hands in his lap and the look of defeat on his face. "I'm sorry. I was…"

"Don't be sorry," I said. "Be better. I should've been paying attention. Let's try it again. You have the controls."

We exchanged control, and he flew the pattern beautifully, nailing the approach speeds perfectly, and we gently touched down exactly where we should've.

"Much better. Always fly the numbers, and never forget which airplane you're in."

"I know. I'm—" He caught himself. "I'll do better."

A small Citation jet parked near our main hangar caught my eye. "Whose airplane is that?"

Gator peered through the windshield. "I don't know. I've never seen it before, but the bigger question is, what's it doing here?"

We taxied in and shut down just as Don Maynard, our airport manager, drove up in the fuel truck.

I filled out the logs and climbed down the ladder. "Hey, Don. Whose Citation is that?"

He glanced at the glistening white airplane. "Oh, that's Ms. Anya's, apparently. She brought Skipper and Dr. Mankiller home in it this morning."

"Did you fuel it up yet?"

"Not without your permission. The fuel isn't mine to hand out."

"Top it off for her," I said. "If she's hauling Skipper and Celeste around, it's the least we can do."

* * *

Inside the op center, Skipper, our analyst, had the rest of the team assembled and awaiting our arrival.

"Sorry I'm late," I said. "We tried to crash the Caravan on the way in, but we failed."

Gator shook his head. "You used the wrong pronoun, Chase. *We* didn't try to crash. *I* tried to crash."

I said, "We're a team, and have I got a story to tell you guys."

I laid out what we knew about the situation concerning the floating body parts and Kenny LePine's father in the bayou. It should've taken two minutes, but I struggled to find the right words to describe what Gator and I saw on our little excursion.

Clark, a former Green Beret and my current handler, knocked on the table. "Great story, but what's it got to do with us?"

"Earl asked us to look into it for Kenny's father, and saying no to Earl isn't something I can stomach."

"What does she expect us to do?" he asked.

I glanced at Gator, and he stared back with a blank expression. Since he didn't have an answer, I did my best to pull one out of the air. "I guess she wants us to figure out who's killing people and dumping their body parts in the bayou around Kenneth LePine's house."

"You guess?" Clark asked. "You don't have a definitive objective?"

I said, "That is the objective, unless Mr. LePine is the guilty party."

Mongo, our big-brained giant, asked, "Are you saying Kenny's father might be killing people?"

I shrugged. "It's possible, and at this point, it seems like the most likely answer. The first thing I learned in this job, though, is that things are rarely as they appear, and if they are, we perceived them incorrectly the first time."

"I'm not finished," Mongo said. "Are you telling us we're doing this gig, or is this just a roundtable to brainstorm some ideas?"

I said, "You know I don't assign missions. I invite you to join me, and that's what's happening here. Gator and I are in. I'd love to have your help, but as always, this one's not mandatory."

Mongo was first to answer. "I've got nothing better to do. Count me in."

Our chief pilot, Disco, said, "It sounds like somebody needs to come along who doesn't try to wreck perfectly good airplanes, so I'll go."

Singer, our Southern Baptist sniper, picked at his fingernails. "They like to mess around with a little voodoo down there, don't they?"

Gator huffed. "That's the understatement of the year. Those people are crazy."

I jumped in. "I just happen to know you don't think all of them are crazy. There's a pretty little Cajun queen you seem to have a great deal of admiration for."

A chorus of "Ooh" rose from the table, and Gator retaliated. "Chase has it all wrong. She came to me. I didn't go after her."

"Yeah? I noticed you didn't push her away."

He groaned. "Why don't we get back to business and leave my love life out of it?"

That scored a second round of reactions from around the table, and I couldn't resist saying, "Oh, so now it's love, is it?"

Gator threw a pencil at me. "Cut it out."

I threw up my hands. "I'm just telling the truth. You know she woke up in your bed two days ago, and you're carrying her rosary beads around."

Singer perked up. "Rosary beads? What are you doing with those?"

"Nothing," Gator said. "I'm not doing anything with them. She gave them to me to ward off the voodoo spirits."

"Oh, for God's sake," Singer said. "Give me those beads."

Gator glared at me. "This is all your fault, and you know it." He pulled the beads from his pack and slid them across the table.

Singer caught them with a hooked finger and held them up in front of him. "Hmm. So, this is your shield against voodoo, huh?"

Gator shook his head. "If I had known what this meeting was going to turn into, I would've stayed in the bayou. This is a tough crowd."

"Don't change the subject," Singer said. "We're talking about this string of beads."

Gator sighed. "Okay, okay. Here's the truth. I like the girl. She's cool. She gave me the beads, and I like that they make me think of her."

Singer slid the icon back across the table. "In that case, put them around your neck. What good are they hidden away in your pack?"

Gator froze, obviously uncertain how to take Singer's advice, and Skipper spoke up for the first time. "I think that's great, Gator. Good for you."

"Thank you," he said as he tossed the beads over his head and around his neck. They disappeared inside his shirt, and I reclaimed the floor.

"How about you, Shawn? Are you in?"

Shawn was the newest member of the team, but far from the least experienced. He was a Navy SEAL special warfare combat crewman, so having him aboard multiplied our team's capabilities exponentially. Having lost Hunter from the team, Shawn quickly became our water-borne operations officer and was already proving his value every time we got wet. His skill set would prove invaluable in the flooded world of the bayous.

Shawn studied the faces in the room and said, "I don't understand."

"What don't you understand?" I asked.

"Does anybody ever opt out of a mission?"

"It hasn't happened yet, but it's always an option."

He scowled. "If I'm an option, why am I on the team?"

I leaned back in my chair. "I understand your confusion now. Think about it this way... If we're on a mission and you get shot in the head, are we supposed to abandon the mission, pack up, and go home? Everybody in this room is a hardcore operator, and we rely on each other every step of the way. However, no one here is so important that we can't work without them. I want you on every mission, but I'll never turn one down just because you aren't coming."

To my surprise, Shawn scribbled on a scrap of paper, quickly folded it into an airplane, and tossed it toward me. I snatched it from the air. "What's this?"

"It's my proxy. If you're in, I'm in."

Clark shoved the SEAL. "Nice! Way to suck up to the boss."

"That's not sucking up. That's commitment."

In seconds, the air above the conference table was congested with tiny paper airplanes full of comments soaring my way.

"I guess that settles it," I said. "Now to the paperwork. Skipper, what do you have for us?"

She struck a key and spun to face the team. "I just sent you the briefing packet. Let's talk about Gator's girlfriend first since she's the most interesting character in this play. She's Cecilia Lachaussee, no middle name. Undergrad in geology and master's degrees in agronomy and soil science. She's put in the hours for her doctorate but apparently hasn't defended or published her thesis yet. I'll keep digging for that. She's a recent contractor for Flambeau Exploration, an enormous oil and natural gas exploration company based in Buenos Aires. And get this... She holds a sixteen-hundred-ton Coast Guard Master's license and a commercial helicopter license." She paused and eyed Gator. "Did you know any of that?"

"Nope, but I do know she can suck the brains out of crawfish faster than anybody I know."

Skipper frowned. "Is that a euphemism for something dirty?"

"No, it's a real thing they do down there. Just wait. You'll see."

Skipper rolled her eyes. "Anyway...back to the briefing. Let's talk about Kenneth LePine the Second. He's almost as interesting as Cecilia. He was a long-range reconnaissance patrol Ranger in Vietnam. He came away with a Silver Star, a Bronze Star for valor, two Purple Hearts, and Airborne and Air Assault qualifications. After nineteen seventy-one, he dropped off the face of the Earth. No driver's license, no Social Security records, and he's never filed a federal income tax return. But..." She looked up, apparently to make sure we were all paying attention. "But, he owns almost six thousand arpents in two parishes in Louisiana."

I raised a finger. "Okay, I'll be the one to ask. What's an arpent?"

Skipper said, "It's okay. I didn't know either. It's like a French acre. It works out to be about eighty-five percent of an American acre, so that means Kenneth LePine owns around five thousand acres of bayous."

Disco said, "Who would want five thousand acres of bayous? That's gotta be worth at least two or three hundred bucks, wouldn't you think?"

That got a chuckle, but I had questions. "Do you have a plat of the property he owns?"

She grinned. "I thought you'd never ask. Feast your eyes on the big screen."

Gator and I stood in unison and approached the monitor. Our fingers landed on the slough at the same instant, and he said, "That's where he claims to have found the body parts."

Skipper widened her gaze. "Okay, that's unexpected, but I'm not finished."

I said, "Hold on a second. Is this all the property he owns?"

Skipper moved the cursor to highlight the boundary of Kenneth's land. "Yeah. Everything inside the yellow line is his."

"And it's contiguous?"

She nodded. "Yes."

I stared at the map for a long time, trying to imagine it overlaying the bayou where Gator and I had spent the past several days. "Did he buy it a little at a time or all at once?"

"It's all on one deed from nineteen sixty-one."

"What about his prison time?" I asked. "Didn't that show up in his background check?"

"It did, but that's the other strange thing I want you to see. He went to Angola State Prison Farm in September of nineteen seventy-four, but there's no record of him being transferred, released, escaping, or dying."

Chapter 12
Jealous Much?

I was intrigued, but I didn't want to get bogged down. We still had a lot of information and planning to cover, so I kept my inquisition brief. "Does Angola have the records from the seventies?"

Skipper huffed. "Yes, but they're not searchable like modern records. Somebody scanned the paper files and turned them into one enormous, old-school PDF document. It's basically a poor-quality Xerox copy of already poor-quality paper files. It's a mess."

"Could you have missed his release?"

"Sure, but I had the computer devour every letter of the PDF, searching for anything relating to anyone named Kenneth and/or LePine. His intake is there, but nothing after that."

I said, "Let's put that one on the back burner and come back to it later. Let's talk about the land. I want to see a map of who owns the land adjoining Kenneth's. Can you do that?"

"Sure," she said, "but it won't be quick. You'll have to give the computer and me a couple of days. Those counties—or parishes—down there aren't exactly on the cutting edge of technology. Most property records are available, but they're mostly handwritten in plat books. I even found one that had been surveyed in nineteen thirty-eight by a guy on horseback. He measured the property lines by counting the horse's strides."

"Most of the land is flooded bayous down there," I said. "How could he survey it on horseback?"

She chuckled. "You'll love this. Apparently, his horse's dry stride was seven-tenths of a yard, and his wet-to-the-stirrups stride was half of a yard."

"That was in the deed?"

"It was. I told you. It's a different world down there."

"Let's move on," I said. "Where's the ship?"

She brought up a chart of the Caribbean and pointed toward the Dry Tortugas with her cursor. "Right there. Captain Sprayberry gave the crew three weeks' liberty so they could go home and spend time with their families. They're on recall, of course, so if we need them, they can be back aboard in seventy-two hours."

I glanced at the location on the chart. "If he doesn't have a crew, what's he doing at sea? Shouldn't he be in port somewhere?"

"Apparently, his crew would rather stay with the ship. A few of them took the time off, but over seventy percent of them stayed on board. They've been playing in the Keys for a week. They're apparently doing some scuba diving and sunbathing as we speak."

"Good. Those guys deserve a break," I said. "Unfortunately, though, we're going to need them. Get the captain on the horn if you would, please."

A few seconds later, Captain Barry Sprayberry's voice filled the air from the speaker on the center of the conference table. "Afternoon, Chase. How's the saving-the-world business?"

"Business is good, my friend. That's why I'm calling. We need you and your boat in Terrebonne Bay, just west of Grand Isle, Louisiana."

"Are you starting a war with the shrimpers?"

"Not exactly. It's not that kind of mission. You'll be a floating hotel and op center more than anything else. Hopefully, you won't have to shoot at anybody, and nobody will be shooting at you."

"That sounds boring," he said. "When do you need us?"

"Skipper tells me you're on a reduced crew at the moment."

"Yeah, but don't worry about that. We've got plenty of folks on board to handle an assignment like you're describing. If you're sure there won't be any need to sink anyone, we can be there in twenty-four hours."

"I can't imagine who we'd shoot at, but don't yank your divers out of the water. Let them play. Have Gun Bunny pick us up at the airport in Houma, Louisiana, in forty-eight hours."

He said, "No problem, boss. Are we trying to hide? If so, that's tough inshore. There are so many oil rigs, crew boats, service vessels, and helicopters out there, there's no way to hide in that bay."

"I'm not particularly concerned about hiding," I said. "Accommodations in that part of the world are hard to come by, so as I said, I'm using your warship as a Motel Six."

"It all pays the same," he said. "We can come in as far as Bayou Lafourche. Halliburton has a port, and we've got carte blanche with them."

I gave his offer some thought. "For now, let's lay off far enough to avoid unnecessary attention. We may change plans, but for now, let's keep a low profile."

"You got it. We'll see you in two days."

Skipper ended the call and asked, "What's next?"

"Let's load out and get ready to head into the bayou."

She spun from her station at the console. "There's one more thing you might want to do before you start packing."

I couldn't put my finger on it, but something about the tone of her voice told me I was about to step to the plate and swing at a nasty curveball. "What is it?"

"It's waiting for you in the gazebo."

The mystery was solved, and what waited for me in the gazebo was far more dangerous than any curveball.

I turned to Gator. "Take Shawn to the armory and load him out."

The former SEAL said, "I'm pretty well stocked for gear, but thanks."

I said, "The gear you have now... Is it your personal kit?" He nodded, and I said, "Go with Gator and build two more kits. One will stay in the armory aboard the ship, and the other will be your daily kit. I don't want you to use your personal gear. We'll provide you with everything you could need or want. Don't be shy. Consider it an all-expenses-paid shopping spree."

He said, "You're the boss."

On my way through the kitchen, I pulled two bottles of water from the refrigerator and headed through the back door. The steps leading from the back gallery and onto the lawn were replicas of the originals that were there for over a century before the fire. I'd stood on those steps beside Penny the day my great uncle, Judge Bernard Henry Huntsinger, married us on a day that seemed like both yesterday and a thousand years in the past.

The carpenters incorporated one of the few pieces of the original house back into those steps during the reconstruction. It was a charred, triangular piece of an original tread, and every time I saw it, the memory of my wedding day flooded my mind.

And now, in spite of who and what awaited me in the gazebo, the memories still came. Her long, blonde hair glistened in the late-afternoon sun and danced on the gentle breeze coming off the North River. The gazebo was the center of my world, the place to which I retreated when everything became too much. Jack Daniel's and I spent countless hours inside that structure, and the instant I saw her, I knew I should've left the water inside and brought the bottle of Old Number 7 instead.

"Hello, Anya."

Anastasia Anya Burinkova had almost been my end, but somehow, we'd both survived each other. She was dispatched from the Kremlin to find, flip, or kill the newly minted American operative fifteen years before, but the Kremlin's plan came apart at the seams. Mother Russia's beautiful sparrow found, enticed, and enchanted me, but instead of flipping me to provide American intel to the *Sluzhba vneshney razvedki Rossiyskoy Federatsii,* the irresistible SVR officer traded in her Russian credentials for a shiny new American passport with the name

Ana Fulton emblazoned across the first page. I had been in love with her back then, and she was still in love.

"Hello, my Chasechka. Is beautiful afternoon, yes?"

"It is," I said. "Thank you for bringing Skipper home."

"Of course."

I was convinced her Russian accent remained by choice. Her English was as good or better than mine, but it would sound and feel odd if she spoke without sounding like a recent export from Moscow.

"It sounds like you guys had a good time. Thank you for doing that for her. She needed the time away."

"I told to her she can come to island anytime."

"That's kind of you," I said. "Nice airplane, by the way."

She'd learned to smile at State School 4 on the banks of the Volga River when the KGB taught her to make American men melt in the palm of her hand. The smile she wore that day hadn't been coached. It was sincere, and even more beautiful than the one she'd learned behind the stone walls of Sparrow School.

She said, "Thank you. It is Citation jet, but you know this already, yes?"

"I guess I didn't know you were type rated in the Citation."

She tilted her head. "There are many things you do not know about me, Chasechka, but I want you to know them."

"You look..." I didn't finish the compliment, but she caught it anyway. Her fingertips explored her jawline, and she brushed the back of her hand against her cheek. "I had cosmetic surgery to restore my face. I am ashamed of my own vanity, but I did not like ugly scars. You think I am again beautiful, no?"

There was no way to escape the trap into which I'd willingly stepped, so I put my psychological education to work. "You've always been beautiful, Anya."

I expected her to take the conversation down a path I wasn't willing to walk with her, but to my surprise, she said, "You have mission, yes?"

"Sort of."

She frowned. "Sort of? What does this mean?"

"We have a self-imposed assignment, but it's not really a mission."

She stared across the river as a pair of pelicans careened into the water from dozens of feet above. "Is time of day for birds to be hungry."

"Why are you here?" I asked.

Her attention didn't leave the pelicans. "I could not leave without seeing you. There will come time when you will not come home from mission. Thought of this day makes me sad, so if I have opportunity to see you, even if only for moment, is ridiculous to cast away this moment. I thought maybe you would need help on this mission that is only *sort of* mission."

"I need help understanding it."

She turned to face me. "Is complicated?"

"Maybe. And maybe it's far simpler than I'm making it out to be. I don't know yet. Somebody is dumping body parts into the bayou southwest of New Orleans."

She cocked her head. "This sounds like perfect place to put body parts. Alligators will destroy evidence, and no one will know. Why is this mission for you? Are you now police officer?"

I laughed. "No, I'm definitely not a cop. I'm just trying to help a friend."

"I am your friend, yes?"

The question hit me like a truck, and I didn't have an answer. I had never tried to define the relationship Anya and I shared. Perhaps *friendship* wasn't the correct word, but it was as good as anything else I could come up with. "Yeah, I guess we are."

"This makes me happy. I am available for mission or helping of friend if this is what you want."

I was, again, caught on my heels. I didn't have any tactical need for which Anya was the answer. She possessed skills none of the rest of the team would ever develop, but I had no way to know if that skill set would be necessary in Louisiana. Ultimately, I had a nice private chuckle inside my head thinking about the chaos a beautiful Russian would create in the bayous of Southern Louisiana.

I finally said, "Can I be completely honest with you?"

She tilted her head and smiled just like she'd done when I watched her walking on the beach in St. Thomas. I believed then, as I believed on the day we sat in that gazebo together, that both of those smiles were purely hers with no pretense of any kind. When she spoke, I'm not certain the words left her mouth, but I watched her lips form the word *always*.

"I don't know what I need on this assignment. I don't know if I need you or a posse of U.S. Marshals. Gator's in love with a Cajun girl who sucks the brains out of crawfish. There's an old guy who thinks the spirits of dead people visit him on their way to Heaven. Oh, and he may or may not practice voodoo. Also, he may or may not be dead. They lasso each other and throw concrete blocks through truck windows trying to kill people who mess with their daughters. There's floating dismembered bodies—not torsos—just arms and legs that alligators won't eat floating in the swamp. They haul two-hundred-year-old dead trees off the bottom of the bayou and sell them for thousands of dollars. And that's just the normal stuff that goes on down there."

She giggled.

"That's not exactly the response I expected," I said.

"You are cute when you do not know what to do, Chasechka. I think I will come with you, and we will make all of this make sense for you. Well, maybe not sucking brains of crawfish, but together, we will find reason for dead body parts."

Stopping Anya Burinkova from doing something she wanted to do was like stopping a freight train with a Q-tip.

"Fine. You can come, but when I tell you to stay on the ship, you *will* stay on the ship."

She shrugged. "We will see. And since we are taking ship, I will have great fun making you jealous when I flirt with sailors."

Chapter 13
War and Love

The echo of gunfire yanked me from the relative tranquility of the gazebo, and Anya and I leapt to our feet, each of us drawing our pistols. Taking cover behind the massive cannon in the center of the structure, I scanned the direction from which the gunfire had come until I saw the long red flag flying at the southern end of our training ground.

I holstered my Glock and relaxed. "It must be Shawn. Gator hooked him up with a new kit, so he's probably zeroing."

She slid her pistol back into concealment. "You should tell to me when this is going to happen. I was not prepared."

I laughed. "You're always prepared. Come on. Let's see if you can still shoot."

We made our way to the range, where Gator and Shawn were zeroing a pair of rifles and his new pistols.

"Mind if we join you?" I asked. It was more of an announcement of our presence than an actual request.

Shawn looked up. "Sure. The more the mightier. By the way, that's some toy store you've got down there."

"It's not mine," I said. "It's ours. If you need a piece of gear and we don't have it, just say the word. I'll make sure it shows up ASAP."

I motioned for Anya to follow me. "Let's shoot the tree."

"Why would we shoot tree?"

"It's a challenge tree," I said. "There are ten steel targets mounted on a vertical hinge. We'll start with five on my side and five on yours.

Every time you shoot one of yours, it'll swing to my side and vice versa. The first one to shoot all of the targets onto the other side wins."

She studied the tree, drew her pistol, and said, "This sounds like fun, but I must first tell to you secret."

"A secret?"

She stepped beside me, placed her left hand on my shoulder, and pulled me toward her until her lips were only inches from my ear. "If I were your wife, we could play very different kind of game."

In the instant that followed her "secret," five rounds exploded from her muzzle, and I lost without ever firing a shot.

"That's not fair."

She stepped back and smiled up at me. "All is fair inside war and love, no?"

"And which one is this?"

Her only reply was that mischievous smile that left men melting in their boots all over the world.

When I recovered from her verbal attack, I asked, "Do you need any gear?"

She patted the grip of the pistol that was already tucked away out of sight. "I have already everything I need to beat you, so, no, I do not need anything else. Besides, I have full kit on ship, so I am ready for part that is not love."

With Shawn's weapons zeroed and operating like clockwork, we closed the training range, brought down the big red flag, and headed for dinner. A meal for our family was a bit like feeding time at the zoo. We weren't poorly behaved, but we burned enough calories in our daily lives to devour most things that found their way onto our plates.

Our horde of hungry faces pulled into the Low Country Landing —St. Marys' newest restaurant—and although it was my first time, I'd heard nothing but praise.

As we filed through the door like a never-ending centipede, the look on the hostess's face turned from bright-eyed enthusiasm to terror in an instant.

I took her hand. "Don't worry. It's not as bad as it looks. We tip well, and we're happy to sit outside."

She mouthed "Thank you" as she led us through the dining room and onto the patio out back, where two rows of picnic tables waited just for us.

She said, "We've got the fans going, but if you don't want them on, feel free to pull the chains. I'll send Carolyn out to take care of you. She used to work in Charleston, so she's really good with big groups."

An unflappable-looking young lady danced her way onto the patio a moment later and showed no fear. "Hey, guys! Beer, Coke, water, lemonade, sweet tea. Those are your options. Who's first?"

I took control. "How about a couple of pitchers of each, and we'll have the low-country boil all around."

"Too easy," she said, and pointed to a hutch by the door. "Grab you some paper for the table, and we'll dump out a couple of pots."

Soon, our tables were covered with brown paper and piles of boiled shrimp, sausages, potatoes, corn, crab claws, and even a few crawfish. Gator gave a hands-on seminar on the proper method of devouring the mudbugs, and he even sucked a head for historical accuracy.

Anya sat beside Skipper, and the two laughed as if they were life-long friends. It was nice seeing Skipper smile again. She'd been through far more than anyone deserved after Tony was murdered six months earlier. Part of me wondered if her smile would ever return.

Anya ignored me throughout the meal, with the exception of one glance to ask if I needed a refill of tea while she was pouring. After her little whispering game on the range, it was a relief to have her attention focused on anybody other than me.

We ate, drank, and laughed for almost two hours before everyone seemed to realize we'd eaten far too much and needed a place to crash. As promised, we tipped well and made our way back to Bonaventure, where we slowly separated and drifted to our houses and bedrooms.

Skipper took Anya's hand. "You're coming home with me. There's no chance I'm letting you sleep in *that* house while Penny's in California."

The Russian gave me a wink. "This is good choice. For Chase, I am irresistible, but for me, he is only friend."

Being relegated to the friend zone was, for me, the perfect arrangement.

* * *

When the sun sliced through my second-story bedroom window, I had been awake for almost an hour. My prosthetic was firmly attached to the metal post protruding from what remained of my leg, and my second cup of coffee was well on its way through my body.

One of the most fascinating characteristics of my team was our innate ability to know when to arrive. That morning's gathering occurred on the back gallery at Bonaventure, and I gave the final status call.

"Gator. Go or no go?"

The youngest and least-experienced teammate gave a thumbs-up. "Good to go."

"Shawn?"

The former SEAL and newest member of the family said, "Go!"

I continued down the list. "Disco?"

The chief pilot nodded slightly. "I'm a go."

"Singer?"

The best sniper I've ever known and moral center of our team flashed the okay signal. "I'm a go."

"Mongo?"

Our giant said, "I'm always ready to go."

"Anya?"

Everybody's favorite Russian rolled her eyes. "This is waste of time. Everyone is ready to go."

Mongo moved with remarkable speed and scooped Anya from her

feet, in spite of her physical and verbal resistance. "Just say the word, boss, and I'll throw her in the river from right here."

I raised both hands. "Be careful. She's getting old and fragile."

"Good point," he said as he gently returned her to the gallery deck.

At the same instant her feet touched down, one of her fighting knives stuck into the decking between my boots. "I am not old, and I am definitely not fragile."

I brushed the edge of my boot against the still-vibrating blade. "If you say so, but I remember a time when you could stick it a lot closer to the toes."

Before she could retaliate, Shawn launched two blades of his own, sticking them within a centimeter of each of Anya's boots. Every eye turned to the SEAL, and he said, "You're not the only one with skills, comrade."

She huffed and kicked both knives out of the decking, sending them clattering across the floor.

I made no effort to hide my amusement. "It looks like you've got some competition. Now, behave." She reclaimed her knife, and I continued. "Skipper?"

"I'm a go, but I want to bring Celeste. Are you okay with that?"

I turned to our technical services officer, Dr. Celeste Mankiller. "Are you in?"

She said, "Always, and I've got a bagful of new toys for you guys."

"That's why you're always invited to the party," I said. "Are you ready to go?"

"I am."

"Clark, are you coming?"

My handler shook his head. "You're on your own for this one, College Boy. I'll be available if you need me, but I'm keeping my feet dry this time."

Operating without Clark would always make me feel as if a piece were missing from my puzzle, but his job description as handler for me and the team didn't include deployment downrange.

I said, "That's everybody. Anya, if you're okay with it, I'd like for you to bring your Citation. The rest of us will take the Caravan."

She said, "Of course. I will bring Skipper and Celeste. It will be girls' plane. Oh, and Shawn, since you throw like girl, you can come also with us."

Shawn waggled a finger. "The three of you can't handle this much sexy in that little airplane, so I think it's safer for everyone involved if I ride with the guys."

We piled into the Suburbans and headed for the airport, where Don Maynard met us at the hangar.

"Morning, Don. Is everything all right?"

He grimaced. "I'm not sure. I was just about to call you. When I got here, the chain was off the sprockets on the drive-through gate, and the door to the office was unlocked."

"That's not good," I said. "Did you forget to lock up when you went home yesterday?"

"Not a chance. I've been locking that door for over twenty years. It's muscle memory at this point. There's no way I would've left it open."

"Was anything missing?"

He scratched his face through his white beard. "That's the thing. Yes, the petty cash box was missing, but there was only about five hundred bucks in it. They didn't take anything else."

"What about the security cameras?"

"They were powered down."

I furrowed my brow. "Powered down? How did that happen?"

"I don't know. I wouldn't know how to power them down if you offered me a thousand bucks to do it. I only noticed because of the little blue lights. They cast an interesting pattern on the ceiling every morning when I open up the office, and they weren't flashing today."

I turned to Gator and Singer. "Take Celeste, and make sure her lab hasn't been disturbed."

Without a word, they press-checked their pistols, hopped into a golf cart, and headed across the airport.

I asked, "How about the hangar? Did you see anything out of sorts when you opened the door?"

"No, but I'd do a thorough preflight before you fly anything. Just because it didn't look like anyone had been inside doesn't mean they weren't."

Disco headed for the Caravan with Mongo only steps behind.

Don said, "Should I call the cops?"

"Not yet. Let us poke around a little before we make it official."

"That's what I thought you'd say. Everything's full of fuel, including Anya's Citation. Is there anything else you need?"

I said, "We've got it from here, but next time, call me immediately when you notice anything out of the ordinary."

"You got it," he said. "I really was about to call you."

"I know. Just keep doing what you're doing. I'll get a security team here later today, and I'll have them report to you. Keep them hidden. I don't want to prevent another break-in. I want to catch them in the act if they come back."

Anya trotted to a spot beside me and held up her index finger. The tip of it was streaked with a gray substance.

"What's that?" I asked.

She looked at Don. "Is graphite from lock on office door. Did you put graphite inside lock?"

"No, it's never needed graphite. It's always been smooth."

Anya said, "This means someone picked lock."

Gator, Singer, and Celeste pulled up in the golf cart, and our resident mad scientist said, "The lab appears untouched, and the security cameras and alarm are all showing normal."

Disco and Mongo galloped up. "Everything's clean in the hangar. No one's been in there except us in the last twenty-four hours."

I ran through the evidence in my skull. "That means whoever it was, they were looking for something in the office. The petty cash has to be a distraction. Nobody picks a lock to steal five hundred bucks. Hey, Shawn. Have you talked with your former team lately?"

"Not in the last month or so. Do you need me to give them a call?"

I pulled out my phone. "No, I'll have Clark handle it."

He answered quickly and said, "That didn't take long. Miss me already?"

I briefed him on the overnight occurrence, and before I could recommend bringing in a security team, Clark said, "I'm on it. I'll have some shooters on the ground before lunch."

"Great. I told Don to keep them tucked away so they can make contact with anyone who penetrates the fence."

"Good idea. And I'll bring a stack for the petty cash box."

I tucked my phone away. "Don, don't call the cops. Let's handle this one internally."

He grinned. "I like your style, boss."

We boarded the Caravan with Disco and Gator in the drivers' seats. Anya could wait an hour to take off, and she'd still beat us to Houma, Louisiana, in her Citation.

I've never been a good passenger. I prefer a front seat, but Gator needed some time up front with Disco to hone his skill in the Caravan.

I took a seat beside the sniper and said, "Let's hear it."

"What do you want to hear? 'The Old Rugged Cross' or 'Shall We Gather at the River?'"

"Both," I said. "But first, let's hear your thoughts on the break-in."

Gator raised the nose after a flawless takeoff run, and we climbed into the bright blue sky.

Singer steepled his fingers. "They're good enough to pick a relatively sophisticated lock, but not good enough to wipe off the graphite. After shutting down the camera feeds, they erased the video of their arrival, so that means they're tech savvy. They took a fistful of cash but nothing else. All of that adds up to a semi-pro hitter who wants us to believe he's a delinquent kid."

"What do you think they were really looking for?"

Singer said, "They weren't looking for anything. They were leaving something behind. When the security team sweeps the office this afternoon, I'd put money on them finding a bug or two."

"That's exactly what I was thinking."

He pulled the lever to allow his seat to recline several inches. "Now, leave me alone. I'm overdue for a nap."

Chapter 14
The Short Stop

Singer got his nap, and Gator delivered us safely back into the bayous of Southern Louisiana. When I climbed down from the plane, we weren't the only Cessna 208 on the ramp. A matching pair of Caravans with probes extending from the rear of each fuselage sat at the east end of the parking apron.

Disco seemed to notice them at the same instant as I did. "Check out those two. What do you suppose the probes are for?"

I shrugged. "No idea, but I'm curious."

"Let's take a look."

We strolled across the tarmac as if walking through our own backyard. I've always been amazed how easy it is to fit in somewhere with nothing more than confidence.

The two Caravans appeared to be exceptionally well maintained. They were far from new, but the ubiquitous black swath of turbine exhaust that was so common on 208s all over the world was missing from the skin of the two glistening planes in front of us.

"Somebody loves these machines," Disco said.

We walked around the aircraft, and I committed the registration numbers to memory. When we arrived at the booms protruding from the tail section of each aircraft, I grew even more intrigued. There were no markings of any kind on the probes, and they were painted an identical color to the fuselage. It looked as if they'd been installed at the Cessna factory.

"Any ideas?" Disco asked.

"Nothing. Maybe it's some kind of an atmospheric research thing. Who knows?"

He reached up and ran a hand across the device. "It doesn't feel like aluminum."

I followed his lead. "You're right, but I don't know what it is. Maybe fiberglass?"

"Could be," he said. "My money's on carbon fiber, though."

"Hey! What are you doing?"

I looked up to see a man and a woman crossing the tarmac in a run directly toward us.

I said to Disco, "This should be interesting."

When the two people were within fifteen feet, the man said, "Can I help you with something?"

I said, "We were just taking a look at these probes. That's our Caravan on floats over there. Are these yours?"

"We're responsible for them, and I'd appreciate you keeping your hands off."

I said, "Sorry. We didn't mean any harm. We were just curious."

"Yeah? Well, you can take your curiosity somewhere else. You don't see us messing with *your* airplane, do you?"

"Again, I'm sorry. There's no need to get upset."

From my vantage point, I watched the great diffuser crossing the ramp, and I couldn't wait to see him at work.

Mongo stepped between the man and woman as if they weren't there. "Hey, boss. Is everything all right?"

The woman never changed expression, but the unnamed man took a step backward. The intimidation factor of a man the size of Mongo is difficult to quantify, but the look on the previously aggressive face of the man said he wasn't interested in pushing the situation any further. The woman, on the other hand, didn't back down.

She said, "No. Everything is not all right. Your boss put his hands on our airplanes, and that's not how we do business. We've got a job to do, and we'd appreciate being able to do that job without worrying about somebody, like your boss, molesting our equipment."

Mongo turned to face the woman. "Ma'am, I'm going to have to ask you to dial back the aggression. We're doing our job, too. If you'd like to see our credentials, we'll be more than happy to produce them for you, but that will only escalate this situation, making it far more unpleasant for you."

"What credentials?" she demanded.

Had we been playing volleyball, Mongo's set would've been perfect for my spike, so I slid my Secret Service cred-pack from my pocket and stepped beside him. I didn't open the pack, but the embossed seal of the Treasury Department on the outside of the black leather wallet was impossible to miss.

I said, "I assume your job entails flying these two airplanes that have been highly modified. I don't see any placards indicating the aircraft are experimental or restricted, so I suppose I'll initiate an investigation to determine their airworthy status. It shouldn't take more than thirty days. In the meantime, we'll chain the propellers and start the paperwork."

The man said, "Wait a minute. I think we may have gotten off on the wrong foot. We didn't know you guys were officials. We have all the necessary paperwork. These aircraft are perfectly legal and airworthy. Why don't we just show you our documentation and call this whole thing a misunderstanding?"

"There's no misunderstanding on our part," I said, "but it sounds to me like you meant to apologize for your aggressive behavior toward..." I bounced the cred-pack in my palm. "Well, toward us."

"You're right," he said. "We saw you messing with our airplanes, and we didn't know who you were. I apologize for the misunderstanding. Would you like to see our paperwork?"

I pocketed my credentials. "That won't be necessary. Feel free to continue your..."

The man said, "'Aerial survey' work."

I nodded, and as if we'd rehearsed the move, Disco, Mongo, and I stepped at the same instant. "All right. Fly safely, and I hope you find what you're looking for during your...aerial survey."

The man appeared relieved and said, "We already found it. Now, it's just a matter of getting to it."

My posture was meant to give the impression that I'd let the comment float away on the breeze, but in reality, I tucked it away inside my head, just in case it somehow tied into Kenneth LePine's body parts situation.

By the time we made it back across the parking apron, Gator had our rental truck positioned beside the Caravan, and the rest of the team was tossing gear into the back.

I laid a hand on the bed rail of the truck. "Hey, guys. Where are you taking this stuff?"

My team froze, and I said, "Gun Bunny will be here soon with the helicopter, and we can transfer the gear straight to the Huey."

Kodiak said, "We're just sorting out what we're taking to the ship and what we're leaving ashore."

Before I could agree with his plan, the unmistakable chirp of tires on the runway caught my attention, and I looked up to see Anya's Citation slowing to make the turn on the taxiway.

Kodiak's eyes followed mine, and he said, "It looks like the beauty and brains of this operation made it."

I furrowed my brow. "Hey! I thought I was the beauty of the op."

He huffed. "Well, of course. I meant the other beauty."

"Good. I'm glad you recognize my value."

Gator tossed a gear bag at me. "Oh, we all recognize your value. It's your signature on our checks."

"There is that..."

Anya taxied beside our Caravan and shut down the turbines. She pulled off her headset, laid it on the panel, and shook out her long, blonde hair.

Kodiak gave me a hip check. "Cut it out, boss. You're a happily married man."

"I was just making sure she shut down the engines correctly."

He laughed. "Yeah, I'm sure. She still gets to you, doesn't she?"

I tossed the gear bag into the truck. "It's not that. There's something going on in her head, and it has her distracted. I've known that woman a long time, and it's not like her to let anything pull her focus off the mission."

"Any guesses what it might be?"

"Not yet, but if this thing turns into a fight, I'll need all hands on deck and laser focus on the objective."

Kodiak said, "Do you want me to poke around and see if I can get an idea what's on her mind?"

I shook my head. "Not yet, but I'll let you know if it comes to that."

The fairer half of our team descended the stairs from the Citation, and I couldn't resist having a little fun.

I checked my watch. "It's about time you got here. If I had a jet that couldn't keep up with a Caravan, I think I'd trade it in for an electric car or something equally useful."

Anya rolled her eyes and laid a palm in the center of my chest. "If we arrived before you, you and your boys would be deprived of watching us walk down the stairs. We would never want to rob you boys of such pleasure."

She stepped around me and whispered, "I know *you* were watching."

Thankfully, the beautiful sound of Huey rotor blades saved me from whatever I would've said next, and Gun Bunny nestled the skids onto the tarmac as gently as a baby's kiss.

We spent the next several minutes sorting and loading gear. When everything was in order, our pilot said, "I can't take everybody *and* all the gear at once, so hop number one will be all girls. Sorry, boys."

We watched them fly away, and Shawn said, "This is a strange life you live."

I laughed. "You're living it too, SEAL."

He shook his head. "Yeah, maybe, but that doesn't mean I'll ever get used to it."

The Huey returned, and the sweaty, grimy contingent climbed aboard. We touched down on the helipad aboard the Research Vessel *Lori Danielle* after a perfect flight over the bayous and oil rigs as far as the eye could see.

* * *

In the combat information center, the nerve center of the ship and our operation, I rolled a chair beside Skipper and passed her the slip of paper.

"What's this?" she asked.

"It's the registration numbers of two Cessna Caravans on the ramp back at Houma. We had a little run-in with them, and I'd like to know everything you can find on them as quickly as possible."

She took the paper and pulled her keyboard from its slot beneath the monitor. "Sure. No problem."

I stood, and she put a hand on my thigh. "Don't go anywhere. I'll have everything you need in seconds."

I replanted myself and waited the promised seconds. She did not disappoint.

"Okay...let's see here. Sequential serial numbers. Cessna Two-Oh-Eight Caravans. They were manufactured in two thousand eight and ordered by Skyways Solutions, Incorporated. The total order was eight identical aircraft."

"Did you find anything about the probes?"

"Hold your horses, Spy Boy. I'm getting there."

"Spy Boy? That's what you're going with?"

She chuckled. "Yeah, for now. Anyway. All eight of the Caravans went to a company called Morgan-Danley Systems to have aerial natural gas, oil, and mineral exploration systems installed at a cost of just over a million bucks per plane."

I let out a low whistle. "Ouch."

"Ouch is right. That puts the price tag on each plane at three point five million."

"And they bought eight of them?"

She said, "Yep, and I can't find any evidence of a lien ever being recorded against any of them, so they paid cash or borrowed against other assets."

I closed my eyes and let the new information dance around in my skull. "So, the probes. Those are the gas, oil, and mineral detection systems?"

She spun a monitor toward me. "Here's the whole system. The probe is just the container for the sensors. The real power is in the computer systems inside the airplane."

I studied the schematic. "This is all new to me. I've never heard of anything like it."

"Neither have I, but it gets more interesting."

"Let's hear it."

She spun the monitor back to its original orientation and leaned back in her chair. "All eight airplanes were immediately leased to Flambeau Exploration."

"Now, that *is* interesting. So, that means Flambeau is sniffing for oil with thirty million dollars' worth of airplanes."

"At least," she said. "These eight may not be the only ones Flambeau is using."

I stood. "That's what I need...one more thing to toss into the mix of this already confusing situation. Thanks. When you have time, do a little digging on Flambeau. I'd like to know where the bodies are buried."

She stared down between her feet. "Uh, Chase. Have a seat for another minute. There's something I need to tell you."

I perched on the edge of the chair I'd just vacated. "Sure. What's up?"

She took a long breath. "I did something without asking you."

"Not everything requires my approval."

"Yeah, but this one probably did."

I rolled a few inches closer. "Just spit it out. How bad can it be?"

She finally met my gaze. "I asked Anya to teach me to fight."

"That's not a big deal. You've trained with her before. Why do you think I would care about that?"

She licked her lips. "Well, it's not just fighting. I want her to teach me everything."

"What do you mean?"

"The whole thing," she said. "The manipulation, intelligence gathering, plotting, and the killing."

I slid myself fully into the seat. "Why would you ask her to do that?"

"It's about Tony. He knew how to fight, and he still got killed. This is a dangerous world we live in. I want to be able to do more than just punch keys on this computer."

I crossed my legs with my right boot resting across my left knee. "Listen to me. I know you're not the bratty little girl in Athens anymore, but what we do outside the CIC is a world no one chooses. We're knuckle-draggers because we're not smart enough to do anything else."

"Come on, Chase. You know that's not true. Everybody on this team has skill sets that can sustain them in a thousand different careers. You're a psychologist, for Pete's sake."

I tapped on the prosthetic where my shin and ankle should've been. "Out there, it's life and death every time we go to work. I made a promise to your father that I'd never intentionally put you in harm's way like that."

"You're not putting me anywhere. I'm telling you that's what I want. I want to do what Anya can do. I don't want to spend my whole life in a dark cave, staring into a computer screen."

"Now, you're the one who's exaggerating. You know you do far more than stare into screens. You're the lifeline we rely on when bullets start flying and blood starts hitting the ground."

"I'm doing it, Chase. It's my decision."

I chewed my bottom lip. "I can't stop you from learning, but my greatest responsibility is to put the best people in positions where they can do the best work. Nobody—and I mean absolutely nobody on Earth—can do what you can with that mouse and keyboard. Nobody's better behind a rifle than Singer. Nobody's better at making men melt down in front of her than Anya. And there's not a finer pilot on the planet than Disco. What kind of leader would I be if I put you behind the rifle, Singer in the cockpit, and Disco in the chair you're sitting in right now?"

She squeezed her eyelids closed. "I get it. I do. But Anya's almost forty. How much longer can she—"

I took her hands in mine. "Do it. Learn everything you can from her. She's got a broader skill set than anyone on this team, and I'd be a fool to let that skill set die without being passed on. I'm not saying I'll put you in the field, but I support you learning everything she knows."

She pulled her hands from mine, leaned forward, and took me in her arms. "I love you, Chase. I had a stupid teenage crush on you when you were the big-shot ball player at Georgia, but you turned into the best big brother anybody could ever have."

I held her for a long moment. "You didn't have a crush on me. You were digging on Randy Cline, the shortstop back then."

She pulled away and shrugged. "Yeah, maybe you're right. I wonder where he is now."

"He's coaching Double-A ball in Tennessee for the Smokies. I think they're in the Cubs organization. Maybe you should catch a game next time you're up there. I'm sure Randy could score you some good tickets."

She gave me a playful slap. "Stop it. Go get to work. We've got missing body parts to deal with."

Chapter 15
I'm Not the One

I left the CIC and turned toward the navigation bridge. Captain Sprayberry's insistence that I could come aboard the bridge anytime I wanted without expressed permission would never feel natural to me, but I gave it a shot.

"Good afternoon, Captain."

"Well, look at you. Just sashaying in here as if you own the place."

I stuck out a hand. "I sort of do own the place."

He shook my offered hand. "Yeah, I guess you do. How was the flight?"

"Perfect. How about your trip around the Keys?"

"Not bad. We've got a couple of small issues in the engine room, but Big Bob is getting them straightened out. We'll be back at full strength by the end of the day."

He suddenly had my full attention. "A couple of issues? What limitations do those issues create?"

"We can only make about eighty-five-percent power, and one of the generators is out of service."

"Can we still run on the foils?"

He said, "We can, but it would take a couple of extra minutes for the engines to get us up since we can't produce full power."

One of the most unique characteristics of the *Lori Danielle* was her ability to deploy four foils and fly the hull out of the water. That capability gave her the guts to make almost sixty knots in smooth seas. I didn't know of any ship in her class who could come close to those speeds.

"Keep me posted," I said. "I don't anticipate the need to run or chase, but I don't like the old girl being crippled."

"She's not crippled," Captain Sprayberry said. "She's just sore."

"Call it what you want, but keep the fire burning under Big Bob."

The captain chuckled. "Bob doesn't respond well to fires under his butt, but I'll stay in his ear. I'm confident he'll have her back on track in twelve hours or less."

"Good enough. If you need me, I've got my radio and sat-phone."

"Welcome back aboard," he said. "It's nice to be in command of a warship instead of a lowly research vessel."

Behind the *Lori Danielle's* demure exterior beat the heart of a lioness on the prowl. Not only could she outrun almost anything at sea, she could also go fisticuffs with any foe afloat. I was proud to have her in our arsenal and even more proud to have Captain Barry Sprayberry at the helm.

My next stop promised to be far less cordial than my visit with the captain, but it had to be done. I found Anya on the stern deck with her face lifted toward the afternoon sun and her hair blowing on the breeze. Everything about the scene took me back to the afternoon on the beach in St. Thomas, where I saw her for the first time without a rifle in her hands.

"We need to talk."

She pulled her hair into a ponytail and slipped a rubber band from her wrist to hold it in place. "This will be talk about Skipper, no?"

"You bet. First, why did you agree to train her before talking with me?"

She leaned against the rail and cocked her head. When Anya Burinkova lied, she had only one tell. Her command of English diminished, and her Russian accent grew. It was no secret she could sound like a native English speaker, but I let her get away with the accent for two reasons: First, she believed she had everyone around her

THE CREOLE CHASE · 125

fooled into thinking the accent was authentic. Second, I thought it was cute.

"What did she tell to you?"

I caught my smile before it materialized. "Just that you agreed to teach her everything from manipulation to murder."

"Is not murder, Chasechka. You know this."

"You know what I'm talking about. Why didn't you come to me when she asked you to train her?"

Anya picked at a flake of paint on the rail. "Tell to me exactly what she said."

That sent my head in a new direction, but I played along. "She told me that she asked you to teach her to fight."

Anya closed her eyes. "This is only part of truth."

"So, tell me the whole story."

"Skipper is friend to me. She has been hurt very badly, and this makes me sad for her. She wants to fight back against world that took her husband. I told to her she cannot win this fight, but she does not care."

She paused, and I prodded. "Keep talking."

"At first, I tell to her I will not teach her these things because she will be killed. She does not have foundation for learning what I know."

"Go on."

She abandoned her paint chip and took my wrist in her hand. "You must first promise to me you will not be angry with her."

I pulled away. "Tell me what she said, Anya."

She finally looked up to face me. "She told to me if I would not be for her teacher, she would tell to Penny you and I are..."

I gritted my teeth. "You and I are what?"

She closed her eyes. "She said she would tell to Penny that you and I are sleeping together."

I swallowed the bile in my throat. "She wouldn't do that because it's not true."

"She is desperate, Chasechka. She will do anything to fight back against all of world that took Tony from her."

I spun on a heel, but Anya grabbed me. "Wait! Do not be angry with her. She is hurting, and you must remember how this hurt feels. Think of young boy whose parents and sister were murdered inside jungle of Panama."

I yanked my arm from her grip and shoved a finger into her face. "No! You don't get to use that against me. That's out of bounds, and you know it." I withdrew my pointed finger. "If you're telling the truth, what Skipper did is unthinkable, regardless of her state of mind. She is not going to threaten any member of this team and get away with it. That's *not* how we play ball."

She softened her tone. "I am not member of team, my Chasechka. I am person who sometimes you ask to help, but I am outsider."

"That's not true. You're just as much a part of this team as any one of us. What Skipper did is the kind of crap that destroys teams and families, and I won't have it."

"Wait," she almost begged. "I can change her mind. I can make her understand this is terrible idea. You must trust me."

I let myself lean against the rail. "I'm not qualified for any of this. I'm a gunslinger at best. I don't know how to investigate floating body parts or deal with threats inside my team. I'm not—"

Before I could finish my own pity party, she drew a knife from some mysterious, concealed location and swung it toward my neck.

I didn't think and merely reacted, capturing her wrist before the blade reached my flesh. I spun her until she was pinned against the rail and stripped the knife from her forceful grip. Taking one long stride backward, I assumed a fighting stance with my newly acquired knife at the ready.

Anya held up both hands. "You may not believe you are qualified, but there are maybe fifty or fewer men on Earth who could survive un-provoked attack from me. You have inside you something others do not. This is why you are here in charge of team...as head also of family. Now, give to me knife and go do job that is yours."

I dropped the knife at her feet. "I'd much rather be stabbed in the face than in the back. You make sure that's the first lesson you teach Skipper."

I left the deadliest woman I'd ever known standing alone by the stern rail while demons danced inside my head. Until that moment, I believed everyone around me would turn their back on me and burn my world to the ground before Skipper would ever betray me. But that belief had imploded and lay in pieces at my feet. I yearned for someone to give me the direction I needed to keep my world together, but the longer I begged for a single name I could turn to, the lonelier the man inside of me became.

Clark never led a team like mine. Dr. Richter was gone. My father was on the other side of eternity. And I was left standing in the darkest of holes...alone.

Everything inside my logical mind told me to walk away and let Anya teach Skipper the one lesson she needed to learn more than any other, but the wounded animal in me couldn't do it.

I thundered through the doorway of the CIC and found Weps— our weapons officer—Dr. Mankiller, and Skipper huddled around a console.

I ordered, "Give us the room."

Two of the three occupants looked up, but the third did not.

Weps cocked his head. "Is everything all right?"

"Give us the room," I demanded again.

Without another word, Celeste and Weps hurried past me and secured the hatch behind them as they made their exit.

Skipper held up a finger. "Chase, don't! You don't understand what it's like. You don't know..."

I drew the deepest breath I'd ever taken. "Put your finger down, and tell me what makes you think for one second that you get to tell me what I'm *allowed* to do on *my* ship with *my* team. What you did is tantamount to treason. You drove a wedge into this team. You made a threat with a lie that could destroy me. Me! Do you get that? I pulled you out of the worst hole you could've ever fallen into, and..." I drove a finger through the air toward the stern. "And *that* woman...the woman you threatened with that lie. She took a bullet for *you* that day and came as close to dying as anyone can. Tell me you're not so blind that you could forget that. You wouldn't be alive if Anya hadn't been there that day. How dare you?"

She didn't raise her voice. Instead, she stared straight into my soul. "Chase, would you have this same reaction if I had threatened Penny?"

My stomach churned, and rage filled my head, but before I could burst into the next tirade, Skipper said, "Your first instinct was to protect Anya. Why don't I deserve the same? Why didn't you immediately come down on my side? I'm the widow here. I'm the one who lost the man she loves forever. I'm the widow here, Chase. Me. Anya's got you. Penny's got you. Neither of them lost the man they love. That was me, and that's what gives me the right to do whatever I have to do to avenge my husband."

The rage softened enough to dull the next words from my mouth. "What do you think would've happened if you came to me and asked for training?"

"I don't have to think about that, Chase. I know what would've happened. You would've given me the same old tired speech about how valuable I am right here in this chair and how you can't afford to lose me."

I wanted to pour out a thousand reasons why she was wrong, but she wasn't.

She continued. "You're going to lose me if I can't do something with all of this anger and hatred and fury. It's going to kill me. Then what will you do? Who's going to answer the phone at two in the morning when one of your crazy ideas won't let you sleep? Who's going to sit in this chair and run your missions in the field? Whose voice is going to ring in your head when you need a way out, a way in, or a way around the problem you can't solve with guns and knives? Huh, Chase? Who?"

I let myself settle onto a chair beside her. "You're right...about all of it. But what you did is still wrong."

"I wouldn't have actually done it," she said. "It was just desperation. I wouldn't have really told Penny you were sleeping with Anya."

"That's the first lesson you have to understand about what we do in the field. We make a thousand threats a minute when we come face-to-face with an enemy who's ready to fight. We put muzzles in their faces and fingers on our triggers. We don't bluff. If you throw around empty threats on the battlefield, your body will be carried off that field if you're lucky. If you're not, there won't be anything left to bury."

She nodded, and I rolled closer. "If you really want to learn to fight, Anya will teach you. But if you ever threaten to stick a knife in the back of anyone on this team again, we'll find a new analyst. Don't make the mistake of thinking that I'm bluffing."

She nodded.

I softened my tone. "When this mission is over, I'm hiring a psychologist to get you through this thing."

She laid a hand on my arm. "I don't want another psychologist. I've got you."

I shook my head. "Not for this one. I'm too close, and you don't see me as an option. If you did, you would've come to me weeks ago before giving Anya an ultimatum. I'm not the one, but we'll find someone who can help you. I promise."

Chapter 16
Kill It or Count It

Ronda No-H called herself "the ship's purser," but she was far too humble. The Air Force paid for her education to become a CPA after she served as a door gunner for six years in uniform. Since becoming part of our organization, she not only served as the financial officer aboard the *Lori Danielle*, but also as the CPA for our entire organization. The look on her face as she rearranged the food on her plate at dinner caught my attention.

"Is everything all right?"

She sliced into a roasted potato. "I was just about to ask you the same thing."

It suddenly became my turn to push my meal around the plate. "Yeah, I'm good."

She leaned forward. "Lie to somebody who'll believe you, big boy, 'cause I'm not buying it. What's going on?"

"Do you really want to know?"

She laid down her fork. "Unless you're about to fire me, yes, I want to know."

I let out a chuckle. "No, you're too valuable, and besides, you know where the bodies are buried."

"I know where the *next* bodies will be buried, and don't you forget it, either. So, what's up?"

"I'm just a little out of sorts, and I've got a little mutiny working."

She raised an eyebrow. "And what did you do to bring this mutiny about, Captain Bligh?"

"Oh, it's my fault, is it?"

"Mutiny is always the captain's fault. That doesn't mean he's wrong, but he always causes it."

I stared down at the pork steak on my plate and considered her position. "That stings a little."

She shrugged. "The truth often does."

"So, what do you suggest I do?"

She took a bite and washed it down with a sip of tea. "Floggings before the mast for the mutineer might do the trick, as long as Disco isn't the guilty party."

I let my fork fall onto my plate. "Your man has nothing to fear. He's one of the loyalists. Perhaps I'm the one in need of a good flogging if I'm truly the cause."

"From where I sit," she said, "you're already giving yourself a pretty good whipping. Maybe cutting yourself a little slack and remembering that these people love you is a step in the right direction."

"You'd make a pretty good psychologist."

She laughed. "I'm an old door gunner who's pretty good at keeping a ledger, so if I can't kill it or count it, it's none of my business."

I stood, and she asked, "Where are you going? You've hardly touched your dinner."

"I'm going to call the chief flogger and see if he can fit me in."

Dr. Frederick Kennedy answered on the first ring as if he'd been waiting with his finger poised over the answer key. "Hello, Chase. To what do I owe the pleasure?"

For a time, Fred had served as the staff psychiatrist and psychologist at The Ranch, where I was trained to become whatever I was. He'd been a student of Dr. Robert "Rocket" Richter and shared my affection for the long-deceased psych professor.

"You may not consider it a pleasure by the time we finish the conversation."

I could almost see him pulling off his wirerimmed glasses and crossing his legs. "I'm listening."

I wasted no time. "My analyst is imploding."

He cleared his throat. "That happens when a young woman becomes a young widow. How can I help?"

"Clearing your schedule for a couple of weeks would be a good start."

"Is she coming to me, or am I making a house call?"

"How do you feel about shipboard living for a few days?"

He said, "If said ship is a luxury yacht, I'm all for it. However, if it's a sailboat, I'm out."

"How quickly can you be in New Orleans?"

"How does the day after tomorrow sound?"

I said, "Let me know your arrival time, and I'll have a chopper pick you up."

"Chase!" Gator's voice echoed down the corridor, and I spun to see him sprinting toward me from the mess.

I said, "I've got to run, Doc. See you in two days."

Shoving the sat-phone into my pocket, I said, "What's going on?"

Gator pointed toward his phone. "Kenneth's house is on fire."

In that moment, every doubt I carried melted away, and I said, "Get the team."

"They're already on their way to the helipad."

I snatched the radio from my belt and thumbed the button. "Bridge, Alpha One."

A crackling voice that wasn't Captain Sprayberry's answered, "Go for bridge."

As I sprinted toward my cabin, I said, "Make ready for helo ops and say ship status."

The voice that came through my handheld radio next was, without question, the voice of the captain. "Helo ops approved. Propulsion ninety percent. Generators sixty."

Instead of questioning why Big Bob in engineering hadn't restored the ship to full strength, I said, "Set MEDCON Alpha. Show eight personnel airborne in ten."

The captain said, "Roger. Shall we be to quarters?"

"Affirmative."

Almost before I answered, the claxons rang, and the captain's voice sounded through the speakers inside the ship. "Attention, all hands. This is the captain. General quarters. This is not a drill. General quarters. Set MEDCON Alpha."

General quarters aboard a ship of war is a perfectly choreographed ballet of professionals moving in sync and preparing for combat. It was possible that I had overreacted, but I'd rather have the ship and crew ready for a fight than resting on their heels.

My first brief stop was in my cabin to throw my kit across my shoulder and retrieve my rifle. I met Skipper in the doorway to the CIC.

She was all business. "What's wrong?"

I pushed her back inside. "Kenneth LePine's house is on fire. This thing just turned nasty. We're going in. Get the satellite linked, and monitor the local emergency response."

Without a word, the weapons officer pushed past the two of us just inside the doorway and planted himself at the weapons station.

Skipper cocked her head. "We're going to quarters for a house fire on land? And did I hear the captain say MEDCON Alpha?"

"Yes, we are," I said. "I don't know what or who started the fire, but I want the medical staff on alert if we have casualties, and we may need to evac Kenneth if this is what I fear."

I shrugged on my plate carrier and slung my rifle while sprinting for the helipad. Press-checking my rifle and sidearm, I confirmed a round chambered in each and ready for a fight. I bounded up the ladder to the pad and watched Mongo, Gator, Singer, Kodiak, and Shawn climb aboard the Huey. Disco was strapped into the cockpit beside Gun Bunny, and the main rotor slowly spun to life.

My boot hit the right skid at the same instant it left the deck, and we were airborne in a climbing left turn toward the bayou.

We synced our radios with our bone conduction devices and performed the comms check on the climb-out.

With the preliminaries complete, I turned to Gator. "Tell me what you know."

"Cecilia called me. She said Kenneth's house is burning, and the volunteer fire department isn't responding."

"Is Kenneth inside?"

"She didn't know."

"Why aren't the volunteers responding?"

"Same answer," he said.

I shuffled forward and stuck my head into the cockpit. "See it yet?"

Disco raised a finger. "We've got a plume of black smoke at twelve o'clock."

I pulled my knees beneath me and raised my head. The landscape looked unfamiliar from the south, but as we flew closer, I picked out a few landmarks. "That's got to be it."

Disco said, "It's the only fire in sight."

I peered around Gun Bunny to study her GPS screen. "Can that thing show the volunteer fire department?"

She said, "Disco, you have the controls."

He replied, "I have the controls."

After repeating the acknowledgment to erase any possibility of confusion over who was doing the flying, Gun Bunny said, "I can pull up that layer. Give me a second." She pressed several buttons, and soon, a layer showing businesses appeared on the screen. She scrolled and zoomed in until a fire hydrant symbol was centered on the screen. "There it is."

I scanned the landscape in front of us and tried to match what I saw with the GPS. Finally, a crossroads intersection and a water tower appeared, and I had my bearings. "That puts the fire department just north of Kenneth's house."

I spun to face the team. "Gator, you take everybody except Shawn and find out what's going on at Kenneth's house. Shawn and I are going to the fire station."

Gator nodded. "Roger. I snagged two Scott Air-Paks and some gear from the ship. Are we authorized to go inside?"

I didn't hesitate. "You make the call on the scene." I checked over my shoulder as the column of black smoke grew ever nearer. "Get ready to go in sixty seconds."

The team moved to the doors and poised as Disco flew the descending approach upwind of the fire.

Gator led the deployment out the door. "Go, go, go!"

Kodiak, Mongo, and Singer followed him from the helo and into the dust storm beneath the rotor blades.

We climbed away from the fire and turned for the concrete block building with a volunteer fire department emblem painted high above its aluminum doors.

I yelled into the cockpit, "Take high cover and report squirters!"

Disco gave a thumbs-up and pulled pitch just as Shawn and I cleared the skids. Although I hadn't seen anyone near the building on our approach, I turned to cover Shawn as he mule-kicked the steel door, sending the heavy slab exploding inward. Unsure what we'd find inside, we pressed through the opening with our rifles at the ready.

Twenty seconds after penetrating the structure, Shawn said, "Clear in the rear."

I lowered my rifle. "Clear up front."

Shawn hit the lights, and the bulbs slowly came alive, casting yellow hues across the concrete floor and the pair of bright red trucks. When the light grew bright enough, there was little mystery left concerning why the trucks weren't spraying water on what remained of Kenneth LePine's house.

"They've all been slashed," Shawn said.

I stuck my hand through a gash in one of the tires. "Not just slashed. It looks like they did it with a chainsaw."

Shawn said, "Look what I found!"

I turned to see him hefting a gas-powered water pump into his arms. He grunted. "Grab a hose and the intake line."

I grabbed the equipment and called Disco. "Sierra Five, Sierra One. Get back on deck outside the fire station."

"Roger," came his reply, and we moved back through the destroyed door with our newfound tools.

Shawn groaned as he raised the enormous pump and slid it through the door of the Huey.

I threw the hoses aboard and stepped onto the skid. "Go!"

As we climbed, I called Mongo. "Meet us at the helo. We'll be on the ground in thirty seconds."

We touched down a hundred yards from the inferno, and Mongo was poised for any task I could assign. He and Shawn muscled the pump and ran toward the bayou. I followed with the intake and fire hose over my shoulders.

"Who's inside?" I yelled over the roar of the flames.

Mongo said, "Kodiak and Gator, and they've been in there way too long."

"Where's Singer?" I demanded.

"He's moving the airboat."

Shawn rigged the intake and tossed the screen into the bayou while Mongo started the engine on the pump. I tucked the nozzle of the fire hose beneath my arm and ran for the wall of flames, where the door to Kenneth's house had once been.

As high-pressure water filled the hose and sprayed from the nozzle, the energy sent me staggering backward. What I hit behind me felt like a solid wall, and our SEAL yanked the hose from my grip and shoved me aside.

Shawn pressed forward, adjusting the nozzle as he went, moving with the practiced patience and skill of a seasoned firefighter unfazed by the force of the stream. He widened the spray until it formed a shield of water in front of him as he approached the door, then he disappeared into the torrent of steam, smoke, flame, and water.

I lunged forward to follow him into the fight, but Mongo caught me by the shoulder. "You stay here with me. Shawn knows what he's doing. This clearly ain't his first fire."

Three of my men were inside a burning shack perched on the edge of the bayou, and my friend Kenny LePine's father was likely burned to death and far beyond recognition.

The rising smoke turned from black to gray and finally white as the fire surrendered to Shawn's assault. I jerked away from Mongo and ran for the remains of the shack. Shawn backed through the partial door frame and closed the valve on the nozzle.

I yelled, "Are they in there?"

He shook his head and wiped a black swath of sweat and char across his face. "I don't think anybody's in there. I couldn't see, but I didn't feel anybody. I'll catch my breath and go back in."

I stepped around him and forced my way through the rubble and blackened debris. Although the fire was out, it was still nearly impossible to make out any shapes amid the smoking piles, though nothing resembled human bodies. I gagged and coughed as I pawed at everything, desperately searching for my brothers or Kenneth LePine.

Several minutes into my search, the floor beneath me collapsed, and I fell through until I spread my arms to stop my descent into the muck below. Two thoughts went through my mind as I dangled through the burnt floor above the bayou: *Are alligators afraid of fire? I hope they don't like the taste of prosthetic legs.*

I twisted and writhed to pull myself back through the floor and make my way from the debris, but the harder I pulled, the more the floor crumbled. Finally, a massive hand hooked me beneath my left arm and hoisted me from entrapment in one smooth motion. It was either an angel or a giant, and I was happy to see either.

When Mongo stepped clear of the black, smoking remains of the shack, with me still in his grasp, Singer ran Kenneth's airboat ashore a hundred feet away. Kodiak and Gator stumbled over the bow and onto the relatively dry ground. I was relieved beyond words to see them alive, but no matter how hard I looked, there was no sign of Kenneth in the airboat.

Seemingly out of nowhere, Cecilia Lachaussee appeared in a sprint. She threw her arms around Gator. "Oh my God! Are you okay?"

He tentatively returned the hug and then stepped away to remove his drenched turnout gear and drop the Air-Pak from his shoulders. "I'm all right. We got pinned in the back and had to fight our way into the bayou. Singer plucked us out of the water, but I don't know about Kenneth. We didn't find him. Have you seen him?"

Before Cecilia could answer, the small camper that had been home for Gator and me three days before exploded as if it'd been struck by a missile.

Chapter 17
The Rule

Everyone jerked, ducked, and instinctually threw up a hand to protect themselves from the explosion and flying debris. The gathered crowd retreated, but my team leapt into action. Mongo reengaged the water pump, and Shawn wrapped a massive arm around the pulsing fire hose. He moved toward the blaze with the nozzle pouring all the water the pump could force from the bayou. The blaze persisted, but Shawn wouldn't surrender. He fought his way forward, delivering a massive volume of water onto the flaming demon in front of him.

Nothing about the fire looked or felt natural, and nothing inside the camper could've created an explosion of that magnitude. A pair of propane bottles fed the camper, and a gasoline generator provided power, but neither of those elements could result in the explosion and towering flames in front of me. The longer Shawn fought, the hotter the inferno grew.

I moved in behind the SEAL and laid a hand on his shoulder. "Pull back and let it burn."

He cast a look across his shoulder that said he wasn't ready for the round to end and for him to return to his corner.

I tightened my grip and strengthened my tone. "Let it burn."

His expression made it clear he didn't share my opinion, but he swallowed his pride and retreated.

When we were far enough away to close the nozzle, he said, "What if somebody's in there?"

"Nobody would've survived that explosion," I said. "That's obviously not just the camper burning. Somebody loaded that thing with something and set it off remotely."

"Could've been a timer."

"Maybe, but why not torch it with the house instead of after the scene calmed down?"

He glanced at the gathered crowd. "Who knows? But I say we pat every one of them down until we find our trigger."

The remainder of the team obviously had the same idea. They were already interviewing the crowd and asking to see the contents of their pockets.

As the camper crumbled beneath the roaring flames, the noise died down enough for me to hear one of the onlookers protesting as Gator tried to search him. The Cajun patois was impossible to understand, but there was no way to misinterpret the man's meaning.

As Gator backed away, Kodiak stepped behind the man and planted a boot in the bend of his knee, sending the Cajun to the ground. Gator moved back toward his suspect, and Mongo stepped beside the downed man to discourage any of his buddies from coming to the man's rescue.

Gator turned out the guy's pockets and shook his head. He scooped up the treasure the man had worked so hard to protect, then tossed the find into the bayou and turned to me. "It was a crack pipe and a couple baggies of dope."

I spoke loud enough for everyone to hear. "Did anybody call the sheriff?" Heads shook, and I asked, "Why not?"

Somebody said, "What da sheriff gon' do, him? He ain't gots no fire truck."

"Speaking of fire trucks," I said, "does anyone know why the volunteer fire department didn't show up?"

The same reaction came, and I grew more frustrated with every passing second.

Turning back to the diminishing flame where the camper had been, I said, "Go ahead and put it out and see if you can find any remains."

Shawn went back to work, and I said, "Does anybody know where Kenneth LePine is?"

"Out huntin' sinker logs. Dat be all he do, him. Pull up dem logs and stack dem dollars. Dat be all."

I spun until I found Cecilia standing next to Gator. "Where's your uncle?"

She sighed. "I don't know, but he ain't pulling logs without me."

"His truck's gone. You must have some idea where he'd go."

"Maybe he went to town. I'm not his keeper. He calls me when he needs me to pull logs for him. Other than that, I see him a couple times a week."

Shawn's skill behind the nozzle had the camper fire drowned out by the time I ran out of questions to ask. He approached the remains and kicked through the still-smoking debris.

He met my gaze and shook his head. "Nobody was in there."

I called Disco. "Any squirters?"

He said, "We didn't see anyone running away, but one of those fancy Caravans with the probe was orbiting at forty-five hundred until we showed up."

"Come on down and pick us up. We're done here." I turned back to the crowd. "Are any of you volunteer firemen?"

A smaller man poked his head around a few people in front of him. "Me do, but only sometime, me. Dem trucks ain't no good."

"So, what do you do when somebody's house catches on fire?"

He looked around as if the answer were obvious. "We do dis. What else we gonna do?"

Every time someone opened their mouth, I felt like I was falling deeper down the rabbit hole with the looking glass well astern.

Disco and Gun Bunny planted the Huey a few hundred feet away in a cloud of sand and dust.

I grabbed Cecilia's arm as the rest of the team headed for the helo. "Keep calling your uncle until he answers. This was no accident. You know it as well as I do. Call Gator the second you hear from Kenneth."

She nodded and grimaced as if fighting back tears. "What if he never answers?"

"Does he ever disappear for any length of time?"

"No, he never goes far, and I don't ever remember him being gone overnight."

"Think of a list of places he's been in the past year. I want you to hit every one of those places and ask if anyone's seen him. If they have, you call Gator. Got it?"

She stared at the ground. "He's not going to be at any of those places, is he?"

"No, probably not. I suspect whoever torched his house and camper took him and his truck, but we've got to cover all the bases. Why didn't you call the sheriff?"

"I'll call him now," she said, "but he'll want to talk to you, and I've got a feeling you don't have a good answer for why you're flying around in a military helicopter and putting out fires down here in the bayou."

"Give him Gator's number. We haven't done anything wrong, so I'm not afraid of the sheriff's questions." I took a step closer to her. "Do you know any of those people who turned out to watch?"

She studied the crowd. "Yeah. I know all of 'em. They're Cajuns. They love to drink, fight, and get loud, but none of them are fire-bugs, if that's what you're asking."

"How about desperate for money?"

She laughed. "Good luck finding anybody within fifty miles of here who isn't. Whoever you are, Chase, you're way outside your backyard. When and if the sheriff agrees to get involved, you can bet the strangers from out of town are going to be the target of his investigation. Uncle Ken never hurt anybody, so nobody around here has any reason to burn down his house...if you can even call it a house."

"That may be true," I said, "but those floating body parts showed up a long time before we did."

She said, "Just don't expect this to play out like an episode of *Law and Order* on TV. We've got a sheriff, one deputy, two constables, and one police truck. That's all we've got to protect and serve down here. We tend to look after each other."

I turned to face the pile of smoking rubble that had been her uncle's house an hour before. "It doesn't look like anyone was watching out for Kenneth."

We flew back to the ship, and I headed straight for the CIC.

Skipper made a terrible face when I walked through the door. "You smell like a fire."

"Imagine that," I said. "Were you listening in?"

"I was. Is everybody all right?"

"We're good, but Kenneth LePine is missing and homeless. He may not know either of those things yet, but if he's still alive, I doubt he's very comfortable."

"So, what do we do now?"

"The first thing I'm going to do is get a shower. Where's Anya?"

She recoiled. "Are you planning on showering with Anya?"

"Not hardly. I just want to make sure she knows why we didn't take her with us."

Skipper said, "I was wondering that myself. So, why *didn't* you take her?"

"I don't know yet, but I'll come up with something by the time I find her."

* * *

I walked through the hatch to my cabin to find a mane of long blonde hair cascading from the edge of my bunk. I gave the bed a kick. "What are you doing in my room?"

She rolled over and smiled. "I did not expect you to be back so soon. I was enjoying moment of quiet and pillow that smells like you."

"Get out. I'm going to take a shower, and you're not involved."

"I can wait here for you."

"No, you can't. Get out. I'll come find you when I get out of the shower and dressed. I need your brain."

"My brain is all?"

"Yes, your brain is all I need. Now, get out and meet me in the CIC in twenty minutes."

Burning my clothes would've made them look and smell better, but instead, I shoved them into the recycling system aboard the *Lori Danielle*. I had no idea how the system worked, and I didn't care as long as the burnt odor disappeared.

I broke the captain's three-minute-shower rule, and it was glorious. Nothing about what was happening in the backwater bayous of South Louisiana made any sense, and I wanted nothing more than to pack up, head back to Bonaventure, and pretend I never heard of floating body parts that alligators wouldn't eat. As much as I wanted to walk away, my obligation to my friends, Earl and Kenny LePine, wouldn't let me. I owed it to them to get to the bottom of the mystery, and maybe, just maybe, mend the rift between Kenny and his father—if that were possible.

Like all good things, the shower had to end, and I had to plunge myself back into the real world...if anything about the world of the bayou qualified as real.

* * *

When I made my entrance into the combat information center, Weps glanced up from the weapons station, and I realized I'd failed to tell the captain it was no longer necessary to stand at the ready.

I lifted the handset that would immediately ring on the bridge, and Captain Sprayberry answered quickly. "Bridge, Captain."

"It's Chase in the CIC. Everyone is safely back aboard."

He said, "I know. I was wondering how long it was going to take you to report in. If you wouldn't mind, I'd like to secure from general quarters if it's not too much trouble."

"Touchy tonight, aren't we?"

"Not touchy. I just don't like leaving my crew on high alert while the away team commander takes a fifteen-minute shower."

"Sorry. I'll make it up to them."

"Sure, you will," he said, and the line went dead.

Seconds later, his announcement came over the speaker system. "All hands, this is the captain. Secure from general quarters. You can thank Mr. Fulton for the prolonged state of readiness. That is all."

The weapons systems officer shut down his console and headed for wherever he goes when he's not shooting at someone.

Skipper said, "You look—and smell—better. I hope you threw your clothes overboard."

Anya spun in her seat and looked up at me with eyes that could melt iron, and I wished I were immune. But no man is that strong.

"Okay, so, anyway. The fire. It was obviously arson. Kenneth's truck is missing, and there was no sign of him in either his house or the camper. Speaking of the camper, it exploded well after the house fire was under control, and it wasn't an accident."

Skipper said, "I know. I debriefed Gator and Mongo while you were in the spa."

"The spa? What's that supposed to mean?"

She shook a finger. "You know the three-minute-shower rule."

I lowered my chin. "And you obviously don't know the I-sign-the-paychecks exemption to that rule. Now, let's talk about the fire."

She said, "Any ideas who might've started it or where Kenneth might be?"

"I've got a theory on the first question. One of the Caravans operated by Flambeau Exploration was circling overhead when we arrived on scene. I'd like for you to do a deep dive into that company and get me every detail you can dig up."

"I'm on it," she said.

"And one other thing. Pull the file on the oil rig job we did. I can't remember the owner's name, but I want to talk to him. If anybody knows about the oil business down here, it'll be him, and he owes me a favor."

Chapter 18
Honeytraps 101

Skipper was good at a thousand things, but she was the best on Earth at the game of efficiency. Without searching a single file or even blowing the dust off the box, she said, "His name is Thomas Meriwether, and he's CEO of Meriwether Energy Systems."

"That's him," I said. "How about a number?"

She blurted out his office, home, and cell numbers as if reading from a teleprompter, and I asked, "How do you do that?"

She smiled. "The same way you fly anything with wings. It's my world, baby."

I dialed the number and stuck the receiver to my ear.

The Texas drawl was heavy when Thomas Meriwether said, "Well, as I live and breathe, if it ain't my favorite double-naught spy. To what do I owe this pleasure?"

"Good evening, Mr. Meriwether. I hope I'm not interrupting anything."

He chuckled. "Just a twenty-two-ounce ribeye medium rare and a waitress who looks like she belongs on the Cowboys' cheerleading squad. What can I do for you, Chase?"

"That sounds delicious," I said.

"If you think she *sounds* delicious, you should see her walking away."

"I meant the steak, Mr. Meriwether."

"Of course you did. Now, what's this all about?"

I cleared my throat. "I'd like to get on your calendar to discuss oil exploration in the bayous of South Louisiana."

"Why, Chase? Are you going into the wildcatting business, son? 'Cause if you are, you're in the wrong place."

"No, nothing like that. We're working a case down here, and things get more bizarre at every turn. Is there a time you could carve out an hour to talk with me and get my head straight on how the whole thing works?"

"I've always got time for you, Chase. You saved my hide and a billion dollars, so I'll scrub whoever's on my calendar. When are you thinking?"

"How about when you finish your steak?"

"Oh, it's that urgent, is it? Well, in that case, I'll forego a glorious evening with the runner-up for Ms. Texas and pencil you in. Are we doing this face-to-face or on a secure line?"

I said, "Surely the secrets to the oil exploration business aren't classified, are they, Mr. Meriwether?"

He laughed so hard I could almost hear him slapping his knee. "Boy, you listen to me when I tell you the oil-hunting business is more classified than anything the Pentagon's got going on. Take down this number and call me in two hours."

I wrote down the number. "Thank you, Mr. Meriwether. Enjoy that steak, and we'll chat in two hours."

Skipper giggled, and I said, "You were listening in, weren't you?"

"Maybe a little," she confessed. "Two hours should be more than enough time to dig up some dirt on Flambeau."

Anya cocked her head, and I asked, "What just happened in your skull?"

She said, "This word, *flambeau*, is French, but in Russian is *fakel*. I think this means in English maybe *torch* or *really big candle*."

"All right," I said. "Should that mean something to me?"

She furrowed her brow. "I do not know, but something about name rings for me small bell inside head."

"Keep chewing on it," I said. "If anything comes to you, don't keep secrets."

She nodded. "Before long shower, you said you needed my brain. It is now yours."

I settled into a chair. "Your brain doesn't work the same way mine or Skipper's does. Because of your KGB and SVR training, you pick up on things we overlook, so I want to lay this out for you and get your initial reactions. Are you good with that?"

"Okay. I will try."

"Don't try. Just tell me what pops into your head at any point while I tell you the story."

"I can do this," she said.

I slid a legal pad from the console and positioned it on my thigh. It took several minutes to take Anya through everything we knew about the situation, and she listened intently to every word.

When I finished, she said, "This is not mission for us. This is mystery for police."

"I couldn't agree more," I said, "but the handful of cops in the parish don't care, and Kenneth is afraid of going back to prison, so he's not willing to push the issue from a criminal perspective."

She twisted several strands of hair between her fingers. "Does he have money?"

"He's got to have some money. The logs he pulls are worth a fortune, and he can't have any debt. His truck is twenty years old, and his house is...*was* little more than a shack."

"Where is his money? If it was inside house, it is now burned away, no?"

"I don't know. Skipper couldn't find a bank account, and you're right about the money if it was in that house. Why does it matter if he has or had any money?"

She said, "I think someone is trying to make him go away without killing him. If he has enough money, it is possible for him to do this, but if he has no money, he cannot go anywhere."

I considered her idea until she said, "We must think of reason someone would want him to go away. Does he have enemy?"

"Not that I know of, but I think that's something we should dig into."

She said, "His niece... Her name is Cecilia, yes?"

"That's right."

"Maybe she knows answers we do not. I think she will tell to Gator everything."

"There it is," I said. "That's why I needed your brain."

I called, and Gator materialized in the CIC.

The hesitant look on his face said he had no idea why I summoned him. "Did I do something wrong?"

"Have a seat," I said. "You've done nothing wrong. In fact, you may have done something very right."

He pulled up a chair, but the worry didn't leave his face. "Okay, so what is it?"

Anya said, "You have relationship with girl Cecilia, yes?"

Gator's eyes danced between Anya and me. "I wouldn't necessarily call it a relationship. I mean, she's fun and cute, but—"

"This is relationship, and you must now get her to tell to you everything about Kenneth. You can do this, yes?"

He turned to me. "I'm not sure I understand what you want me to do."

I took the reins. "What Anya means is that you have a closer connection with Cecilia than any of the rest of us. She's comfortable with you. That means she won't have her guard up if you start asking questions."

Anya jumped in. "Is like honeytrap, except with boy instead of beautiful girl like me."

"Honeytrap?" he said. "You want me to sleep with her to get her to talk?"

Anya said, "No, this is not necessary. Is very different for women. She is very pretty girl in world of men, so it will not be unusual to her if you want to sleep with her. What is unusual is that you want to talk and listen and spend time with her. These are the things she does not get but she wants."

He ran a hand through his hair. "So, I'm supposed to pretend to like her and get her to spill her guts. Is that what you're saying?"

Anya smiled. "I do not believe you have to pretend. I think you do like her. This will make it even easier for you, but there will come time when you are alone with her, and she will offer herself to you."

Gator stiffened. "This is getting uncomfortable. It's like talking about sex with your parents."

Anya placed a foot on the side of Gator's chair and shoved him across the floor. "I am not old enough to be mother for you. This is insult, and I do not like you now."

He dug his heels into the deck and stopped his backward momentum. "Dad, would you do something with Mom? She's getting cranky again."

I chuckled. "Roll back over here, and we'll tell you where babies come from."

He said, "No, thanks. I'm good right here."

Anya bit her lip. "You have not already slept with her, have you?"

"We slept in the same bed in the camper one night, but it was perfectly innocent, and nothing happened. Chase was there. He was three feet away."

Anya smiled. "This is very good. This means she thinks you do not like girls, or you are gentleman. Either of these is good. She believes already she can trust you."

Gator stared directly at me. "I like girls."

"Relax," I said. "I wasn't planning to ask you to snuggle."

He rolled himself backward two more feet, and Anya giggled. "Come with me, silly boy. I will teach to you how to ask correct questions and to let her know you also like girls...especially her."

I couldn't resist throwing a departing jab. "Make sure you teach him that thing women like with the spatula and oven mitt."

Anya said, "Yes, I could teach to him that, or"—she leaned toward me—"I could teach to him that thing you like."

I held up a hand. "That's enough! Just go do the honeytrap class with Gator, and leave me out of it."

* * *

When two hours passed, Skipper established a secure connection with the number Thomas Meriwether gave me, and the Texan started talking.

"That's impressive timing, son. Most folks don't respect other people's time these days. I appreciate your courtesy."

I said, "There's nothing more valuable than time."

He let out a chuckle. "Well, maybe, but black Texas crude comes mighty close. So, what can I do for you, son?"

I didn't love him calling me *son*, but I was in his world and needed his wisdom, so I brushed it off. "I'd like to start with a company called Flambeau Exploration. Have you ever heard of them?"

He let out a long, low whistle. "What have you gotten yourself mixed up in, Chase? Them boys over at Flambeau ain't got a sense of humor at all."

"I'm learning that. There are a couple of Cessna Caravans—"

Before I could finish, he said, "Yeah, I know about those Caravans. You're talking about the ones with the telephone pole sticking out of their tails, ain't you?"

"I am. I'm working a situation with a guy who owns six thousand arpents in two parishes in South Louisiana."

Meriwether said, "Wait a minute. Hold on there, boy. That's nearly five thousand acres if my French math ain't all screwed up."

"Your math is right on the money."

"Yeah, right on the money is right. Does this guy of yours own the mineral rights to those six thousand arpents?"

"He does."

"Let me guess. Them boys over at Flambeau are trying to scare your man off that land, and you're wanting to start a fistfight with 'em."

"You know me, Mr. Meriwether. I love a good fisticuffs."

"I know you do, son, but let me tell you a thing or two about spitting into the wind. Those Flambeau boys are rumored to be mobbed up. Nobody's ever crossed them and lived long enough to prove it, but they're a powerful force in the world."

"In the world?" I asked. "Do you mean they're international?"

"You can bet your bolo they're international, and if they get wind there might be a drop of oil on the moon, they'll be interstellar."

I said, "Before we get too excited, tell me about these probes they've got. Can they really find oil?"

A sound like his boots falling from his desk and onto the floor came through the receiver. "No, they can't find crude with any degree of accuracy, but they can find natural gas, and where there's gas, there's usually crude. Five thousand acres of bayou might be worth more money than I've ever spent on ex-wives, especially if somebody like Flambeau sniffed some methane bubbles. Are you ready for a little geology lesson, son?"

"Sure, let's have it."

In an instant, the cowboy-hat-wearing oil man turned into a geology professor. "Sometimes, natural gas finds its way into large cracks and spaces between layers of overlying rock. This gas is called conventional natural gas. In other places, you can find natural gas in small pores of shale, sandstone, and other types of sedimentary rock. That's called tight gas. You've heard of fracking, right?"

"Of course."

He continued. "That's what they're after when they harvest by fracking. But the kind of gas we're talking about occurs with deposits of crude oil. We call that associated gas, and that's what Flambeau's after. They can bleed off all the natural gas and still have millions of barrels of crude to harvest. We're talking about real money now, son."

I said, "Thanks for the lesson, but I'm afraid we're getting a little ahead of ourselves. Where else does Flambeau explore?"

"Where *don't* they explore is a better question. They kicked off in Eastern Europe a bunch of years ago. That's where most of the commie money comes from in the Soviet Union."

"There's no such thing as the Soviet Union anymore."

He laughed. "Maybe not, but there's still billions of cubic feet of gas flowing behind what used to be the Iron Curtain, no matter what you call it now."

I said, "I've taken up too much of your time already, but I'd like to ask one final question. What's your advice for me if I do start a war with these people?"

"Have you still got that crazy Russian chick on your crew?"

"Yes, sir. She's still with us."

It sounded as if his boots landed back on top of his desk. "Then I recommend siccing her on 'em and getting out of the way."

"That sounds like sage advice, Mr. Meriwether."

"It is, son. Trust me. Now, I've got one more question for you before we wrap this thing up. How much does your man want for that five thousand acres of swamp gas?"

"If I can find him, I'll ask him. Thanks for your time."

"Wait a minute, Chase. Did you say you can't find him?"

I caught the handset just before I handed it back to Skipper. "Yes, sir. He's missing after his house burned to the ground earlier today."

He groaned. "Then don't waste your time looking for him. Just notify the next of kin and tell them you've got a buyer. You should throw in a nice finder's fee for yourself while you're at it. A man's got a right to have his expenses covered and to get paid for his time and trouble."

"Thank you, Mr. Meriwether. I'll be in touch."

Chapter 19
Something I Understand

"What are you smiling about?" Skipper asked after closing the connection on the secure line.

"I'm smiling because this thing just became a war, and war is something I understand."

She spun a monitor so I could see it clearly. "It's about time. Let's do some of that black ops stuff."

I rolled forward and focused on the screen. "What's this?"

"This, my favorite spy, is the home and gentleman's ranch of one Sidney Barbour. It's just outside Hockley, Texas, northwest of Houston."

I asked, "Who's Sidney Barbour? And why do I care?"

She zoomed in on an overhead view of a palatial estate on the outskirts of Houston. "Sidney Barbour is the CEO of Flambeau Exploration North America."

I grinned, and she rolled a few feet away. "Don't do it."

"Don't do what?" I asked.

She waggled a finger in the air between us. "You were about to hug me, kiss me on the forehead a thousand times, and tell me I'm a genius. You're welcome to proceed with the genius part, but let's skip the rest of it."

"You know way too much about me."

She pulled off her glasses. "I know *everything* about you, and I can prove it."

"You think so?"

She spun the monitor away and typed furiously for several seconds before saying, "Okay, let's hear it. Who are you taking on the raid?"

"What raid?"

She planted her hands on her hips and raised an eyebrow. "Don't pretend you're not already planning to hit Sidney Barbour's house. Now, tell me who you're taking with you."

I extended a finger for each teammate. "I'll take Kodiak, Shawn, and Gator inside the house."

"Keep talking."

"Singer will stand overwatch, Disco will drive, and Mongo and Anya will travel with us as alternates and quick reaction force in case one of us gets hurt or it turns unnecessarily ugly."

She spun the monitor back toward me, and the exact list of operators and their assignments I'd created on the spot appeared in the center of the screen.

She crossed her arms. "I told you."

"Okay, I concede. You know everything about me. I'd love to see a—"

She cut me off and struck a key. "Floor plan and security system schematic, including cameras and motion detecting sensors?"

Before she could escape, I had her in my grasp, and I planted half a dozen wet, sloppy kisses directly on her forehead.

She squirmed and jerked until I finally let her escape.

"Stop doing that! You know I hate it, and it's unwanted affection in the workplace. There's a law against that, you know."

I lowered my head in mock shame. "Go ahead. Turn me in to HR. Maybe they'll fire me this time."

She wiped her forehead. "When are you leaving?"

"Tomorrow morning. Line us up a pair of Suburbans at the closest small airport and overnight lodging for us and the airplanes."

"Consider it done. Plan for Houston Executive Airport."

"You're the best," I said. "Now, where did Anya take Gator?"

She rolled her eyes. "I'm not a Russian zookeeper. Stop asking me where she is."

I leaned in for another forehead kiss, but she stuck her pen beneath my chin. "It may not be a knife, but it's still going to hurt."

I surrendered and went in search of the honeytrap training class.

I found the professor and her student in Gator's cabin. "Don't you two look cozy?"

Gator jumped, pulling away from Anya, but the Russian didn't flinch.

I said, "I didn't mean to interrupt whatever that was."

Anya looked up at me with those eyes. "I am teaching to him art of touch. You remember, yes?"

Oh, I remembered, and something down deep in my body felt the tiniest twinge of jealousy. I forced it down and tried to laugh it off at Gator's expense. "If you have to be in a training class, this one isn't so bad, is it?"

He stammered, and Anya came to his rescue. "I think he definitely likes girls."

"I'll get out of here and let you get back to...that. But I need both of you ready to go at zero four hundred."

Anya asked, "Where are we going so early?"

"We're going to a place called Hockley, Texas, to visit a guy named Sidney Barbour."

Gator scowled. "Should that name mean something to me?"

"Not yet," I said. "But it will soon. He's the CEO of Flambeau Exploration's North American division. I'm sure his perfectly manicured hands are clean, but I'm convinced that somebody working for him burned Kenneth LePine's house. We're going to pay him a little unscheduled visit tomorrow night and see if we can't shake a few answers out of him."

Anya got that look she only gets when it's time to put her perfectly honed skill set to use. "This sounds like very much fun."

"Calm down," I said. "You're backup and QRF with Mongo in case it goes sideways. I'm not ready to unleash you on these guys yet."

Her shoulders dropped. "I told to you I will do whatever you need, but is waste of skill to leave me outside."

"Don't worry. You'll get your time at bat, and who knows? Maybe we'll get wrapped up in Barbour's house and you'll have to pull us out."

Her eyes lit up again, and I stepped back through the door. "Continue your little lovey-dovey session, but hit the sack early...and alone."

I called the rest of the team together in the CIC and gave them the full briefing.

When I finished, Mongo said, "You're leaving me outside with Anya?"

"That's right. Somebody has to control her, and you're our best shot at that."

He nodded. "Roger that."

* * *

The ship's cooks had breakfast waiting at three thirty the next morning, and the whole team ate as if they'd never have another meal. The typical pre-mission banter didn't happen, and I wrote that off to the early hour.

The Huey had no trouble handling our weight and size, and Disco pulled her off the helipad and into the dark, humid morning air. Flames burning atop the vent stacks on oil rigs in every direction dotted the landscape as we soared over the black bayou. We'd done more than our share of scaring the life out of wealthy executives all over the world, but something about the day's mission left me questioning our readiness to kick down Sidney Barbour's front door.

My hesitance vanished in an instant the second I stepped from the Huey and saw our formerly beautiful Cessna Caravan sitting on her floats with all four tires slashed, just like the fire trucks a mile from Kenneth's house. But the damage didn't stop at the tires. Most of the windows were broken, and the bracing cables between the pontoons had all been cut.

I closed my eyes and focused on just breathing until Mongo laid a massive hand on my shoulder. "It'll be all right, boss. We'll make them pay."

I turned to Anya. "It looks like we're in need of a ride to Texas. Do you happen to know anybody who's got a Citation jet we could borrow?"

On the short flight to Houston Executive Airport in Anya's plane, I called Skipper. "They got to the Caravan. It'll need all four tires, new glass, and a ferry permit to get it back to the factory in Wichita."

"These guys aren't messing around," she said. "I'll get Cotton on his way and a security team in place. You must be in Anya's plane."

"We are. Well, most of us are. Gator and Disco are bringing the Huey. We'll beat them there by at least ninety minutes, but I couldn't leave the chopper on the ground. God only knows what they would've done to it."

"Anything else?" she asked.

"Not yet. Are the Suburbans..."

"Do you really think you have to ask if the Suburbans and lodging have been arranged? Who's your girl Friday?"

"You're my girl every day."

She said, "No, that was a *Robinson Crusoe* reference."

"Yes, I know. I was just messing with you. I'll let you know when we're safe on deck in Houston."

"No need," she said. "I'm tracking you. But Chase..."

"What is it?"

"Just be careful, okay? I know you're mad about the fire and now your airplane, but keep your head on straight."

"It's not *my* airplane. It's *ours*, and I promise to keep my focus."

Houston Executive was busier than I expected, but just as promised, our matching pair of black Suburbans waited beneath the portico at Henriksen Jet Center. The gentleman behind the desk allowed us to drive one of the rented SUVs onto the parking apron to unload what he called "bags" from the Citation.

Some of our gear was in bags, but I was thankful we could park close enough to the jet to mask our movement of enough tactical gear to support an infantry platoon.

Our first stop was the rented house Skipper arranged, and once again, she hit a grand slam. The house was perfect, with an oversized garage for the Suburbans and enough privacy to avoid attracting unwanted attention.

By the time we had our gear arranged in the vehicles and we finished arguing over who got the master bedroom, it was time for Gator and Disco to show up. They landed two hundred feet from the house, and no one seemed to notice. I was beginning to believe that Texas may soon change its nickname from the Lone Star State to Mind Your Own Business, and I liked it.

We pulled up beside the Huey, and Disco stuck his head in the window. "Your boy got all the helo flying he wanted and then some. The autopilot wet the bed about ten minutes into the flight, so we had to hand-fly the thing all the way out here."

"I guess that means you don't feel like driving, huh?"

He huffed and replaced Mongo behind the wheel.

Finding Sidney Barbour's "gentleman's ranch," as Skipper called it, wasn't a challenge. The white painted fence around the property probably cost more than our beat-up Caravan back at Houma.

"That's quite a place," Kodiak said.

I surveyed the property. "It sure is. Tell me what you see."

Kodiak said, "I see a man who doesn't know squat about personal security. The gate on the main drive is a joke. I could push it open with a tricycle, but he does have a couple of decent cameras mounted up high."

"I wasn't planning on using the driveway. Keep looking."

We circled the property twice and memorized every detail. We even stopped at the two service entrances and picked the locks holding the simple metal gates closed. That would save us a little time and avoid the necessity of picking locks in the dark.

Shawn asked, "Can Skipper get us some satellite photos? It would be nice to see the place from God's perspective."

I gave him a grin. "We don't need no stinking satellites. We've got a helicopter."

We piled ourselves back aboard the Huey and flew three passes over the target property.

"This is going to be a piece of cake," Gator said, and the whole team groaned.

Mongo planted a size sixteen boot against Gator's hip and threatened to kick him out the door. "Now you've doomed us. You never say stuff like that, rookie."

Shawn leaned toward Gator. "Don't listen to those superstitious jokers. When you've got mad skills like you and me, who's got time for that business?"

Gator said, "Thanks. I appreciate that."

Shawn's cordial expression and tone turned ominous, and he grabbed Gator by the shoulders. "I was just playing. If you ever start a mission with a phrase like that again, I'll throw you out of the bird myself."

Chapter 20
My Dragon

The house Skipper rented for us was nothing short of spectacular. Gator's youth and computer prowess demanded that he be our IT guy, and he embraced the role. It took him less than half an hour to convert the great room into a war room. By the time the rest of the team planted themselves on the plush sofas and chairs facing the massive television above the mantle, Skipper was on a secure satellite link and filling the screen. A pair of cameras perched on the hearth and mantel delivered our image back to her in the CIC aboard the *Lori Danielle*.

Skipper kicked off the meeting. "Nice work on the aerial shots. I compiled them into a mosaic. You should see that on the television screen as well as on each of your tablets."

"Yep, we've got it," I said.

She continued. "I'll do the zooming from here, but if necessary, you'll be able to do the same on your tablets in the field."

The picture on the TV expanded until the roof of the house filled the screen. "Now I'll turn on the floor plan layers. We'll start with the ground floor. Keep in mind that the floor plans I have are what were submitted for the building permit. They should be reasonably accurate, but there could've been some remodeling or changes during construction."

We studied the layout and moved through the second and third floor.

I asked, "How about the security system schematics? Can you overlay those?"

"Of course," she said, and in seconds, the entire security system was displayed over the floor plans as well as the circuits to the exterior cameras.

I said, "Great job, Skipper. I wish we had intel like this on every op."

Anya squinted and leaned toward the screen. "What is that symbol at top left of schematic?"

Skipper said, "I saw that, too. It says 'stub' in the legend, but I don't know what it means."

Mongo, the big brain in the room, said, "It could be a stub-out for future expansion if they decide to build on or add another exterior circuit."

Skipper said, "That's as good as anything I could come up with, but I can check with a couple security system guys if you think it's important."

"Make that happen," I said. "I don't like loose ends."

She said, "Consider it done. Now, there's one more thing I want to bring up that might qualify as a loose end." The picture on the screen zoomed out until we could see several hundred feet around the house. "Take a look at the structure northwest of the main house. It's not on Google Maps, so it's likely new construction."

"It's a barn," Disco said. "A nice one, but it's just a barn."

Skipper said, "The barn isn't as interesting as what's between the house and the barn. Look at the grass."

I pinched the picture on my tablet until I was zoomed in on the area. "It's new grass."

Skipper said, "I don't know about new, but it's definitely a different color than the rest of the property. Maybe it's a septic drain field and the grass gets more nutrients there than anywhere else. I don't know, but there's something different about it."

"We'll keep that in mind," I said. "What else do you have?"

"I'm sure you already know, but I marked the obvious ingress and egress routes from the northeast."

"We picked those up, as well, but I'd like to come up with some alternates. Do you see anything that would prevent us from egressing to the west?"

She said, "There appears to be a fence running north and south, about a thousand feet to the west of the house, but it doesn't look substantial on the aerials. If you can get through, over, or around the fence, there's a county road running south. That could be a way out if things fall apart inside."

I took the floor. "Here's the plan. We'll recon that fence before sundown, and if necessary, we'll weaken or dismantle it. We'll hit the house from the northeast."

Singer raised a finger. "The only high ground I saw was the barn, so if you want me on overwatch, I'll put myself on the roof."

"Hold that thought," I said. "Disco, how close can you get the Huey to the house without waking anybody up?"

"Not close enough to be a sniper platform if that's what you're thinking. It's loud in cruise flight, but at a sustained hover outside ground effect, it would sound like thunder."

I sighed. "So much for that idea. I guess we're stuck with the roof."

Singer said, "Let's take a look at this from a tactical standpoint. There's no way Barbour is expecting us. There was no evidence of physical security other than a couple of toy gates. This place isn't Fort Knox, and who am I supposed to shoot?"

"Are you suggesting that we don't need overwatch?" Kodiak asked.

Singer shrugged. "Can you come up with a scenario that would result in me pressing a trigger tonight?"

I knocked on the arm of my chair. "I hear you, but I'm putting you on that roof. I want your eyes on the environment while we're inside."

Our sniper nodded. "That settles it. Drop me in a direct line with the house and barn. I'll move in just after dark and be in position within two hours, undetected."

I said, "Let's talk about QRF. Mongo, that's you and Anya. Where do you want to stage?"

He glanced at the Russian. "Are we staging with the chopper or an SUV?"

Anya said, "You can fly Huey, yes?"

Mongo shook his head. "Absolutely not. But I assumed you could."

"I can fly helicopter, but I have never flown Huey. Flying strange machine in darkness is not good idea. We should use vehicle."

"Let's make it plural," I said. "We'll take the seats out of the back of both Suburbans and stage the two of you at opposite ends of the property. That way, we can all quickly mount either vehicle. If you're staged together and get cut off, that leaves us without support."

"This is very good plan," Anya said. "Who will bring Singer out for egress?"

"That depends on how Barbour wants to play it. If he gives us what we want, Singer will stay in place to cover our retreat. We can pick him up with the chopper or either vehicle. At that point, it won't matter who sees us. We'll have the goods, and we'll be on our way home."

"What if he doesn't want to play ball?" Shawn asked.

"That's when we get to have a little fun with him. I doubt it'll take much persuasion to get him to tell us everything he knows. He's a CEO, not a SEAL."

Shawn lowered his chin. "You and I need to talk privately."

I glanced around the room at the team who was as much a family as a fighting force. "I don't know how you did it in the SEAL teams, but here, anything you need to say to me is perfectly fine to say in front of all of us."

Shawn's face hardened. "It would probably be better if we talked privately."

A thousand scenarios poured through my head. Was Shawn unhappy on the team? Did he disapprove of how we planned missions together? Perhaps he was accustomed to having orders come down from some unseen officer, but I would never run my team on that formula.

"Can it wait?" I asked.

He never looked away. "It shouldn't wait."

I stood. "Excuse us for a minute."

Shawn followed me through a set of double doors and onto the deck overlooking the stand of weather-beaten trees in the distance.

"What is it?"

He glanced back across his shoulder as if someone from inside might be listening in, and he seemed to consider what was about to come out of his mouth.

"Come on, Shawn. We've got a lot to do. Whatever's on your mind can't be as bad as you seem to believe. Let's hear it."

He took a long, deep breath. "It's just something you need to know about me. We should've discussed it before now, but I haven't been in a position with you guys for it to matter before this mission."

"Spit it out. Whatever it is, we'll deal with it."

He said, "I don't have limits."

I stared through his eyes in search of the depth of his revelation. "We all have limits. What are you talking about?"

He dusted off the top rail around the deck. "I mean, when it comes to interrogation, I don't have limits. I'll do whatever has to be done to get the information we need."

I leaned against the rail. "I think you may have the wrong idea about what's going to happen tonight. We're going to wake up a man who's most likely unarmed, and most certainly unprepared for a team of operators in his bedroom. He'll be scared, confused, and most likely more than willing to tell us whatever he knows to get us to walk away. It's not like we're going to waterboard the guy."

The newest member of my team shrugged. "I just want you to know how sharp the tools in your tool chest are. I don't know if you've got an interrogator, or if maybe you are that guy, but I need you to know that I'm that guy if you need me."

The emptiness in his eyes left me questioning my decision to bring him on board. Had I missed the signs of severe PTSD? Had I invited a psychopath inside my sacred circle?

I said, "Listen, if you need some time off to get your head straight..."

"My head is fine. I just need you to know that when you need a fire-breathing dragon, that's what I am."

The timing was wrong. I needed hours, and maybe days, to explore the inside of his head, but I had to take advantage of what little time I had. "Were you trained as an interrogator?"

"Yeah, but like all the meaningful lessons we learn in our world, the brutality of war was my teacher. I didn't become a monster in a class-room. It happened in a cave in Afghanistan."

Sometimes, just listening is the best way to ask a question, so that's what I did.

Finally, he said, "I pushed a Taliban fighter to my limit instead of his, and I let him lie to me because I didn't have the guts to push him over the edge of my cliff. I believed him when he spit out the location of his team through bloody lips and a broken body. I believed him, and we made our move based on what I pulled out of that lying, god-less piece of trash. We made our move straight into the ambush his team had planned from the moment that bastard let himself get captured."

He caught his breath and looked out over plains where I saw scrub brush and trees begging for water under the Texas heat, but what he saw was something impossibly different. He saw a cave in a mountain in Afghanistan, ten thousand miles from home, and a million miles from humanity.

He spat over the rail and drove his fist into the wood. "Six men. Six badass, hardcore frogmen died because I wouldn't break one more bone and deliver just one more punch to make sure my pris-oner was telling the truth. It should've been me. I should've been on point, but I wasn't, and I survived while my six brothers died in that hellhole."

Perhaps out of frustration or self-loathing, Shawn grabbed my shirt with a fist of iron and stared through me. "I killed those men. That's on me because I was too weak to push that seventeen-year-old kid just a little further. Their bodies died that night, but part of me went with them. The part of me where limits live... That part of me is gone forever. And that's what you need to know."

Chapter 21
Penetration

Shawn and I made our reentry, and it was only slightly less uncomfortable than that of the space shuttle returning from orbit. Every eye in the house locked on us, and it was obvious they were placing wagers on whether we were going to explode in a spectacular fireball or touch down and gently roll to an uneventful stop at our very own Cape Canaveral. My money was on something in between.

I tried to ignore the bevy of questions floating around the room, but the more I wanted to change the unspoken subject, the more I wanted to stare it into submission. So, I said, "I apologize for the sidebar, but Shawn was absolutely right. I was looking at things from a bit of a skewed perspective, and you deserve better from me."

I paused to down a swallow of water and the sting of extemporaneity of my next sentence. "I was thinking about this mission from my heels rather than my toes. We may not be rolling up a premier assassin or maniacal zealot, but we're dealing with a character who's motivated by the oldest and one of the strongest pursuits of mankind...greed."

I let the revelation hang in the air for a moment before saying, "He'll fight to hold on to his god just as fiercely—"

Shawn interrupted. "You can stop, Chase."

He turned from me to face his brothers- and sister-in-arms. "What he's doing is noble but unnecessary. He's right. Barbour will fight to hold onto what he holds most dear, but that's not what our conversation was about. Just like all of you, I've seen, experienced, and done things we don't talk about. The talk Chase and I just had was about one of those things, and I'm sorry for not being brave enough to bring it straight to all of you."

Curiosity on the faces of my team turned to concern as Shawn continued. "Most people live in a world of boundaries. There's one particular area in my life in which I have no such limits. Please don't take this as ego on my part. It's hardly that. It's far more confession than swagger. I'm one of the world's most effective extreme interrogators. I can't sit in a boardroom and negotiate a deal, but in a dark hole, face-to-face with evil, I'll tear the soul out of a man's body to get the intel I need, and I won't let anything—and I truly mean anything—stop me from getting what I need. What happens inside us when we're forced to erase the line between our own humanity and the demons we have to exorcise is a switch that can never be un-flipped. I needed my team leader to know what I'm capable of doing when human lives lay in the balance."

Singer laid his arm across Shawn's shoulders. "We've all got our crosses, and none of them is light, but together, we can carry them all."

Suddenly, I was ashamed of the pitiful excuse I tried to hang in front of my team, but I had done it to protect our newest brother. The lesson I learned in that moment was that we don't need protection from people who truly know, love, and understand us. That is the essence of family.

Mongo pretended to check his watch. "We're burning daylight."

I was thankful for the redirection and said, "You're right, big man. Anyone else have anything to add to the night's adventure?"

Gator grimaced. "I'm sorry for asking, but how about the rules of engagement if things go south in there?"

"Never be sorry for questions like that," I said. "I should've covered it. The ROE are simple for this one. Press forward to our target with minimal required force. Do not start a gunfight, but more importantly, don't lose a gunfight if somebody else starts one. I'm not expecting any armed resistance. There's no evidence of any human security measures. It's a soft target by any metric."

Gator nodded, and I said, "Anybody else?"

No one spoke up, and no one wore a look of concern, so I closed the briefing. "Get some rest and calories in your bodies. We'll hit the ground running an hour after sunset."

The team dispersed, but I kept Skipper on the line. "What have you accomplished on the Caravan back in Houma?"

She said, "I sent you an email, but I guess you've been busy. First, I need to know if you want to file an insurance claim. If you do, we'll need a police report."

"I'd rather leave the cops out of it. Can we get the Board to pay for it?"

"If we were on an officially sanctioned mission, I'm sure they'd cover it, but we're out on a limb on this one."

"Ouch," I said. "I guess we'll have to eat it."

"Okay. Twenty-four-hour security is on-site now, and Cotton will be there tomorrow. He says he can carry most of the parts and tools he'll need in one trip, but depending on how significant the damage is, he may need to make more trips."

"Tell him he's got a blank check. We'll cover whatever he needs and double his hourly rate. We need that plane."

"Yeah, I already told him all of that. I like it when our heads are in the same place. Do you want to ferry it to Wichita, or should he arrange that?"

"Have him take care of it if it isn't too much trouble. One of us can fly it up there when this is over if it's absolutely necessary."

"I'll pass it along," she said.

I stepped back onto the deck to continue the talk. "Are you doing okay?"

"As long as I'm working, I'm good. It's those hours when I try to close my eyes and sleep that kick my butt."

"I get it," I said. "We're going to take care of that very soon. Don't overdo it. We shouldn't need too much support on this one. It's pretty cut-and-dried."

"Chase Fulton!" Skipper said. "You know better than to say something like that."

"Yeah, yeah, I know, but—"

"But nothing. You keep your head in the game. Do you hear me?"

"Yes, Mother."

I could almost see her smile. "I'll mother you. Seriously, Chase. Be careful. I can't go through it again."

"I promise. I have to run. I'll let you know when we get underway tonight."

Based on the snores echoing through the house, I was the only one who couldn't drift off, so I lay on my bed playing through every possible scenario the night might bring. Every scene ended the same way, and for the first time in months, I felt like I was on top of my game and my ducks were lining themselves into a perfect row. Perhaps I slept for moments at a time, but my mind did very little resting in the two hours I spent horizontally.

An hour before sunset, I dropped Singer off at the spot he chose to begin his slow, methodical trek to his overwatch position atop the barn. While I was depositing our sniper into position, Disco pulled the camo netting from the blades of the Huey and moved the bird into position.

As I arrived back at the house, the sun slipped from the western sky, and like the predators of the night they were, my team came alive, seemingly fueled by the absence of the sun's glow. The lighthearted personalities who'd walked out of the afternoon's meeting were transformed into the hearts of warriors, and no matter how great our advantage would be in the coming night, every eye carried the look of determination and refusal to fail.

We donned our gear, stuck our com radios into their assigned pockets and opened the channel with the combat information center back aboard the ship.

"CIC, Sierra One. Radio check."

Skipper answered. "Loud and clear. How me?"

We continued down the line of operators until every radio was confirmed to be functioning perfectly.

We positioned Mongo and vehicle number one in a location from which the house was visible, but the SUV was not. Anya's position was a bit more precarious, but we managed to get the Suburban far enough off the road that it wouldn't be a glaring sign of a tactical operation underway only a few hundred yards to the south.

Just before ten thirty, Singer said, "Sierra Six is in position, and there's motion at the front gate."

I twisted in my seat, but I couldn't get a clear line of sight to the gate. "Roger, Six. We're blind to the gate, so report further movement."

"Roger."

A few seconds later, he said, "It's a vehicle in the drive and approaching the house."

"Can you see passengers?" I asked.

"Negative, and I'll be blind in a few seconds when the vehicle moves closer to the house."

"I've got a garage light," Mongo said.

"I've got it, too," Singer confirmed.

I said, "Get ready to move. I want to make our initial egress while they're moving from the vehicle and into the house."

"Vehicle is inside, and the door's coming down," Mongo said.

I gave the order. "Let's move."

We dismounted the vehicles and crossed the fence in silence, spreading out into a wide formation as we pressed forward across the field under the cover of the moonless night. Lights came on and went off at irregular intervals over the next few minutes as we slowly grew closer to our target.

When we reached the house, Kodiak silently turned the corner and pulled open the heavy metal box mounted on the side of the garage. "Ready to cut power on your mark."

I took a knee at the rear door and slipped a tensioning arm and pick into the deadbolt lock. The twist came quickly, and the bolt slid from the jamb and back into the housing of the lock. The knob that should've been easier to pick proved more of a challenge than I expected, and I believed for a moment I may have to force open the door. That would be far from optimal, but if it became necessary, I certainly wouldn't call off the operation because of a sticky lock.

I refocused my attention and pressed harder against the tensioning tool. The pins of the mechanism clicked, bound, and released just as they should, but the lock didn't turn. I glanced up at Shawn, and he raised the toe of his boot, but I shook off the offer and pressed the opposite direction on the tensioner. The barrel moved, and I probed at each pin again until the lock turned smoothly in the opposite direction of every knob lock I'd ever picked.

Shawn pressed the blade of his knife between the door and the jamb at the top left and gave me a nod. With the trigger for the door alarm still depressed beneath the blade of our SEAL's knife, we slipped silently into the kitchen, and I said, "Kill the power."

A second later, the few lights remaining in the house went dark, and we waited to hear the chirp of the alarm system's battery backup. The high-pitched tick sounded just as Kodiak stepped through the door.

Our night-vision devices gave us the ability to see clearly, and Kodiak moved like a cat across the kitchen to the entry door of the pantry, where the alarm panel waited just inside. I held my breath as he worked inside the panel.

When his work was done, he leaned back through the doorway and gave the okay signal. Shawn released the switch on the door, and nothing happened. There was no beep, no horn, not even so much as a click, and we were inside with the alarm system disarmed and darkness consuming the interior for everyone who was wearing nods.

The floor plans we committed to memory were perfect, giving us the ability to clear the first floor of the house in minutes. With no apparent movement inside the structure, we took our first strides up the stairs. I led the way up the front staircase with Gator to my left while

Kodiak and Shawn climbed the rear stairs. We reached the second floor simultaneously and continued down the hallway to the location of the master suite.

Just before I reached for the doorknob, Singer said, "One, Six. I've got movement in the barn."

We froze, and I took a knee. Talking wasn't an option, so I clicked my tongue against my teeth three times.

Singer said, "It's definitely human."

I had a thousand questions, none of which I could ask in the moment, but the best intel analyst on Earth lived inside my head, and she came on the line right on cue. "Visual or audible?"

Singer said, "I'm on the peak of the room. I hear the movement through the ridge vent."

"Single?" Skipper asked.

"Affirmative. Stand by."

No one made a sound, and the seconds passed like hours until the sniper said, "Someone just flushed a toilet."

Skipper asked, "Are we sure that's a barn?"

Singer said, "It looks like a barn, but there's definitely someone inside, and they have a toilet."

Skipper said, "Do you want any further intel, One?"

I clicked my tongue once, and she said, "Roger. Continue mission."

I turned the knob and lifted upward to take the weight of the door off the hinges. The last thing I needed was for Sidney Barbour to hear us coming and draw a weapon on us as we came through the door.

The hinges didn't squeak, and we moved through like ghosts. What I saw inside the bedroom made my heart sink, and I held up one finger.

Gator moved beside the bed and watched for my signal, even though our target clearly wasn't where we expected him to be.

I studied the room compared to the floor plan and moved into the bathroom. Barbour wasn't there, either, so I gave the signal, and Kodiak mounted the dressing bench situated at the foot of the enormous bed. He pressed the switch on his rifle and sent a flood of punishing white light pouring down on the only apparent occupant of the house.

At the same instant, Gator covered the woman's mouth and said, "I'm only going to hurt you if you don't give me what I want."

She whimpered and kicked at the mattress, sending the covers rippling in every direction. Shawn yanked the billowing covers from the bed, leaving the woman exposed, trembling, and obviously terrified.

Gator spoke in soft, measured tones. "I'm going to remove my hand from your mouth, and you're going to tell me where your husband is. If you make any sound other than that, I will put a bullet through your skull. Nod if you understand."

She nodded rapidly, and Gator kept his word. He slid his hand across her chin and pressed the muzzle of his suppressed 9mm to her temple.

She spoke between gasps and jerks. "He's not here."

Gator pressed the muzzle deeper into her flesh. "We know he's not here. Tell us where he is, and we'll let you live."

"Who are you people? What do you want?"

"Don't make me kill you, Mrs. Barbour. Next time you open your mouth, you will determine your fate. You'll either tell us exactly where your husband is, or you'll never hear the shot that will turn your brain into liquid. Now, tell us exactly where your husband is or die."

"He's..." She choked on the fear she was feeling as she tried to form the words.

Gator was doing well, and I was pleased, but I wasn't sure we could get Mrs. Barbour calmed down enough to tell us where Sidney was.

"He's where?" Gator asked in his continued gentle voice.

"He's... He's in the..."

"He's in the what?" Gator asked.

She took a ragged, jerking breath. "Back. He's in the back. Please don't—"

I planted a knee on the vacant side of the bed and pressed the hypodermic needle into her arm. As her struggling subsided and her breathing returned to something near normal, Gator said, "You're going to sleep for a while, and you'll be fine. You did well, and we're not going to hurt you, but we will stay with you until we're certain you're sleeping soundly."

I hooked two fingers beneath Shawn's arm and pulled him toward me. The two of us slipped from the room, leaving Kodiak and Gator to rock Mrs. Barbour back to sleep. We couldn't afford to have her making a phone call to anyone, especially not her husband in the back.

Chapter 22
Calling an Audible

Shawn and I descended the main staircase and paused inside the foyer. Our open channel comms gave us the ability to speak to every team member as if we were all in the same room. The system is a remarkable tool, but like all tools, it has its limitations. Gunfire, hand-to-hand fighting, and extremely loud environments led to communications chaos using the system. As I took a knee just inside the door of the Barbour's house, I wished our comms would allow me to hear the thoughts of the rest of the team and not just their words.

No battle plan survives first contact, and that statement never rang truer than it did that night in East Texas. Instead of the simple mission to enter the house, subdue the occupants, and interrogate Sidney Barbour, the operation turned into a two-pronged assault without intel on the interior of the second structure. As daunting as that challenge would be, we also had an innocent bystander tranquilized upstairs and no plan to deal with her after we rolled up her husband.

The combat information center aboard the *Lori Danielle* was the brain of our existence and the clearinghouse for the massive collection of intelligence we gathered in the field. However, the minute-by-minute operational decisions were made by the tentacles of the beast my team had become. Ultimately, those decisions were mine, and I alone bore the responsibility for their results and consequences.

I took a knee and announced the revised plan. "Attention all Sierra elements. Our target has changed. We have one secondary target subdued, but our primary is inside the structure to the north of the house. I need Anya and Mongo to close on the structure on foot. Gator and Kodiak, I need you to prep the secondary target for helo transport. Disco, stand by for two targets and two operators back to the ship. Acknowledge."

Gator said, "Roger. Packing for shipping."

Mongo said, "Closing on new objective."

Anya echoed, and Disco said, "I'll need two minutes to be airborne, so a heads-up call would be great."

"Expect it," I said.

The new plan fell together like pieces of a puzzle in my mind, and the clarity reinforced my confidence.

I mentally ran through the team, ensuring everyone knew their assignment. When I came to our sniper on my mental checklist, I said, "Singer, hold position and cover squirters."

His calm, confident tone added to my comfort level in calling an audible in the middle of the operation. "Roger. Holding position."

Shawn and I reached the barn just before Mongo and Anya and took a knee near the east entrance. When the others arrived, I said, "Gator and Kodiak are now the quick reaction force. Shawn and I will make entry through the west entrance. The two of you will enter here, and we'll work inward and upward depending on what we find inside. Noise and light discipline are key. We want to catch Sidney sleeping or at least lying in bed. We have no reason to believe he'll offer much resistance, so don't hurt him beyond what is necessary. Got it?"

Mongo and Anya nodded, and I said, "Skipper, how quickly can you get a floor plan for the barn?"

She said, "I've been working that, but there's no record of a building permit, so that probably means they built the barn without a permit and maybe without floorplans."

"It doesn't matter. We're still going in."

Anya pulled her pick kit and went to work on the doorknob.

I said, "It may turn backward. The lock on the house did."

She nodded without a word and kept working. Shawn and I sprinted for the opposite end of the building, and I had the lock open seconds after we arrived at the door.

"We're in," I said, and Anya replied, "Same."

I checked the area for prying eyes and gave the order. "Execute."

Our night-vision devices made the interior of the barn look like an operating room. The few dim lights were enough to give us perfect visibility. The ground floor of the barn was a collection of horse stalls, but they all appeared to be empty. The floor was clean, and a set of stairs appeared on the north wall.

We could see Mongo and Anya moving like cats toward the stairs at their end of the barn, so I timed our ascent with theirs. Reaching the top, the collection of dim lights on the ground floor no longer gave us the clear visibility we had before climbing the stairs. The infrared floodlights mounted on our rifles replaced the light we'd enjoyed downstairs, and we slowed our pace to match the new environment, planting each foot as gently as possible as we progressed toward the center of the barn.

Mongo and Anya pressed inward at the same pace Shawn and I made until we met at a pair of double doors near the center of the barn. If we expected armed resistance beyond the doors, we'd form a column and burst through the opening in a dynamic entry designed to overwhelm the fighting force inside, but we had no reason to believe we'd encounter anything other than a snoring multi-millionaire.

I turned the knob and lifted as I pulled the door toward us. It swung open, and Anya led the silent penetration into the interior room. Shawn followed, and I took third position through the door. Mongo always played the anchor man because of his size. Although he'd make a great shield, it was impossible to see over or around the monster.

The lighting conditions changed again when we cleared the door, and it took our nods and eyes a few seconds to adjust. A pair of doors appeared out of the fog to our left and right with a single door straight ahead. A slice of light bloomed from beneath the single door.

The mindset of stepping through a door with no idea what waits on the other side is the core of close-quarters combat, but combining the psychology of stepping into an arena of potential gunfire doesn't leave a lot of mental bandwidth to study the architecture. When I was convinced there was no immediate danger of incoming fire, I tried to picture what lay behind each door. The single door straight ahead was most likely a bathroom. People tend to leave dim lights on in bathrooms to make midnight stumbles to the head less treacherous.

With the point of a finger, I dispatched Anya to clear the small room, and she moved as if she were part of the environment. Every stride landed silently, and the building seemed to absorb her rather than resist her advance. A few feet from the opening, she placed one hand on the floor and lowered herself until she could see through the sliver of space beneath the door. Searching for feet beyond a door when given the opportunity is an invaluable piece of early intel about what awaits on the other side.

She rose back to her feet, lowered her rifle against her chest, and drew her pistol. In one fluid motion, she grasped the knob, swung the door outward, and stepped inside. Silence continued, so I had my answer before she emerged. The small room was unquestionably clear.

The instant Anya stepped from the room, Singer's voice filled my head. "I hear Anya moving directly beneath me. The previous movement was northwest."

I clicked my tongue against my teeth twice to let our super-hearing sniper on the roof know I heard and understood. Anya, Shawn, and Mongo all made eye contact with me, and I held up two fingers and pointed toward the doors to the northeast. They cleared the empty room almost as quickly as Anya cleared the bathroom, and they rejoined the SEAL and me.

Still determined to remain silent until we made our entry, I signaled toward the target door where Singer heard the footsteps. Each member of my team nodded, and I formed a fist. We were going dynamic.

We formed the same column we'd used to enter the enclosed section of the second floor, and Mongo squeezed my shoulder. I laid my left hand on Shawn's shoulder and gave him a squeeze. He did the same to Anya, and everyone in the column knew we were a second and a half away from scaring the religion out of Sidney Barbour, who was no doubt sleeping like a baby on the other side.

Anya turned the knob and yanked open the right door. She exploded through the opening, turned right, and scanned for targets. Shawn powered through one step behind her and turned left, establishing an intersecting fan of fire with Anya. Mongo and I cleared the opening and joined our teammates with practiced speed and precision.

I focused on the bed with the headboard centered on the exterior wall and yelled, "Hands! Hands! Hands! Show me those hands!"

The form beneath the blanket never moved, so I lunged forward, grabbed the cover, and yanked it from the bed. To my horror, a pair of pillows lay end to end, giving the appearance of a body, and the air left the room.

We had just stepped into an ambush.

The realization hit my teammates at the same instant, and each spun, covering the room with their muzzles. I dropped to the floor and sent my infrared light cascading beneath the bed. Nothing was there.

"Find him!" I ordered.

Looking straight up as if I could see through the roof, I said, "Singer, report movement or squirters."

The sniper said, "Roger. There's no exterior movement."

Our situation was bad, but we were still alive, and no one was shooting at us.

"Gator, Kodiak, get out here and cover the exits from the barn."

"Moving," came their one-word reply.

I backed to the corner of the room as my mind churned trying to piece together what I'd missed. "Disco. Spool it up and get in here."

No matter what scenario would unfold in the coming minutes, our cover was blown, and our advantage of silence was in the wind.

Two sounds hit me simultaneously.

Singer said, "Movement interior. Are you running?"

The second sound was the thud of an object striking the floor a few feet in front of me.

I didn't answer my sniper. Instead, I yelled, "Grenade!"

I threw myself to the floor, praying the shrapnel cone would miss me, but I was close enough for the concussion alone to rip me apart. To my horror, Shawn dived directly toward the grenade with both arms outstretched.

The SEAL had been with our team only a few months, but he was making the ultimate sacrifice to keep the rest of us alive. Every fiber of my being cried out for him to run and let me absorb the blow, but even though the scene played out in ultra-slow motion, there was no time for either of us to survive the coming blast.

Shawn's left hand landed squarely over the grenade, and he rolled, hurling the killing device through the air and open door. Through my nods, I watched the black, baseball-sized orb sail over the railing and fall toward the first floor.

The blast came, and it felt like thunder from within my chest. Shrapnel filled the interior of the barn, and the world around me waved in and out of focus for a long second.

Singer yelled, "Interior, report!"

I could barely make out the words he'd shouted, but I shook off the ringing in my head and said, "We're alive. He's in the attic."

Chapter 23
Great Minds

With rolling echoes of thunder still pounding in my skull, Skipper said, "Sitrep. What's going on in there?"

A thousand answers to that question floated somewhere above me, but the truth was a phrase I couldn't bring myself to say. "Unclear, but all four inside are still operational."

Before she could respond, automatic weapons fire roared from the overhead, and I watched for the rounds to tear through the ceiling and rip us into shreds, but they didn't come.

A thousand scenarios raced through my mind, and I called, "Singer, report."

The sniper's breathy response came. "Shots fired through the roof. He knows I'm up here. Egressing now."

Anya pulled open a narrow closet door, revealing a ladder protruding from the ceiling inside. She and Shawn stood with their eyes trained on me, obviously waiting for the order to give chase.

I spread two fingers, pointed to my eyes, and then to the ceiling. Shawn started up the ladder with his rifle leading the way. Getting eyes into that attic was the only way we could know what or who we were facing.

Near the top of the ladder, our SEAL pulled out a small telescoping rod with a round mirror affixed to the end and extended it through the opening above. He made a three-hundred-sixty-degree sweep of the space and then glanced back at me while shaking his head. He stowed

THE CREOLE CHASE · 185

the mirror and signaled with a raised thumb that he wanted to go up, so I gave a nod.

Shawn's muzzle was first through the opening as his boots made slow, deliberate progress up the ladder. He twisted his massive shoulders to squeeze through the opening as he took one more step upward. Then, to my surprise and utter terror, both of his boots left the rungs of the ladder, and he yelled, "Get down!" as he fell back through the opening.

Mongo, Anya, and I dived for the deck, but I couldn't take my eyes off the scene unfolding in front of me. Before Shawn's boots hit the floor, the overhead exploded into a billion shards of wood, sheetrock, and insulation. Shawn landed on his side with a massive cloud of dust boiling around him and hundreds of pounds of debris raining down on him.

With lumber still flying and the roar of the explosion still echoing through the building, Mongo lunged for Shawn. The giant gripped the unconscious SEAL by the collar of his plate carrier and dragged him from the rubble. Mongo stumbled and fell backward, dragging Shawn's limp body on top of him. I shoved two fingers against the flesh of our newest team member's neck, begging for a pulse.

His helmet and nods were gone, and his rifle hung from its sling around his neck and shoulder. His face was a bloody, dirty expanse of nothing.

Finally, a weak thud touched my fingertips, and Shawn's nostrils flared slightly.

I yelled, "Get him out of here."

Mongo scampered to his feet and hefted Shawn across his shoulder, leaving Anya and me to continue the fight.

I grabbed the footboard of the bed and dragged it beneath the gaping wound in the ceiling where the tiny closet and ladder had been only seconds before. Using the bed as a step, I leapt upward and planted both arms on the framing of the destroyed ceiling. Anya stepped onto the bed and grabbed each of my boots, placing them on her shoulders. With her effort from below, I hauled myself into the attic and scanned every direction in search of any sign of Sidney Barbour, but the smoke and dust from the explosion reduced the visibility to mere feet. Reaching beneath my plate carrier, I yanked my T-shirt up and over my mouth and nose to avoid breathing the dust that filled the air.

Convinced that Barbour had to be at least as blind as me in that environment, I abandoned my search and spun around to grab Anya's arms. I pulled the Russian through the opening and deposited her beside me.

Hoping my comms were still operational, I said, "Anya and I are pursuing into the attic. Shawn is down, and Mongo is bringing him out. Hold your fire, and somebody cover the exfil."

Singer said, "I'm on the ground and covering the northeastern corner."

Gator said, "I've got the southwest, and Kodiak's moving to cover Mongo and Shawn. Where are they coming out?"

Mongo huffed. "We're moving to the west end."

Disco's calm voice came over the radio. "The bird's ready to fly if Shawn needs dust-off."

Mongo's breath was coming hard, and he said, "Get that chopper in here. Shawn needs more help than I can give in the field. He's down hard."

I leaned toward Anya. "How many mags do you have?"

She whispered, "Eight. Do you want me to pin him down?"

I pulled four thirty-round mags from my rig and slid them into her hand. "Great minds think alike. I'll stay low, and I want every ounce of lead you can fire to fill the air above me. I'm going hunting."

The telltale *womp-womp* of the Huey settling into ground effect reassured me that Shawn was only minutes away from an emergency room somewhere near Houston, but the sick feeling that followed reminded me that we no longer had a helo for extraction. In that moment, I had no way of knowing that neither of those things was true.

Staying as low as my gear would allow, I crawled on my belly toward the east end of the barn's attic. The holes Barbour had shot in the roof allowed just enough light into the space to give my nods something to magnify. My visibility wasn't great, but it was better than nil. The deeper I crawled into the space, the more I could see, but if Barbour had access to grenades and explosives, I had to believe he had his own set of night-vision goggles. If I turned on my infrared light or laser, it would point directly back to me, giving him a perfectly lit target to destroy. Darkness, in that moment, was both my friend and my enemy.

When I was ten feet from Anya, she raised her M4 and sent a flurry of 5.56mm rounds screaming over my head. The projectiles were mindless killing machines at that point, and they'd be just as happy to tear into my back as they would to find the flesh of Barbour's body somewhere in the dark. Anya wouldn't lower her rifle, but the supersonic lead slicing through the air just a few inches above me was enough to keep my attention focused as low as possible.

Counting full auto rounds leaving a muzzle is impossible, but the pause in the gunfire made it clear Anya was changing magazines. That gave me two seconds to scurry forward as quickly as possible, and I gained ten feet of advantage just before she opened fire again. This time, though, two sets of automatic weapons sounds pierced the air. Barbour was shooting back.

The sound of his submachine gun against the thunder of Anya's M4 was like a violin competing with a bass drum. He was clearly ahead and right, and in that moment, I wanted his neck in my hands. Crawling onto his dead body full of Anya's rounds would be a disappointment. I wanted to look into his eyes and make him beg to stay alive. I couldn't call off my gunner, though. If she let up, he'd fill the attic with lead until neither of us was alive.

It was time for a fresh magazine for Anya, so I braced the toes of my boots against a rafter and prepped to charge Barbour when the pause came. It came, but Anya's wasn't the only gun that fell silent. Barbour's weapon hushed as well, and the eerie silence made my blood run cold.

Did she hit him? Am I on the verge of explaining to the police why I was in a gunfight in somebody else's attic a thousand miles from home?

Anya's fire returned, but it wasn't rifle fire. It was the dull thud of her 9mm instead of the sharp crack of the M4. She was alive, but her rifle clearly was not.

A wedge of light exploded from the southeast corner of the attic, and the shadow of a figure flew into the beam.

I yelled, "Cease fire!"

Anya's pistol fell silent, and I raced toward the opening through which the light had come. I dived to the deck and stuck my head through the hole. It was a small ladder affixed to the wall. Barbour was nowhere in sight, but he had to be there. He had to be somewhere near the base of the ladder.

I spun and forced my body through the narrow opening and onto the ladder. As I descended, I made the radio call. "He's on the ground floor at the east end. Take him alive if possible."

When I hit the ground at the base of the ladder, the world around me exploded into bright white light. I threw a hand against my nods, shoving them up and over my helmet on their hinge. Someone had turned on the lights, and my eyes were paying the price.

As I shook off the confusion from the flood of light, I heard Anya descending the ladder above me. She hit the ground to my right, and I said, "Clear the stables."

She started down the right side, and I moved left, kicking open stall doors as we went. We were no longer in a capture mindset. We were fighting for our lives, and I was determined that either Barbour's body or mine would be carried out of that barn.

Every stall was clear and looked as if the concrete floor had just been scrubbed and disinfected. If there had ever been a horse in that barn, there was no sign of him left. With only four stalls remaining for

Anya and me to clear, the thundering report of Singer's .338 Lapua roared through the night.

Singer said, "Do you still want him alive, boss?"

I stopped my search through the stalls. "If you can take him without casualties, take him alive. Say position."

He said, "You'll find a burning Jeep two hundred yards east of the barn, and your target is pinned to the ground."

"Hold him," I ordered. "I'm on my way."

Anya and I sprinted from the barn to find the scene just as Singer had described, with the Jeep in flames. Kodiak stood six feet away from Barbour with his rifle trained on his head.

Kneeling on the man's back was our SEAL with his sidearm pressed into his prisoner's neck. "Come on, boss. Please let me kill him."

I took a knee and grabbed a handful of Barbour's hair. With his head twisted far enough for him to look into my eyes, I said, "I've got a few questions for you, but why don't you take a little nap first?"

A butt-stroke to the temple sent him into the spirit world, and Kodiak stuck him with the same tranquilizer that had his wife sleeping like a baby.

Shawn relaxed and settled to the ground beside me.

I watched him squint and reopen his eyes several times. "I thought you were dead."

He twisted his neck, popping his spine in both directions. "I'm pretty sure I was, but I rubbed a little dirt on it and sucked it up. I feel better now. Are we taking this guy back to the ship? I'd like to have a little prayer meeting with him. Just the two of us."

"We're taking both of them," I said. "Gator, you and Mongo get the wife while we load this heap on the chopper."

Disco touched down a few yards away, blowing fire from the burning Jeep in every direction, and we had both detainees strapped inside in no time.

I yelled into the cockpit, "Do you have the fuel to make the ship nonstop?"

Disco gave me the thumbs-up, and I patted the door.

I turned to the team. "I want Mongo and Kodiak on the bird. The rest of us will clean this up and meet you back at Houma after you drop off our guests in their suite aboard our luxury ocean liner."

Chapter 24
Always Faithful

Disco lifted off and turned to the northeast to avoid the complex airspace of Houston, and the remainder of the team was left in a field of grass beside a still-burning Jeep.

I tossed a rock at Singer. "Did you kill the Jeep?"

He rubbed the barrel of his favorite rifle with great affection. "She and I didn't think you wanted him to get away, so we politely invited him to stick around."

I shook my head. "Remind me never to ask you to hand out invitations. Let's get this mess cleaned up and head back to the ship. I don't care how many lives our resident cat has left. I want to get Shawn in front of Dr. Shadrack before his brains start dripping out of his ears."

We put out the fire and pushed what remained of the Jeep back into the small garage attached to the east end of the barn. After restoring power to the house, from the street, the property looked just like it had the day before, and we were eastbound in Anya's Citation at four hundred miles per hour.

* * *

Einstein wrote a great deal about space-time, and although I'll never be smart enough to understand anything he wrote, I'll always agree that time passes at variable rates depending on what's happening around me. Time stands still when bullets fly, but even at four hundred miles per hour, downtime aboard someone else's airplane feels like an eternity.

When we finally landed back at Houma, I trotted across the tarmac and toward the Caravan with her new wheels and armed guards.

It was, in fact, one of those guards who stepped in front of me with one hand raised and said, "Stop right there, sir."

I put both hands above my head. "I'm Chase Fulton, and that's my airplane."

"I'll need some identification, sir."

I liked that guy immediately, and I produced sufficient ID to get his permission to approach my airplane.

He followed my every step as I walked the perimeter of the Caravan.

While tugging on the new rigging between the pontoons, I asked, "Have you heard Cotton mention anything about how long it'll take to have her ready to go to Wichita?"

The young man said, "When he left last night, he said the ferry permit should be approved today. I don't know what that means, but that's what he said."

"It means she's headed north very soon. What time does your shift end?"

"I don't know, sir."

"You don't know? How do you not know what time your shift ends?"

"It's a variable rotation, sir. Only the watch commander knows the schedule. We stand our post until we're relieved. That way, nobody can figure out our schedule and hit us when we're most vulnerable."

I furrowed my brow. "You're doing a variable relief watch for an airplane?"

"Yes, sir. We'd do the same if we were guarding a rock. It doesn't matter what we're protecting. It only matters that we keep it secure."

I stepped from beneath the plane. "You were a Marine, weren't you?"

"No, sir. I still am. I may not be on active duty anymore, but once a Marine, always a Marine."

"I admire the dedication. Semper Fi."

He shook his head. "Don't do that, sir."

"Don't do what?"

"Unless you live it, don't say it."

"Fair enough. Thanks for keeping her safe."

He shined his light along the row of broken windows along the fuselage. "If you don't mind me asking, sir, who did this?"

"Funny you should ask. We invited a gentleman to come over and have a talk with us tonight about that very subject. In fact, I should get to it. I wouldn't want to keep him waiting. That'd be rude."

He said, "Good luck with that, sir. Oh, and if you need somebody to rough him up and make him talk, my name is Pendleton."

"I'll keep that in mind, but I'm sort of a pacifist. I'm not into violence. Make love, not war, right?"

He checked his watch and walked away.

* * *

Back aboard the *Lori Danielle*, I delivered Shawn to Dr. Shadrack in sick bay.

The doctor met us at the door to his office. "Welcome back. It's nice to see nobody got blown up this time."

I eyed Shawn. "Well, now that you mention it, he did, but he's too stubborn to complain."

Shawn squeezed his temples between his palms. "It's nothing. Just a little headache."

"A headache, huh?" Dr. Shadrack said. "Have a seat, and let me take a look."

Shawn took a step back. "Seriously, Doc. It wasn't that bad."

I laid a hand in the middle of Shawn's back and encouraged him forward. "He took an explosion less than three feet away and fell about eight feet. I pulled him from beneath a few hundred pounds of lumber and sheetrock. He was unconscious for several minutes."

"I was just resting my eyes," Shawn said.

The doctor motioned toward a chair. "Don't worry, Shawn. I'm getting really good at treating late-night concussions for these guys. It seems they always pick on the new guy, and tonight's your night."

I left our SEAL in Dr. Shadrack's capable hands and took a stroll to the belly of the ship, where we kept our most special guests. I found Mongo watching over Sidney Barbour, who was hogtied and lying on his belly on the cold, steel deck.

"How's he doing?" I asked.

Mongo motioned toward our prisoner with his chin. "He wanted to wrestle, so I pretended to let him win for three seconds before doing that to him. He's all yours now, but I'll stick around just in case he gets feisty again."

I stepped through the open door of the brig cell and pressed my boot against Barbour's shoulder, rolling him onto his side. "You doing all right, Sid? Need anything? A cup of coffee? A cyanide capsule, perhaps?"

He spat blood and ire, and I stepped aside. "That's not very nice. You're a guest in my house, and you're making an ass of yourself. Show some basic human courtesy."

He spat again, so I pressed the sole of my boot against his face with a significant portion of my two hundred thirty pounds applied. "Listen to me, Barbour. We're going to play nice, or things are going to get very uncomfortable for you."

He bucked and shook his head like an animal until I lifted my boot. Staring back at me from the deck wasn't an oil man. He wasn't a mere exploration company CEO. The eyes of the man at my feet were mine. They were Clark Johnson's. They were the eyes of determined defiance, the eyes of unbreakable fortitude, and for the first time in my life, I questioned if I possessed the resolve to draw out the secrets he held inside the vault of his iron will.

"Let's try another approach. If I untie you, are you going to behave?"

Mongo stood from his chair, stepped into the doorway, and blocked the light from the corridor. Without a word, he had just warned me that untying Barbour was a bad idea.

With my giant five feet away, I didn't fear what an unarmed man might do to me, so I knelt and drew my knife.

"I'm going to cut you free, and you're going to show some respect. Are we clear?"

He growled like a cornered beast, and something primal inside of me shivered. Mongo stepped closer, and discretion—the better part of valor—embraced me in her merciful arms.

I folded and pocketed my knife, stood, and left Sidney Barbour bound on the deck. Motioning for Mongo to follow me, I led him from the brig with Barbour's door secured behind us. "What's happening in there?"

Mongo glanced back, and I thought I saw a glint of trepidation in his eyes. "I don't know, but that guy isn't what we expected."

"Where's the wife?"

"She's locked up on deck three, but she was still unconscious last time I saw her."

"How long has that been?"

He checked his watch. "Maybe an hour or a little less. I think it's time to wake her up." Mongo glanced between me and the brig. "Do you want me to keep an eye on him?"

"No. Get some sleep. We'll let him stew in his own juices for a while before we take another shot at him."

"You're the boss."

I called the CIC, and Skipper answered.

"Go for CIC."

"I need you to send a couple of security guys down to watch Barbour in the brig. Make sure they know not to go inside his cell for any reason. Just report back to you if he does anything crazy."

"No problem," she said. "But aren't you going to interrogate him?"

"Not yet. I'm going to talk to his wife first and see what I can get

196 · CAP DANIELS

out of her. He's not showing any signs of being interested in talking with me."

Mongo was right. I found an armed security officer sitting outside the door where Mrs. Barbour was sleeping off the tranquilizer.

I said, "I need to talk with her."

He stood, pulled a ring of keys attached to his belt by a spring-loaded retractor, and unlocked the door. "I'll be right here if you need me."

I stepped through the door. "Thanks. I'll only be a few minutes. If you need a break, feel free to go for a walk or whatever. I won't let her escape."

He said, "Thanks, but I'm good. I'll be right here."

I met his gaze and said, "Semper Fi?"

He chuckled. "No, sir. Coast Guard. You?"

"No. Me neither. I won't be long."

After closing the door behind me, I planted myself on a stool beside the bed. I squeezed her shoulder and gave her a gentle shake. "Mrs. Barbour?" She didn't stir, so I shook a little harder. "Mrs. Barbour, I need you to wake up."

She groaned and blinked against the light. "What? Where am I? What's happening?"

"Relax, ma'am. You're perfectly safe."

She jerked away, pinning herself to the wall behind her bed. "Who are you?"

I held up both hands. "I don't plan to hurt you. I just want to talk. Now, I need you to gather your wits and relax. You're not in any danger at the moment."

She pulled herself even farther from me. "Who are you? What do you want?"

"Who I am isn't important. I need some information your husband has, and he isn't willing to give me that information yet. I'm sorry that it's necessary for you to be wrapped up in this, but I need you to come with me."

Tears poured down her face, and her voice cracked. "I'm not going anywhere with you until—"

I stood. "You're coming with me. That's not in question. You can either walk beside me, or I'll sedate you again and carry you. That's up to you."

She wilted, sobbing and curling herself into a tighter ball, and I reached for her hand. "Come with me, and nothing bad will happen to you. I promise."

Her crying continued, but she forced herself from the bed and followed me through the door.

The guard stood, and I said, "Come with us. We're taking her down to see her husband."

The man didn't hesitate and fell in locked step with us.

We descended three flights of stairs to the brig, and I stopped at the outer hatch. "Listen to me, Mrs. Barbour. The only purpose of you being down here is to prove to your husband that we have you in our custody. That's all this is about. We'll have you back in your room in just a few minutes. Now, come with me."

I led her through the hatch and in front of Sidney Barbour's cell.

With three powerful kicks to his door, I had his attention. "Look at me, Sid. We've got your wife. You may be a tough guy, but trust me, you don't want to know what we'll do to her to get the information we need."

He glared through the bars from his bound position on the deck and hissed like a viper.

Mrs. Barbour recoiled and threw herself into my arms. "That's not my husband!"

Chapter 25
The Puppet Master

I shoved Mrs. Barbour into the guard's arms. "Get her out of here."

He vanished, leaving me staring down at a man cuffed and tied who already knew more about me than I knew about him. But that was about to change.

The man rolled onto his back and laughed. Nothing about the move made any sense. With both his feet and hands tied behind him, the closest thing to comfort he could experience in that condition would be lying facedown, but the masochist in him must've enjoyed the pain.

I don't know how many stairs and strides it took to get to the CIC, but I didn't remember a single one of them.

"The guy in the brig isn't Barbour. We grabbed the wrong guy."

Skipper spun to face me. "What?"

"We've got the wrong guy. Mrs. Barbour said that's not her husband. Show me the shot."

Almost before I finished the demand, six headshots of Sidney Barbour appeared on the monitor. I studied the shots, scrutinizing every detail of the man's face.

"That's him," I said. "There's no way we grabbed the wrong guy. Print out the first one in color."

She pulled the printout from the tray and stuck it in my hand.

I continued my study of Barbour's face. "That's him. Wake up the team. Get them down to the brig ASAP."

"You got it," she said. "You're going to fingerprint him, right?"

"Absolutely."

I sprinted through the corridor and down the ladders, but I stopped myself just short of the heavy steel door separating the brig from the rest of the ship. Waiting for the team to arrive gave us the psychological advantage of superior numbers, and I needed all the advantage I could get.

Instead of filing down the ladder individually, the team arrived in mass.

I held up Sidney Barbour's picture. "When I brought Mrs. Barbour down here to show her off to our prisoner, she said he wasn't her husband, and the man we snatched tonight laughed."

Shawn piped up. "We ID'd the guy at the scene. That dude is our guy. We didn't screw that up."

"I know," I said. "Somebody's playing a game we don't understand yet, but they're going to learn we can play any game as long as we know the rules. We're going in there together as a show of force. We'll run his prints and get at least five good shots for facial recognition. I expect him to be uncooperative, so we may get to have a little fun with him. Don't be gentle."

The smile on Shawn's face told me Sidney Barbour wasn't going to enjoy the next few minutes of his life.

"Let's move."

I passed the biometric scan and keycode test, sending the heavy bolt receding into the door. We filed into the bay like the hardened warriors we were, but nothing I'd seen on any battlefield anywhere on Earth prepared me for what was happening inside Barbour's cell.

"Get that door open!" Mongo yelled, and I shoved my thumb into the reader.

The instant it took for the electronic lock to read and verify my print felt like hours as Barbour pounded his face against the deck where it met the bulkhead. Blood flew from his face with every strike, and the back of his shirt was covered with crimson stains.

When the door finally clicked open, Mongo and Shawn flooded into the cell and yanked Barbour to his knees. The man's face looked like sausage. His nose was badly broken, and blood flowed from his brows, cheeks, and chin. No bare-knuckle boxer had ever lost a fight as badly as the one Sidney Barbour had endured of his own creation.

I pulled my phone from my pocket and brought up the fingerprint scanner app Dr. Mankiller created. "Break his wrists if you have to, but I'm getting his prints."

Mongo held Barbour in place while Shawn muscled his wrists into compliance, but their efforts were in vain. As I stared at his fingertips, his bizarre behavior of rolling himself onto his back when I left the cell suddenly made sense. While I was in the CIC, Barbour had ground his fingertips against the concrete cell deck until only ground beef remained where his fingerprints had once been. Whoever the man was, he was determined to defeat our efforts to ID him.

He was good, but we were better.

I said, "Somebody get me a four-by-four and some gloves from the med kit."

Gator hustled from the cell and returned in seconds with exactly what I requested. I slipped the gloves onto my hands and opened the sealed package containing the four-by-four gauze pads. "Hold his head still."

Mongo and Shawn made short work of controlling the man's skull while I took a sample of blood and tissue from his face.

I folded the gauze and slid it back into its package. Placing the sample in Gator's waiting hand, I said, "Get that to Dr. Shadrack and tell him to run the DNA."

Barbour spat, sending blood, spittle, and mucus into my face.

Instead of wiping it away, I moved within inches of his demolished nose. "You're out of your league. No matter how hard you fight, I will win, and you will give me what I want."

He inhaled to spit again, but Shawn shoved the muzzle of his Glock into Barbour's mouth until he gagged and convulsed at the assault.

"Spitting on people ain't nice. Spitting on my boss is a capital offense, and you just met the executioner."

Barbour jerked and tried to retreat from the muzzle scraping his tonsils, but between Mongo and Shawn, escape for our guest wasn't in the cards.

I turned from the scene and said, "Get him trussed up someplace he can't hurt himself anymore. I don't want him to steal all of our fun."

We reconvened outside the brig's main hatch, and I said, "Somebody explain what's going on. I've never seen anything like whatever that is."

Kodiak let out a long sigh. "What's happing in there is a level of insanity they never put in any psychology books. That's an animal, not a man. Whatever his end goal is, he'll achieve it, and it looks like hiding his true identity is step one in getting there."

"What could he possibly be hiding?" I asked. "He's the CEO of an oil exploration company, for God's sake. What would make that kind of personality do what he's doing?"

Mongo said, "That's no CEO in there, Chase. That's a madman, and right now, he's winning."

"What do you mean he's winning? He's a bloody mess, and he's tied to a chair."

Mongo shook his head. "He's winning because he's controlling us. We're spending a lot of time trying to figure out who he is. That makes him the puppet master for now."

"Maybe you're right. I say it's time to cut those strings."

I posted a guard on Barbour, with direct radio comms with me and the CIC, and headed to sick bay.

Dr. Shadrack was yawning and pawing at his eyes.

I said, "Sorry to drag you out of bed, Doc, but this one's important."

He poured a cup of coffee and turned to me. "Want some?"

"No, thanks. I just want to get the DNA analysis done ASAP."

He took his first sip. "You could've done that without waking me up. I can stop blood from pouring out of your body, but I can't run the DNA tests on that blood. That knowledge belongs to a pair of technicians who are worth a lot more than you're paying them."

I said, "Tell those two techs that I'll double their salary if they get a DNA match before the sun comes up."

"Nice offer," he said, "but that can't be done. If everything goes perfectly, it'll take eight hours."

I sucked air between my teeth. "Make it happen in six hours, and the offer stands."

"I'll tell them, but I wouldn't expect it to happen."

I said, "When you get them started, bring your bag of doctor tricks down to the brig. I've got a guest with a boo-boo on his face. He'll probably need a Band-Aid."

"Did you give him the boo-boo?"

"Nope. Believe it or not, it's entirely self-inflicted."

He took another sip. "I'm not buying it, but I'm on your team, so I'll come down and take a look. Give me ten minutes. He can stay alive that long, right?"

"Probably."

* * *

In the brig cell, Mongo and Shawn stood beside Barbour, who'd been tied to a restraining chair with a mesh spit bag secured over his head.

Dr. Shadrack walked in and pushed his glasses up the bridge of his nose. "My God! What happened to this guy?"

Shawn said, "Nothing yet, but it's coming. We just need to know if he's healthy enough for a little special kind of love."

The doctor grimaced. "Love hurts."

Shawn grinned. "It doesn't hurt me a bit."

Dr. Shadrack leaned down to Barbour. "Take off the bag. I can't see how bad it is through the mesh."

Mongo said, "That's not a good idea. This one's a spitter."

Shawn pulled a five-pound hammer from his ruck and rested the head against Barbour's knee. "If you spit on the doc, I get to play whack-a-mole with your knee. Please test me."

Through the bloody hood over his eyes, Barbour glared at Shawn but didn't say a word, so our SEAL bounced the hammer somewhat gently against the kneecap. The man flinched under the tapping, leaving me to believe he would howl when Shawn played a little rougher.

Mongo untied the bag, slipped it off of Barbour's head, and grabbed a handful of his unruly hair. "Go ahead, Doc. If he misbehaves, we've got your back."

Dr. Shadrack leaned in with his penlight in hand and examined Barbour's eyes and facial wounds. He pocketed the light, pulled off his glasses, and asked, "Why did you do this to yourself?"

Barbour didn't answer. Instead, he thrust his head forward, ripping a handful of hair from his head in Mongo's grasp. Dr. Shadrack dodged the incoming headbutt and sent a crushing elbow strike to the man's temple, sending stars circling his already battered head.

Mongo clamped his massive hand around our prisoner's neck and shoved him back against his confinement chair, making breathing impossible.

As the man's face turned blue, Doc leaned back in. "Have you ever heard of the Geneva Conventions?"

Barbour's eyes struggled to look in the same direction, but he remained silent and stoic.

So, Dr. Shadrack gave him a pat on the shoulder. "Good. Neither have we." He turned to me and shrugged. "Go ahead. Do what you need to do. If he's still alive when you're finished, I'll take another look, but for now, I'm going back to bed. Have fun."

Mongo bagged Barbour's head again and wound a strand of 550 cord beneath his nose and tied it to the headrest. The headbutting was over.

Anya stepped in front of our man and gripped the handle of

Shawn's hammer. "Is not necessary for any of you to stay. Tell to me what you want to know, and I will bring to you information."

Hearing the cold tone of the Russian's bitter threat sent chills racing down my spine. Shawn released the hammer and stepped back. Anya was far more terrifying than any of us...including our SEAL.

I said, "I don't care about his name, rank, or serial number. I want to know where he put Kenneth LePine. If he won't tell you, we'll feed what's left of him to the sharks."

For the first time since we threw Sidney Barbour into the helicopter in Hockley, TX, his eyes twitched. Perhaps it was leftover trauma from the doctor's elbow shot, but to me, it looked a lot more like recognition.

Chapter 26
Peg Leg

Before I left Sidney Barbour's brig cell, I locked eyes with the most terrifying woman I would ever know, and she stared back through the cold blue-gray eyes of her father, Dr. Robert "Rocket" Richter. I gave a shake of my head that was more of a thought than an action, and she read the gesture perfectly. Her eyes softened, but they did so with a subtlety almost no one else in the world would notice. I'd fallen into those eyes more times than I would ever admit, and yet, I'll never regret those tiny moments so far from everything and so powerful that my heart may never heal.

As the echo of the steel door closing behind me rang in my head, I feared everything. I feared we had the wrong man tied to a chair. I feared I might unleash Anya and Shawn to drag me descending into depths so near to Hell that the clawing demons might grasp my very soul. I feared I'd become wrapped inside a world I couldn't understand —a world in which greed reigned on high and victims were somehow less than human—somehow nothing more than mere stones in the path beneath the feet of men so driven by excess and so consumed by lust for more that they would destroy any innocence and any purity that lay before them.

I climbed the ladder back to the decks above the dungeon of my own creation and saw the first beams of morning light streaming through the portholes and hatches of the *Lori Danielle*. Somehow, that light gave me hope and reminded me that no matter how dark the night, the dawn will come, and the creatures of the darkness will retreat into their dens to await the coming of another night when they can, once again, unleash their fury.

Had I become one of them? Had I longed for the darkness to envelope me and hide me away from the light as I plied my gruesome trade?

I collided with Dr. Shadrack near the hatch to sick bay and stumbled from my introspection and back into the reality of my world.

"Take it easy, Chase. Are you all right?"

I held up a hand. "I'm sorry, Doc. I'm pretty tired, and I was a little lost in my thoughts."

He wiped the coffee from his wrist that had abandoned the mug in his hand. "It's okay. You looked a little out of it. Do you need something to help you get some sleep?"

I shook him off. "No, I don't have time to sleep. How's the DNA match going?"

"The preliminary analysis is done, and we're comparing it against every known profile we have access to. It'll return fifty thousand hits or so."

"Fifty thousand? That doesn't do us any good. I need you to narrow it down to one guy."

He took a sip. "Relax, knuckle-dragger. It's just the preliminaries. If we used a detailed sample to search every database in the world, that would take weeks. We start with a general preliminary sample and find a few thousand possibilities. That way, when we run the detailed search, we're looking through fifty thousand potential matches instead of a billion."

I rubbed my eyes. "Fine. Whatever. But I need a definitive answer two hours ago."

"Without a time machine," he said, "you'll have to wait. We'll likely get a match in a few hours, but there aren't any shortcuts in science. You need some rest. Let me give you—"

"Not now. Let me know the instant you have a match. In fact, when you get your general sample pool or whatever, let me know if Sidney Barbour's name is in the pool of possibilities."

"That's not really how it works," he said. "It's actually—"

I cut him off again. "Just let me know."

My next stop was inside the CIC, where Skipper looked like a zombie. I stepped behind her and laid my hands on her shoulders. "Hey, go get some sleep. We need you fresh when the DNA match comes back."

She sighed and laid her head back against me. "Rub my shoulders, please."

Her neck and shoulders felt like gravel. The knots were hard and endless.

I lifted a handset from the console and pushed the medical button.

A voice came through the earpiece. "Sick bay, Shadrack."

"Do you have a tech or a nurse who's also a massage therapist?"

"We do."

"Good. I'm sending Skipper down. She's been at her computer way too long, and her back needs some attention."

He said, "Send her down. We'll take care of her."

Skipper looked up at me from behind puppy-dog eyes. "Thank you." She stood from her chair, groaning as she went. "Celeste will be here in a few minutes. I told her to expect to work the day watch."

"I've got it until she gets here. Enjoy your massage."

She kissed me on the cheek and turned for the door.

As I sank into her chair, fatigue overcame me, and I weighed a thousand pounds. Thankfully, Dr. Celeste Mankiller came through the door minutes later before I collapsed.

"Where's Skipper?"

I stretched. "I sent her down for a massage and a nap."

"A massage? Do we have a masseuse on board?"

"We do. One of Dr. Shadrack's nurses is a massage therapist."

"I want to get on that list."

I waved a hand. "The ship and her crew are at your disposal."

She grinned. "I like the sound of that."

I asked, "Do you know anything about DNA?"

She laughed. "I'm a scientist, Chase. Of course I know about DNA."

"I thought you might. Keep pushing medical to get a match, and wake me up when it comes."

When I made it to my cabin, I found Gator knocking on my door. "You don't have to knock. I'm not home."

He flinched. "Oh, hey, Chase. Have you got a minute?"

"Sure. Go on in. I never lock it."

He pressed through the door and planted himself on my footlocker. I shucked off the boot from my one remaining foot and disconnected my prosthetic from the other leg.

Gator quivered. "That still freaks me out."

I raised my stump toward him, pretended to jab him with the titanium rod protruding just beneath my knee, and put on my best pirate voice. "Yar, matee. Ye capt'n be pegleg."

He slapped at the rod. "Have you heard the saying about being as busy as a one-legged man in a butt-kicking contest? You're about to find out how busy that is if you don't get that thing away from me."

I plopped down on my bunk. "What's on your mind?"

"I want to go see Cecilia."

I cocked my head. "What's going on in that head of yours? This isn't a love-sick schoolboy request, is it?"

"No, nothing like that. I've got a feeling she knows more than she's telling, and after my sexpionage class with Anya, I think I can get it out of her."

"Sexpionage? Is that what that's called?"

He blushed. "Yeah, well, we didn't...you know."

I wanted to jab a little more, but I gave him a break. "Yes, I know. She's very good at..."

It was apparently his turn to throw a jab or two. "You'd know."

"That was a long time ago, in a galaxy far, far away. So, tell me about this gut feeling of yours."

He said, "You were a catcher. You remember what it was like to look out on the field and know what's about to happen. I was a safety. It's the same thing. I see stuff nobody else does. I can read a quarterback's thoughts before he has them. I know when a wideout is about to break. Cecilia's no receiver, but she might just be a tight end who's wide open."

I was intrigued. "Okay, go see her, but let me give you a piece of advice. Calling her a wide receiver isn't the best move."

He shrugged. "It was an analogy."

"I'll let the captain know you need the Huey. Go find Disco or Gun Bunny to run you ashore."

"Actually, I was thinking I'd take the RHIB. You know, take her for a boat ride and a picnic or something to get her guard down."

"Did Anya teach you that?"

"No. I'm just a romantic guy, you know."

"Yeah, I know. Take the RHIB, but don't get lost. Those bayous are puzzles with a bunch of missing pieces."

He stood. "Thanks. Do you think maybe Dr. Mankiller could hook me up with a wire? If I get Cecilia talking, it'd be nice to have it recorded."

I pushed myself from the bunk and balanced on one foot. "You're learning, kid. Celeste is in the CIC. Now, get out of here."

I swung my stump at him, but this time, instead of quivering, he grabbed the metal rod and shoved me back onto my bed. "Anya didn't teach me that, either."

To my surprise, sleep came quickly, and I avoided picturing what Anya may have taught the new kid.

* * *

I didn't hear my cabin door swinging open, but I felt the soft touch of the obviously feminine hand resting on mine.

"Chasechka, you must wake up."

Maybe it's a dream. I'm not ready to wake up.

The gentle touch strengthened and morphed from a soft squeeze to a shake. "You must wake up. We have problem."

Nope, it's not a dream.

I opened my eyes and stretched. "What time is it?"

"Two thirty," she said.

"In the morning?"

"No, in afternoon. Get up and put on leg. This is very important."

I chuckled at the absurdity of putting on my leg. "Okay, I'm up. What's the problem?"

She handed my prosthetic to me. "I had thought about telling truth."

"What are you talking about?"

"Perhaps we have correct person inside jail, but we do not have correct woman."

I locked my leg in place. "I'm going to need coffee or alcohol if you don't start making this a lot clearer."

"Is simple," she said. "Woman said, 'That is not my husband.' Perhaps she was telling truth. Perhaps man is Sidney Barbour, but she is not Mrs. Barbour."

"I'm starting with coffee."

The machine accepted the pod, and soon, the wonderful aroma of freshly brewed coffee filled my cabin. "Want some?"

She scowled. "You know I do not drink coffee, but I would like tea."

I threw the coffee pod in the trash and slipped a tea into the machine. When the cup was full, I said, "I don't have any honey."

She took the mug from my hand. "Is fine without."

Back on the edge of my bed, I said, "So you think we've got the wrong woman and she's telling the truth about Barbour not being her husband. Is that right?"

"This is possible," she said, blowing across the surface of her tea.

"So, fingerprint her and find out who she is."

"This is happening now," Anya said.

"So, what's the problem?"

She sipped. "When doctor did preliminary comparison for DNA match, no one with name of Sidney Barbour was on list of eighty-five thousand people."

"I may have to switch to alcohol."

"No, listen to me, Chasechka."

"Are you ever going to stop calling me that?"

She shook her head. "Do not be silly. Of course I will never stop because you like this, even though you say you do not."

"Go on with your story. Barbour is not in the pool of possible matches, but you still believe we've got the right guy."

"This is correct," she said. "I believe we have correct person. This means we know *who* he is, but we do not know *what* he is."

Chapter 27
Little Red Bow

Anya and I finished our tea party and headed for sick bay, where we found Dr. Shadrack hanging upside down from a bar.

Anya tilted her head uncomfortably far to the right. "This does not look normal."

"Nothing aboard this ship surprises me anymore," I said.

The doctor said, "Hey, guys. You should try this. It feels amazing."

Anya continued to scowl. "Do you have plan for getting down?"

He groaned. "I hadn't really thought it through yet, but now that you mention it, would you mind giving me a hand?"

I hefted our chief medical officer from his predicament and placed him on the deck. He twisted his neck and stretched. "Thanks. I guess you're here about the narrowed pool of possibilities."

I nodded. "We are. So, tell us what's going on."

He motioned for us to follow him into the lab, where a pair of techs in blue scrubs sat on raised stools in front of computer monitors. "This is Tina and Ericka," the doctor said, and the techs stood.

We shook hands, introduced ourselves, and the younger of the two said, "Oh, yeah. We know who you guys are. You own the ship, and she's the Russian badass, right?"

I chuckled. "Only half of that is correct. I don't really own the ship. Tell us what's going on with the DNA matching."

Ericka, the older tech, said, "When we received the initial cut pool, Sidney Barbour's name wasn't in the pool."

"We know that much," I said. "What are we doing now?"

She said, "We're trying to determine if his name appears in any DNA database. Of course, there are dozens of people with that name on Earth, so it's slow work. When we get a hit, we check that hit against other databases like property tax records, driver's licenses, passports, etc. It's slow-going, but we're on it. I guess we failed the challenge, so we're not getting the raise, huh?"

I opened my mouth, but Anya beat me to it. "Like you said, Chase owns ship, so he can give to you raise whenever he wants, and I think he wants."

Tina grinned at Anya. "Oh, I think *you* are what he wants."

Anya glanced at me from the corner of her eye. "Do you really think so?"

Dr. Shadrack saved me. "Ericka is being a little modest. They're not just checking public databases. Thanks to Skipper, we have access to a few lists that aren't exactly public information, if you know what I mean."

I said, "My guess is that he won't show up on those lists, either, but somebody taught him some tradecraft, so he's likely former military, and I have to assume Sidney Barbour isn't the name on his original birth certificate."

My phone chirped, so I thumbed the button and stuck it to my ear. "Hey, Clark. What's up?"

My handler's voice didn't bear its usual lighthearted tone. "Get to the CIC and pick up the secure line. I'll be waiting."

Before I could respond, the line went dead. "That was Clark. Something's up, and he wants to talk to me on a secure line. Let me know if you get any hits."

Anya trailed but kept up as I sprinted to the combat information center. When we pushed through the hatch, Skipper lifted the headset, and I pulled it over my ears.

With the boom mic pulled to my lips, I said, "All right, I'm here. What's going on?"

Skipper handed Anya a second headset, and she pulled it in place without bringing the mic to her mouth.

Clark said, "That's what I'm calling to find out. What are you doing?" His tone changed from concerned handler to angry father in an instant.

I asked, "What are you talking about? You know what we're doing. We're trying to find out what happened to Kenneth LePine and who burned down his house."

He said, "Yeah, well, you're doing it a little too well. Is Skipper responsible for hacking into the black sites?"

Our analyst took that one. "I didn't exactly hack. It was more of a side entrance kind of thing."

Clark said, "Your little side entrance has bells going off all over the world, and my phone won't stop ringing."

"What are you talking about?" Skipper asked.

Clark huffed. "You're not running the DNA database searches, are you?"

She said, "No, I got in for the lab techs, but I'm not running the searches. They're doing that on their own."

Clark growled. "Get them out of there, right now. They're like loose cannons in a china shop, freezing the balls off a brass monkey."

Skipper quivered. "What?"

I covered my mic and whispered, "Don't worry. I speak Clarkinese." Returning to Clark, I said, "We'll stop them now, but we still need to—"

He said, "By *now*, I mean *right* now."

I shoved one of the ear cups from my ear and lifted the handset to call sick bay, but Dr. Shadrack was already on the line.

"We found him, Chase."

As understanding overtook Skipper. She threw her hands onto the keyboard and typed furiously. Line after line of computer code scrolled across her monitor, and she got faster with every keystroke.

I spoke into the handset. "Have the techs take a picture of the screen, but do not print anything. Just take pictures and get out of the databases."

The doctor gave the order and returned to the line. "We got busted, didn't we?"

"We sure did. Bring the finding to CIC."

I pulled the ear cup back over my ear. "We're out of the databases, Clark."

Skipper held up a finger. "That's not exactly true yet, but we will be in seconds."

She kept typing, and I asked, "How bad did we screw up?"

Clark made a noise like an angry bear. "Bad...real bad."

"I'm working on that," Skipper said. "I'll have it cleaned up in seconds."

"What are you doing to clean it up?" Clark asked.

Skipper struck one final key and leaned back in her chair. "I made it look like the brass monkey in the china shop was a Russian hacker named Kolzak Zaytsev. He's a notorious snake on the world-hacking scene. The NSA bloodhounds will be chasing their tails all night."

Anya smiled. "Is his name really Kolzak?"

Skipper shrugged. "Who knows? That's what most people call him."

"Do you know what this name means in English?" she asked.

Skipper and I shook our heads, and she said, "In English, Kolzak means *slippery*. This funny for me."

Skipper grinned. "I like it. Anyway, Clark, we're out, and we're clean."

Clark said, "You better be, and don't do stuff like that without telling me first. If I have to run interference for you, I need to know what lies to tell."

Skipper grimaced. "I'm sorry. I should've called you. I know better. It won't happen again."

Clark sighed. "Next time, I want you to do the snooping. Don't give a couple of science geeks keys to the castle. They puke on the floor and burn the curtains."

"That's quite a visual," I said. "I apologize for not keeping a thumb on things. Like Skipper said, it won't happen again."

Clark cleared his throat. "Consider yourselves appropriately scolded. Now, tell me how it's going."

I briefed him on the events of the past thirty-six hours, and he said, "It sounds like I missed quite a party."

Ericka came through the hatch with an old-school digital camera in her hand. Skipper took it and plugged it into her computer, and we watched closely as the picture filled the screen in front of us. I read through the gibberish that looked more like a bowl of alphabet soup than a DNA database record.

Skipper covered her mouth and gasped. "Oh, my God. He was a PMOO."

I suddenly felt like a third grader in a college calculus classroom. "What's a PMOO?"

Anya answered before Skipper could. "Is paramilitary operations officer for Central Intelligence Agency. This means he is like you, Chasechka, but making only small salary for government."

"This guy was a spook?" I asked.

Skipper said, "No, not a spook. He was a hitter. Give me a minute."

She opened several windows and typed furiously. Sixty seconds later, she said, "This guy is wanted all over the world. He apparently went rogue on an operation in South America in nineteen eighty-eight. It looks like he's been out in the cold ever since."

Clark moaned. "Of course he is. Why wouldn't my team break into some guy's house in Texas and apprehend the most wanted former ops officer on the planet? Why do you drag me into cesspools like this, Chase?"

I threw up both hands, even though Clark couldn't see me. "Hey, I'm innocent here. I broke into the house and barn, and I rolled up a couple of people, but I thought they were an oil exploration company CEO and his wife. I had no idea we were sparring with a rogue former CIA officer."

Clark chuckled. "Yes, you're practically an altar boy. Squeaky clean and innocent."

I ignored my handler and asked, "What's his real name?"

Skipper said, "Steven McDuffy from some place called Vonore, Tennessee." She continued typing until a new stream of text scrolled across the monitor. "He graduated from the University of Tennessee with a bachelor's degree in political science. He was on the wrestling and swim teams. Officially, he's listed as killed in action in Honduras. His mother got the two hundred fifty grand in life insurance, but she died six weeks after her beloved son from a home invasion gone bad."

I leaned back and stared at the ceiling. "We've got a professional killer gone rogue from the CIA who probably iced his own mother. What am I supposed to do with that?"

Anya said, "We have now ultimate bargaining chip. If he does not tell to us everything we want to know, we will give him to Central Intelligence Agency with little red bow on top of head."

I pulled off my headset and stood. "Let's go down and have a little chat with our new friend."

Skipper held up a sheet of paper with the gibberish from her screen. "Here. Sometimes a visual aid makes things easier."

I took the printout and headed for the dungeon.

On the way down, I asked Anya, "Did you and Shawn do any irreparable damage while I was sleeping?"

She said, "We did not harm hair on outside of his head."

I stopped in my tracks. "That's an odd thing to say...even for you. What do you mean by outside of his head?"

She shrugged. "Maybe I whispered into his head for three hours. Not even you can repair damage I did on inside of his head."

"That's terrifying," I said. "Did you get anything out of him?"

"He never spoke single word, but muscles inside neck were strained many times. This is good sign, yes?"

I laughed. "It's a good sign when you're not the guy with the strained neck muscles. He's not going to chew off his own tongue or anything like that, is he?"

She shrugged. "Maybe. Or I could cut his tongue into two pieces. I have done this before. You remember, yes?"

"How could I forget?"

We cleared the high-security door into the brig and then the hatch into the cell, and I held Skipper's printout in front of me and gave it a shake. "You've been a very bad boy, Mr. Barbour." I made a show of scanning the page. "Or should I call you Steven McDuffy?" He showed no reaction, so I continued. "Swim team, wrestling team, poly-sci, go Big Orange. Is any of this ringing a bell?"

The man remained stoic, so I pulled my red-hot poker from the fire and held it to his eye. "Maybe this will jog your memory. After going rogue in Honduras, you murdered your own mother for the two hundred fifty grand they paid her to convince her you were dead."

His head snapped sharply, and he bore holes through my eyes with his. "I did *not* kill my mother. That was a CIA hit team. They tortured her to get her to give me up, but she didn't know where I was. They pushed too hard, and now every one of them has a star on the wall at Langley."

"You killed the hit team? The whole team?"

"They chose a dangerous profession...just like you did."

Chapter 28
Mandarin for Fun

We'd been playing full-contact checkers until I accused McDuffy of killing his mother. After that, the game became something akin to Russian roulette with baseball bats.

I turned to Anya. "Do you mind giving me a little one-on-one time with Mr. Barbour?"

She glared at me for a moment before locking eyes with our prisoner. "*Ty budesh' vesti sebya khorosho, da?*"

He never looked away. "*Da.*"

I hadn't spoken Russian with anyone for months, but I didn't need a refresher to understand that Anya was asking Barbour if he was going to be nice.

She stepped from the cell and slid a chair inside.

I took a seat a few feet in front of my well-bound friend. "Let's have a chat," I began. "It appears I have three advantages at this moment—physical, psychological, and legal. You're tied to *my* chair in *my* brig on *my* boat. Anya spent the day filling your head full of demons who'll never stop dancing. And we now know the CIA would do almost anything to get you back in their hands."

I wasn't expecting a response, but I gave him plenty of time just in case he felt the desire to open up. He apparently did not.

"I'm going to lay all the cards on the table for you to see, Sidney. Or do you prefer Stephen?"

He licked his lips. "I'm thirsty."

Playing head games with a master requires constant focused attention, so I wasn't about to let him distract me with requests for anything—not even water. "Here's what I want, Sidney. I want to know if Kenneth LePine is still alive, and even if he's not, I want to know where he is. That's the only key that could possibly open the locks required for you to leave this ship alive and free."

For an interrogator, showing surprise is all seven of the deadly sins rolled into one, but it took every ounce of will I could summon to avoid showing my disbelief when he laughed.

Of all things, he laughed and said, "I haven't been free since my junior year in college when I was recruited into the pig stye called Langley, Virginia. You offering me freedom is like a fish jumping in your boat to escape a shark. The fish is dead either way. His pea-sized brain just isn't big enough to think it through."

With great effort, I maintained my calm demeanor. "I'm going to locate Kenneth LePine, with or without you. If you cooperate, you may get to be Sidney Barbour again, but if you don't, I won't lose a minute's sleep over handing you over to your old friends at the Agency."

He laughed again, and I was growing tired of the sound.

"Kid, you're too young and naïve to know how deep you're digging your own grave."

I closed one eye and stared at the ceiling. "You threatening me isn't productive, and I'm too busy for you to waste my time, so either tell me where Kenneth LePine is, or I'm calling Virginia. Pick one."

He closed his eyes and sighed. "I've got about a million reasons to lie to you, but I'm not going to do that. You're obviously a serious guy, so here's the truth. Of course I know who Kenneth LePine is. I want to buy the mineral rights to his property, but he's not interested in selling. I don't know why. We've been more than fair. *Far* more than fair, to be honest. He's sitting on a bunch of oil and natural gas, but he's clearly not motivated by financial gain. The man's mind is different than yours and mine."

I was taught, and I've learned it to be true, that saying nothing is often the most effective interrogation technique. Barbour or McDuffy or whatever his name was had been through much of the same training as me, so I wasn't going to surprise him with any tactic. I gave waiting a try, and to my surprise, it worked.

He kept talking. "Here's the rest of the truth. There have been times when I, or people who work for me, have been a bit aggressive—physically aggressive—in negotiations, but not with LePine. He's an old man, and he'll die soon. That means all I have to do is wait him out."

I continued listening, and he continued spewing. "Look, I don't know what happened to your buddy, LePine, but I do know that whatever it is, we didn't do it."

My patience reached its terminus. "That's it? All you've got is you don't know?"

"I'm telling you, I know him. I've spoken with him. I've made offers face-to-face, but he's not interested. It's not worth the trouble to push him. Like I said, he's old. What do you want from me?"

I made a show of checking my watch before making eye contact again. "Anything else?"

He changed tack. "We're the same, you and me. We are. You'll see. Someday, it'll be you tied to a chair. You don't have to do this to me."

I smirked. "I've been tied to more chairs than you can count, but nobody who ever tied me to one is still breathing, so you and me... we're not the same."

"You may not believe it now, but here's an example of how you and I are two peas in the proverbial pod. If you were trying to track my movement over long distances, what would you do?"

This time, he waited, and I remained silent.

He said, "Here's what you'd do. You'd locate my typical means of transportation and plant trackers, cameras, transmitters, and listening devices until I needed an exterminator to get rid of all of those bugs. That's exactly what you'd do, and you know it."

I wanted to put up an argument, but discretion prevailed, and I didn't flinch.

Barbour smiled—a reaction almost as bizarre as laughing—and said, "I know that's what you'd do because that's what I did to you. I bugged your airport, your boats, your airplanes, and even that piece-of-crap Volkswagen Microbus. You found most of the bugs. So, one operator to another, I have to give you credit for that."

Sucking me into his world wouldn't happen, but my refusal to take his hand on a stroll down Espionage Lane didn't stop him from beckoning for me to follow.

He cleared his throat. "When you're my prisoner, I won't deprive you of water."

"Tell me where Kenneth LePine is, and you can have all the water you want. I'll even feed you and fly you back to Texas if your story checks out. It's that simple."

He licked his lips. "Give me ten million dollars, and I'll let you live."

Nothing about his strange threat made any sense. "What are you talking about?"

He said, "I'm proving a point. I don't know where Kenneth LePine is. I don't know if he's gator bait or partying his ass off on Bourbon Street. I can't give you what I don't have, and I don't have LePine—just like you don't have ten million dollars."

It was my turn to laugh, so I did, and I made it a good one. When I regained my composure, I stood and patted Sidney Barbour, or Stephen McDuffy, on the cheek. "Nice try, but I could drown you in hundred dollar bills, and it wouldn't change my lifestyle one iota. You're boxing out of your weight class, McDuffy, and I'm the reigning heavyweight world champion."

I gave my chair a push with a boot and let the grating sound of metal on metal reverberate from the deck. "So, the woman I've got upstairs, I'm going to throw her over the stern rail. I obviously can't just apologize and send her home. I'm in this thing a little too deep to leave a loose end like that hanging around. Since she's not your wife and you think we're the same, I'm sure you understand that men like us have no choice in situations like that."

A rookie would've watched Barbour for twitches, or pupil dilation, or even a verbal reaction, but my rookie days were long gone, and I was in the heart of my career. I never looked back. I didn't care if Barbour reacted. In that moment, I was a farmer planting seeds and hoping one would take root and grow.

On my way to the CIC, I stopped by Mongo's cabin and found him hidden away inside a noise-canceling headset. He tapped his phone and pulled off the headset. "Hey, Chase. What's up?"

"What are you listening to?"

He shook his phone. "Oh, I'm just trying to learn Mandarin. It's tough, but I'm picking it up."

I shook my head. "For fun, you're learning Mandarin?"

"It's not so much for fun as it is something to keep my mind sharp."

"I think I'll stick with good bourbon and Cubans, but good luck with the Mandarin thing. When you need a break, run down to the brig and water your dog. He's complaining about being thirsty."

He tossed the headset onto his bunk. "Aww, poor baby. I'll take care of it. Did you get anything meaningful out of him?"

"Maybe. Either he's the best liar on the planet, or he doesn't know where Kenneth is."

"Interesting."

I said, "Maybe he's just playing me. I don't know yet, but he admitted to breaking in and bugging the airport and planes. Why would he give that up?"

He stood and consumed most of the space in his cabin. "He's trying to build trust by feeding you morsels of truth. There's an old Chinese proverb that says, *Xiǎokǒu tūnyàn zhēnxiàng gèng róngyì.*"

"I'm sure that means something profound, but I have to admit I have no idea what you said."

He chuckled. "It means the truth is easier to swallow in small bites."

"Is that really what you said?"

He slugged me on the shoulder as he stepped past me and into the corridor. "I have no idea what I said. I made it all up, but the confidence was solid, right?"

"Solid, indeed. Feel free to have a little fun with our guest while you're down there."

He said, "I think he's been through enough for one day. From what Shawn told me, Anya did a number on him. I think I'd rather have her gut me like pig than have her whisper in my ear for five hours."

I closed his door and followed him down the corridor. "You're a wise man, my friend. Don't ever change."

With Barbour's thirst resolution in good hands, I made my way to the CIC. Once inside the secure compartment, I discovered three of the four most important women in my life huddled around a monitor with headsets of their own firmly positioned over their ears. I was instantly certain none of them was learning Mandarin, but whatever was happening inside the devices had their absolute attention.

When my hand landed on Skipper's shoulder, she jumped as if she'd been shocked.

She yanked off her headset and screamed, "Don't do that! You scared me to death."

"Sorry. I wasn't trying to sneak up on you. What's so engrossing?"

She hit a key to stop the audio, and Celeste and Anya yanked off their sets.

The Russian huffed. "Do not turn it off. It is wonderful. He is perfect student. I will kiss him again, but this time for reward and not for learning."

Skipper frowned down at Anya. "You've got to stop kissing people as a reward. Not all of us are Eastern European goddesses. We can't compete with that, so keep your tongue in your own mouth and give the rest of us a chance."

Anya smiled and tilted her head. "You are jealous. I think you have maybe crush on Gator. He is very good kisser, and I could teach him other things to make him perfect for you if you would like."

Skipper's face flushed bright red. "I do not have a crush on Gator or anybody else, and no, I don't want you teaching him anything else to make him perfect for me. He's fine just like he is. I mean, he doesn't need... Never mind. Just leave him alone, would you?"

Anya raised both hands. "I am sorry. I did not know you already think he is perfect."

"That's not what I said!"

As much as I enjoyed whatever was happening before my eyes, it wasn't productive, so I pulled Skipper from the fire. "Are you listening live, or is it recorded?"

Skipper said, "I paused it, so it's not live anymore, thanks to your interruption and Anya's offer to molest Gator. We're at least two minutes behind."

"Can you catch me up?" I asked.

Celeste said, "He's doing great. I think Cecilia may have some information that she doesn't even realize could be helpful, and Gator is pulling it out of her piece by piece. I agree with Skipper. He's pretty perfect."

Skipper growled. "That is *not* what I said. Cut it out!"

"Give me an extra headset," I said. "I should probably nestle up with this hen party and see how Romeo's doing."

Skipper handed me a set and restarted the audio. The quality was astonishing. Celeste outdid herself with the setup, and I was immediately enraptured by the soap opera unfolding through the comms.

Chapter 29
You're Completely Insane

Dr. Celeste Mankiller had indeed outdone herself with the quality of comms for Gator's covert picnic date. His voice was crystal clear, and Cecilia's was only slightly below face-to-face quality. It only took seconds for me to become as captivated by the audio as the others.

Cecilia's voice grew louder but not harsh. In fact, her tone softened. "Nobody's ever taken me for a picnic before. I mean, I've been to picnics, but never with just one person. It means a lot that you'd do this for me."

Gator sighed as if feeling Cecilia press against his body. "It's nice to escape sometimes. I know it has to be tough with your uncle still missing. I thought you might like to get away and have a couple hours of—"

She said, "Shh."

The next sound was impossible to decipher. It came through like wind whistling through a valley. No matter how hard I tried to picture the sound, it wouldn't come to me until I saw Anya smile.

She said, "They are kissing. I taught him to do this."

Skipper huffed. "Hush. I'm sure he knew how to kiss before you taught him."

The Russian shrugged. "Maybe, but he is now better."

The muffled sound became a sound of submission, and Anya's smile broadened.

Skipper held up a finger toward Anya, and she didn't take credit for teaching the techniques that led to the sound.

"We should've done this a long time ago," Cecilia whispered, and Gator released a guttural noise that could've been agreement or even a demand for Cecilia to never stop.

Anya giggled. "Come to me, Chasechka. I will show to you what is happening."

Skipper slapped the Russian's hand. "No! You can't have Gator or Chase. They're not yours to play with. Now, shut up and listen."

"We found him, you know."

The sounds of pleasure were gone, replaced by Cecilia's gasp. "What?"

"We found him."

The sound of rustling rang through the device for a moment.

"You found him? You found my Uncle Kenneth?"

"Yes."

Skipper drove a fist into her thigh. "What's he doing? This wasn't part of the plan."

It was my turn to smile. "Anya didn't teach him this part. I get the credit for this one."

All three women looked at me, and Skipper spoke for the group. "What's he doing?"

"He's baiting her. Just listen."

Cecilia said. "You found him? Where? Is he..."

"That's an interesting response," Celeste said.

I closed my eyes and silently begged Gator to keep his mouth closed.

My student didn't make a sound, but Cecilia asked again, "How'd you find him? I mean...where?"

She'd pinned my protégé into a corner, leaving him with no way out other than answering, and he did it masterfully. "I don't know. I wasn't with them when they found him. I was working on another project."

"What is it you do?" she asked.

Gator said, "I'm the new guy, so I just do what they tell me."

"I'm talking about the company you work for. Surely you don't just go around hunting missing people, right?"

"No, that's mostly what we do. We find people and things that aren't supposed to be findable. Is *findable* a word?"

"He's dead, isn't he? Did your guys notify the police?"

I could almost see Gator shrugging. "I don't know. Like I said, I'm the new guy."

"Did they say how he died?"

Gator was doing well, but his temporary girlfriend was dragging him down a well, and he needed a rope. I plucked my phone from a pocket and tossed him a line.

His voice came on the line. "Gator."

"Keep her talking," I said. "I don't know where she's taking you, but let her lead."

"So, he's still alive?" Gator said.

I said, "Did her expression change?"

"Yes, sir."

"Does she appear pleased?"

"No, sir. Not at all."

My heart plummeted into my stomach. "Get out of there, Gator. Get away from her, and get back to the ship now!"

The line went dead, and through the headset, the crack of a pistol shot rang like a thousand screaming demons. A second shot rang out, but neither of them was Gator's nine-millimeter.

I grabbed the arm of Skipper's chair. "Show me where he is!"

She had an aerial photo on the screen in an instant, and a small green triangle rested on the edge of an island about a mile from Kenneth LePine's former home.

"That's his sat-phone," Skipper said.

I studied the aerial shot as the sounds of a struggle echoed in my head and the green triangle disappeared. "What's happening?"

Skipper typed feverishly. "I don't know, but I'm working it."

"Send those coordinates to everybody's phone," I demanded as I jerked the set from my ears. "We're going after him."

I yanked the handset from the console and thumbed the 1MC. "Attention all Sierra elements. This is Sierra One. Report to the helipad immediately with full kits."

As I ran from the CIC, I yelled over my shoulder, "Get the Huey out of the hangar bay!"

By the time I made it to the elevated helipad, the chopper was already unchained, and one of the mechanics had the twin turbines spooling up.

My team arrived seconds after me in full battle rattle. They hit the chopper like a horde of charging buffalo, and I replaced the mechanic in the right front seat. Long before anyone was strapped in, I pulled pitch and climbed away from the *Lori Danielle*.

Through the open channel comms, Skipper said, "I'm still not tracking his sat-phone, but the RHIB is moving west at fifty knots."

"Keep pinging the phone," I ordered. "And send us the track on the RHIB."

Disco fumbled his way from the cabin and into the cockpit and climbed onto the left seat. "What's going on?"

"We're going after Gator," I said. "I sent him in to question Cecilia, Kenneth LePine's niece or great-niece, whatever. Celeste had him wired for sound, and things got dicey. Shots were fired, but none of them was from Gator's Glock. We've lost his sat-phone track, but we've got a fix on the RHIB."

"He was in the RHIB?" Disco asked.

"Yeah. It's a long story. Program the coordinates for his last-known position into the GPS."

He went to work, and seconds later, I was following the magenta line directly toward the last position Skipper had received the sat-phone's signal.

An enormous hand landed on my shoulder. "What's the plan, boss?"

"We're going to find Gator and grab Cecilia. Lock and load. There's already been gunfire."

One of the most remarkable traits of my team is their ability to take action without asking a thousand questions. Nobody cared why. They only cared that one of ours was in trouble, and we were going to pull him out of the fire.

The Huey's airspeed indicator showed one hundred eighteen knots, and I begged her twin turbines and main rotor for just one more knot—anything to get me to Gator an instant faster. I double-checked our position against the coordinates of his last ping of the sat-phone. The tiny island where Gator and Cecilia's picnic had taken place lay under our nose less than a mile away.

"Take the controls, and put us at a close hover right over that strip of land."

Disco placed his hands on the collective and cyclic. "I have the controls."

I removed my seat belt and twisted the latch on the door. As Disco brought the chopper to a hover a few inches from the sandy shore, I stepped from the skid and onto the beach. The boots belonging to Mongo, Kodiak, and Shawn hit the ground only seconds behind mine, and we fanned out in search of any evidence of what might have happened to our brother.

Disco pulled pitch and took the Huey several thousand feet above our heads. I didn't have to look up to know he was scanning the horizon for the wake left behind by our RHIB. Based on Skipper's report, whoever was at the helm knew exactly how to handle a boat.

"I've got a line!" Kodiak yelled, and I hustled to his side.

He held a black line identical in diameter and color to the one we used on every boat we owned. One end was still tied to the trunk of a tree, and the other end bore the telltale signs of having been sliced cleanly with an incredibly sharp knife.

The scar on the sand at the water's edge looked exactly like the impression our RHIB would've left, and I said, "They were here."

I glanced up, following the Huey's unmistakable *whop-whop*, to find Disco diving for the island. Almost before he came to a hover, we reboarded, and he climbed the heavy machine back into the air.

"Did you see them?" I asked.

"I think so."

He spun the chopper and lowered the nose, accelerating to the west, and I brought up the tracking app on my phone. I studied the screen and looked up to compare it to the maze of waterways in front of us. "Do you see them?"

"Not yet," he said, "but I believe they're just around that big bend to the south."

Disco made the chopper dance as if she were a puppet in his hands, and I stared through the windscreen.

We made the turn to the south, and the faint wake trail appeared in the dark water. Around another bend, the stern of our RHIB came into view in front of the billowing water spraying from the tubes with every turn.

"There they are!" I yelled.

Disco lowered the nose even more and descended toward the swamp as he pushed the Huey well beyond her designed limits. We closed the distance between us and our boat in seconds, and when we were within a hundred feet, I couldn't believe what I saw.

Gator wasn't aboard the racing craft, but neither was Cecilia. The RHIB was empty and running at full throttle across the black surface of the winding bayou, and I couldn't make my mind understand how that was possible.

I spun in my seat and called for Shawn. "Get up here!"

The SEAL leaned between the cockpit seats. "Yeah?"

I pointed through the windshield. "See that RHIB?"

He nodded, and I said, "That's ours, but nobody's aboard."

He furrowed his brow. "How?"

"I don't know, but it doesn't matter. We have to stop it without sinking it."

He glanced over his shoulder at our sniper. "Singer can kill the engines."

I shook my head. "Too much chance of sending a round through the hull, and we're going to need that boat. If I put you five feet above that RHIB and match its speed, can you board her?"

"Sure. Piece of cake. What do you want me to do when I get aboard?"

I said, "I want you to get that thing stopped and rigged for sling loading."

He grinned through one corner of his mouth. "Oh, this sounds like a lot of fun. You're completely insane, and I love it. Get me down there, and I'll have that thing ready to fly in less than sixty seconds."

Chapter 30
Splash and Grab

I situated myself squarely in my seat. "My airplane."

Disco didn't release the controls. "How many times have you dropped SEALs on moving boats?"

"Counting this one," I said, "it'll be one."

He shook his head. "My airplane. Which side is he going out?"

I glanced over my shoulder. "He's set up in the portside door."

Disco lowered the nose. Our airspeed increased in the dive, and the distance between us and our self-driving RHIB melted away. Our chief pilot slid open the window on his door and stuck his head through the opening as he raised the nose to match the speed of the RHIB.

With one eye on Shawn and one on our pilot, I waited to see the delicate dance the two were about to perform. Disco's attention was focused on the RHIB, so I kept my head on a swivel, scanning ahead, astern, and through the open portside hatch.

A grove of trees materialized in front of us, and I said, "Big sweeper to the left, coming up in three...two...one."

Disco turned his head ever so slightly and banked the Huey to match the RHIB's long, skidding turn through the bend.

I called out, "Long stretch. Now's the time."

He gave no reply other than descending to three feet above the racing boat. A second later, Disco said, "Send him!"

I flashed the signal, and Shawn shoved off from the deck and disappeared past the skid. I wasn't expecting the maneuver that followed Shawn's exit, but Disco aggressively raised the collective and climbed away from the bayou. My stomach sank in my gut as the G-forces pulled on my body in the high-speed climb. The next maneuver was even more aggressive. Disco crushed the left pedal and yanked the chopper around with the nose pointing directly at the RHIB.

I gathered my wits and focused on our boat slowing to a halt in the bayou below. "He did it."

Disco said, "You didn't have any doubt, did you? He's a SEAL."

Kodiak's voice rang through my helmet. "He's rigged for sling loading. I've got your ground calls."

"Send it," Disco said.

Kodiak sounded as if he'd done it a thousand times. "Down thirty... Ahead ten."

Disco maneuvered the chopper with the precision of a surgeon.

"Ahead five... Down three... Hold... Hold... Secure, haul away."

"Haul away," Disco repeated, and we slowly climbed from ten feet above the bayou to five hundred with our SEAL cradled comfortably in our flying RHIB.

"Where now, boss?" Disco asked.

"The other way."

He said, "Do you want to fly?"

Flying with three thousand extra pounds hanging twenty feet beneath the Huey was a little more precarious than flying slick, but that was no time for practice. Finding Gator and Cecilia was far more important than me learning a new skill.

I said, "Negative. It's all you."

We accelerated slowly and reached ninety knots.

Disco said, "Everything looks the same out here."

I pointed through the windshield. "Keep running southeast. That's the only direction that makes sense."

Everything inside me wanted to lean out the door and check on Shawn and his magic flying carpet, but scanning the water ahead was priority number one. Disco was right. The bayou seemed to be an end-less landscape of repeating sites.

I called the CIC. "We recovered the RHIB, but there's no sign of Gator or Cecilia. If you've got any ideas, we're all ears."

Skipper said, "I'm tasking a satellite, but it's taking longer than it should. I got an intermittent hit on Gator's sat-phone, but it was just a flash."

"Give me the coordinates."

She rattled off the numbers, and I programmed the GPS. "We're headed there now. If you get that satellite up and running, designate every target within five miles of their last-known position. We'll run them down one by one if we have to."

"Roger," she said. "The satellite is coming online now. Is Mongo with you?"

"Affirmative. He's in the back."

Skipper said, "Sierra Six, CIC."

"Go for Six," Mongo answered.

"There's a drone in a Pelican case on the rear bulkhead. Get it run-ning, and I can fly it from here. That'll add one more layer to our search."

"On it," Mongo said.

Even as powerful as the Huey was, we could feel the weight shift when our giant moved to the back of the cabin to retrieve the drone. He had the device's propellers spinning in seconds.

He said, "CIC, Sierra Six. Drone is operational."

Skipper said, "Sat link is complete. Launch it."

I looked over my shoulder to see Mongo throw the carbon fiber fly-ing machine out the door.

An instant later, Skipper said, "Got it. We're flying. I'll have targets for you shortly."

With three surveillance platforms operational, we had hundreds of square miles covered. All that remained was to locate, identify, and pursue likely targets.

Disco beat me to the punch. "Tallyho! One o'clock low and running south."

I stared along the imaginary line of his extended finger and spotted a roiling wake behind a boat. "Got 'em." I fumbled through the helmet bag beside my seat and pulled out my binoculars. Tracking a moving target from a moving platform isn't easy through glass tubes, but I managed to center the boat in my optics and bring it into focus. "I've got two on deck. Keep closing. It could be them."

Disco continued working his way ever closer to the boat. It couldn't outrun us, but we had to keep the ride as smooth as possible to keep Shawn inside the RHIB suspended beneath us.

"How about now?" Disco asked when he'd closed half the distance to the fleeing vessel.

I pressed the binoculars back to my face and refocused. "I still can't tell."

A few seconds later, the back of the driver's body and head came into clear focus. "It's not them. Break off."

We turned to the northeast and continued searching for any sign of life that wasn't an alligator. We had a different kind of Gator in mind.

Skipper said, "Contact! Ten o'clock to you and four miles. I'm locked on with the drone."

"Have you got video?" I asked.

"Working on it."

Less than a breath later, the screen of my phone lit up with the video feed from the drone.

"You should have it," Skipper said.

"Got it, but it's small on my phone. How many do you see on board?"

"I've just got one," she said, "but from the looks of the driver, it's definitely female."

"Nice work," I said. "Vector us to intercept."

She said, "Turn ten degrees right and hold that course."

Disco followed her instructions, and the boat soon came into view.

"There they are," I said, "and I know that boat. That's Kenneth's log-retrieving craft. It's strong and fast."

"What's the plan?" Disco asked.

"Stay behind her, and don't let her see you while I map the bayou in front of her."

"Roger. Holding back."

I studied the map on the GPS against the real world unfolding before us and found it to be dead-on. "Swing to the north, and maneuver in front of her, out of sight. We're going to drop the RHIB to intercept her."

Disco gave me a nod, but he didn't say a word. His skill at the controls was second to none, and his level of concentration was unlike any other pilot I'd ever known. We slipped behind a grove of tupelo trees well north of Cecilia and three miles ahead of her.

Kodiak threw himself back to the deck with his head and shoulders hanging out of the Huey. "I've got ground calls. Continue... Down thirty... Twenty... Ten... Easy... Easy... Splash. Jettison the hook."

Disco pulled the handle, releasing the rigging that had held the RHIB beneath the chopper, and the lines fell.

"Who's going?" Kodiak asked.

I released my seat belt and pulled off my helmet. "Me and you. Let's go."

As I squeezed between the seats and into the cabin, Kodiak kept giving calls. "Down ten, right five."

Disco lowered us to within feet of the RHIB, and Kodiak and I stepped from the skid and onto the starboard tube.

Shawn grabbed each of our wrists and steadied us until we were solidly on deck. He brought the twin engines to life, spun the boat in its own length, and powered to the west on an intercept course for Cecilia and Kenneth's boat.

Rounding the first bend, our target came into sight far closer than I expected. Cecilia seemed to know it was us, and she aimed her bow directly for ours. She was determined to ram us with the larger, more powerful boat, but Shawn had a different plan.

He yelled, "Get ready. We're doing a splash and grab."

I looked at Kodiak, and he shrugged.

"We don't know what that means," I yelled over the roar of the wind and engines.

Shawn never took his eyes off the oncoming craft. "It means jump on her boat as soon as I lay us alongside."

"How are you going to do that?" I asked.

"Just get ready to board. You'll see."

Cecilia kept coming, and the bow of the massive boat grew ever larger, blocking out the trees and the sky beyond. I grabbed the rail beside the center console and prepared to abandon ship. It was obvious we were an instant away from a massive collision that would likely slice our RHIB in half, but Shawn appeared unfazed.

Kodiak met my stare, and it was clear he felt just as uncomfortable as I did. I don't know what made me do it, but I looked up to see the Huey laying off to the north with Mongo hanging from the starboard door and the M134 Minigun in his hands. He was ready to cut Cecilia down if she didn't surrender.

"Don't shoot her," I yelled, hoping my bone transmission device glued to my mandible would carry the sound to my transmitter and into our giant's ear.

The collision was imminent, and Kodiak looked just as ready to jump for his life as I did, but Shawn yelled, "Hold on. Here comes the splash. Kodiak, get ready to take the wheel when we come about."

He spun the wheel hard over to the left and crushed the right throttle, steepening the turn even harder than steering alone. A massive wall of water rose, obscuring the oncoming vessel.

Shawn's next move was something right out of the movies. He yanked the RHIB back to the right and crushed both throttles. Before my brain could visualize what he was doing, we performed a figure-eight and came out of the maneuver, running only inches beside the timber boat.

The SEAL yelled, "Kodiak, take the wheel!"

Kodiak slipped between Shawn and the wheel and assumed command of the RHIB. Shawn joined me at the portside tube, and we leapt from our craft and onto the starboard gunwale of Kenneth's boat. We hauled ourselves over the combing and onto the deck behind Cecilia.

She wiped away the face full of water Shawn dumped on her during the turn, and it was suddenly time for the second half of Shawn's splash and grab.

Disoriented from the wall of water, Cecilia shook her head and caught the first glimpse of her aggressors. She reacted in an instant by spinning right and yanking both throttles full aft.

The action sent the gears of the transmission grinding and screaming against the assault. When the machinery finally surrendered, the stern of the boat rose in violent opposition to the bow that was diving for the bottom of the bayou. Cecilia braced herself for the force, but Shawn and I did not. Her brilliant tactic threw both of us from our feet and headfirst into the console. I rolled my head to the left and pinned my chin to my chest, praying the collision of cranium against console wouldn't result in unconsciousness, but even remaining conscious wouldn't provide me with any defense against the pistol Cecilia raised in her left hand.

Chapter 31
I Didn't Know

My collision with the console felt like I'd been hit by a train, but my world didn't turn black. Everything in front of me faded out of focus and slowly back into crystal-clear reality. At the center of my temporary new reality was the 9mm muzzle of Cecilia's pistol trained on my face.

I blinked away the pain and raised both hands between her and me. "Take it easy."

Shawn's words dripped from his mouth with an ominous ring. "To hell with easy. Go ahead and flinch. I'll drop you where you stand."

My partner's diversion gave me the fraction of a second I needed. Cecilia spun to redirect her muzzle toward the SEAL, and I ripped my Glock from its holster and centered it on her chest. "You can't win, Cecilia. Put it down."

She spun back to me, panic in her eyes. "No! You put it down!"

"Listen to me. If you shoot me, you'll be dead before the bullet hits me. You can still walk away from this. Just put down your pistol."

Her breathing quickened, and her eyes darted back and forth between Shawn and me. Terror filled her face, but she made no move to surrender. That concerned me. A terrorized, gun-wielding killer is exactly the opposite of predictable, and I needed something to make sense.

She sidestepped her way down the starboard gunwale with her pistol still raised in an effort to improve her angle on both of us, but Shawn and I weren't going to let that happen. He had the positional advantage, so I provided the distraction that would make his next move possible. With my head clear and my vision strong, I hopped to my feet, landing in a crouch. The commotion drew Cecilia's eyes and muzzle, opening Shawn's window, and he took full advantage of her mistake. The SEAL planted a palm on the deck and swept her feet with an outstretched leg. As she battled to catch herself, Shawn attacked, shoving his shoulder beneath her left arm and driving her pistol hand high into the air above her head.

When a man the size and shape of our SEAL establishes a bear hug, the recipient is powerless to break free. Hurting Cecilia wasn't our intention, but controlling her was absolutely essential, and we were one move away from establishing that control.

It was my turn to strike. From my crouched position, I thrust forward and ripped the pistol from Cecilia's hand, rendering her practically harmless—or so I thought.

I believed the fight was over, but she clearly had other ideas. Using Shawn's forward motion, she let her body fall backward and over the gunwale. Shawn's bear hug never weakened, and they disappeared into the black water as if welded together.

A thousand thoughts blew through my mind in that instant, but the memory of chopping a Russian assassin to death with a propeller in Havana Harbor took center stage. I grabbed both throttles and shifters and shoved them into idle and neutral to stop the spinning blades of the props. I had no doubt that Shawn would win the aquatic battle, but I didn't let that confidence pull my eyes from the water. One or both would surface soon, and I would join the fight.

"CIC, Sierra One."

Skipper said, "Go ahead, One. What's happening out there?"

"Shawn's in the water with Cecilia. She pulled a pistol on us, but she's disarmed now."

"What about Gator?"

"We don't know yet, but we'll question her as soon as Shawn gets her calmed down."

"Did you say they're in the water?"

"Affirmative. She pulled Shawn overboard."

"Wait a minute," she said. "Cecilia, all one hundred pounds of her, pulled a two-hundred-fifty-pound SEAL overboard?"

"It happened pretty quickly," I said. "It'll be over soon."

"That explains why I lost his sat-phone."

"Could that be what happened to Gator's phone track?"

Before she could answer, a muffled gunshot sounded from just beside the boat, and a shockwave bubbled to the surface. I leapt to the starboard tube and stared into the roiled, murky filth. A discoloration surfaced, but it was almost impossible to tell the difference between the shades of black. I couldn't imagine what was happening beneath the surface, but everything inside me wanted to dive into the murk and join the fight. Manning the boat in that moment was the priority, but that didn't stop me from itching to get wet.

"What's happening?" Skipper asked again with significantly more force than before.

"Stand by."

She groaned but didn't ask again.

Just when I thought I might never see either of them again, Cecilia's head and shoulders popped out of the water at the stern of the RHIB. I instinctively threw out a hand to grab hers, but she didn't reach up. Instead, she bobbed on the surface like a cork with no sign of her hands or Shawn.

Still unsure how she was capable of floating upright with her head a foot above the water, I slipped two hands beneath her armpits and dragged her over the transom and onto the deck. To my utter disbelief, her hands were flex-cuffed behind her back.

She coughed and spat bayou water from her lungs as I positioned her upright against the back of the seat. "Are you all right?"

She jerked and fought against the restraints. "Untie me! Now!"

"Just calm down and hold still while we sort this out."

A rustling in the water caused me to turn, expecting to see Shawn climbing from the bayou and into the boat, but instead, I watched an alligator carcass float to the surface with the top of its head bearing a massive exit wound. The next item to surface was, thankfully, Shawn's head, which bore no exit wounds, but he wore the look of an angry, injured man.

"Are you okay?" I demanded.

"She bit me!"

I glanced between the deceased gator and Cecilia. "Which one?"

"The dead one," he said. "Now, help me aboard."

Shawn asking for help was so far outside his typical behavior that I feared he had joined me in the missing limb category. We clasped wrists, and I hauled him aboard. His left calf bore the wounds of a mouthful of alligator teeth.

"That doesn't look good," I said.

He motioned toward the water. "Take a look at the other guy. I'd say I won."

I wrapped a towel around his leg and asked, "Does it need a tourniquet?"

"No, I shot her before she could clamp down. It just needs to be cleaned and sewn up."

He turned to Cecilia, still flex-cuffed and dripping wet. "Did she bite you?"

She shook her head. "Why are you doing this to me?"

I abandoned Shawn's wounded leg. "What?"

"Why are you doing this? It's wrong."

"Why are *we* doing this?" I said. "We're not doing anything except trying to get our man back. You shot Gator. We heard you do it. If you tell me exactly where he is, this will go a lot better for you."

She squinted and shook water from her hair. "Yeah, I shot him because I figured out what you're doing. I should've seen it right from the start, but I believed you were really here to help us."

I planted a knee between her feet. "What are you talking about? You should've seen *what* from the start?"

Kodiak nestled the RHIB alongside the timber boat and wound a line around the midship cleat. "Is everything all right?"

I placed a hand on Cecilia's knee so I could look away and still know if she was on the verge of trying something foolish. "Shawn took a nasty gator bite, but he fared better than the gator. As you can see, we've got Cecilia trussed up, and we're having a little conversation. Any word from the CIC?"

Cecilia flinched, and I pinned her knee to the deck with just enough force to get her undivided attention. "Don't move, and don't make me hurt you."

"Why would you hurt me? I didn't do anything."

I held up a finger toward Kodiak, and he seemed to fully understand the necessity of my dealing with our prisoner before continuing our chat.

I said, "I'm going to make this real simple. You tell me where Gator is, and you get to live."

She trembled, and that surprised me. She was genuinely afraid of me. "I don't know where he is. Yeah, I shot him, but only because you —whoever you are—and the other guys are down here to kill Uncle Kenneth so Kenny can inherit the land and the mineral rights."

I furrowed my brow and leaned in. "What are you talking about? We're not here to kill Kenneth. We're here to find out who's trying to run him off his land with the body parts."

"Yeah, that's the story you tell, but I know it's not the truth. You're working for Kenny, and this land isn't his. It's not his. Do you hear me?"

She squirmed and struggled against the restraints, so I said, "Calm down. We've got a lot to figure out, and we're starting with Gator. Where is he?"

"I told you I don't know where he is. I just barely hit his arm when I shot him. I wasn't trying to kill him. I just needed to get him away from me when I put it all together."

I shook my head. "All of this has gotten out of hand, and we need to slow down and focus. We're going to find Gator, and you'd better pray he's alive. Otherwise, you're going to prison."

She bucked even harder. "You can't send me to prison."

I pulled my credentials pack from my pocket and flipped it open for her to see. Even though I'd never be a real Secret Service Agent, the Department of Homeland Security would still claim me if anyone called to check the validity of my creds.

I said, "You might be surprised what I can do."

"You're a fed? Oh, my God. Did I shoot a fed? Is Gator...?"

I folded and pocketed the badge and ID. "Where is my man?"

The fear she seemed to have of me appeared to deepen for a whole new reason. "I swear I didn't know. I swear. He never identified himself as a—"

"Listen to me. Tell me exactly where you were when you shot him. If anything other than that comes out of your mouth, the flex-cuffs become stainless-steel cuffs, and you'll sleep on a federal government cot every night for a very long time."

Her voice broke. "We were on a sandbar. It doesn't have a name, but I can take you there. I swear I didn't—"

"That's enough."

I glanced up. "Disco, head back to the sandbar and start an expanding radius search. We'll be there in less than ten minutes."

The chopper headed off, and I turned back to my captive. "I'm going to put you in that seat behind you, and you're going to behave. Right?"

She nodded, and I helped her to her feet. We shuffled around the seat, and I deposited her on the cushion.

"I've got one more question. How did you get my RHIB to run the bayou autonomously?"

"It's a function of that kind of autopilot coupled with the radar. This boat has it, too. You just program it to keep itself centered between the banks and open the throttle. It'll run until it hits something or runs out of gas."

I huffed. "I knew that."

Kodiak turned from RHIB pilot to combat medic and dressed Shawn's wound after a liberal dousing of iodine and a tetanus shot.

I stepped behind the console and familiarized myself with the controls. My hand landed on the throttles at the same instant Skipper's voice filled my ear.

"Uh, Sierra One, I've got a guy on the phone who says he needs to talk to you. He says his name is Cory Campbell."

I tried to match the name to my mental Rolodex, but it wasn't coming to me. "I don't know anybody by that name. What does he want?"

"He says you took him to the hospital in New Orleans."

"Oh! I do know him. Patch him through."

After a collection of clicks, Cory said, "Is this Chase?"

"It is. What's going on, Cory?"

"I'm sorry to be calling you like this, but, well... Truth is, I didn't know who else to call."

"What is it?" I asked. "I'm kind of busy at the moment."

"Yeah, I figured you were, but me and Billy... You remember my brother Billy, right?"

"Yes, I remember. Now, what is it?"

"Well, me and him found this old Cajun guy talking out of his head and saying all kinds of stuff about his house burning down and a whole bunch of other stuff that didn't make no sense."

I cut him off. "Where is he now?"

"Well, he's with us in the truck."

"Is he hurt?"

Cory said, "He ain't exactly in good shape. Somebody done a real number on him, and he kept telling me to call you. Look, I don't want to get wrapped up in—"

"How far are you from an emergency room?"

"I don't know. We're maybe an hour from Houma."

I was suddenly and violently being tugged in three directions. Finding Gator wasn't optional, and neither was getting Kenneth LePine to a hospital. The third tether tugging at me was a terrified girl planted on a seat six feet behind me who may have burned down her uncle's house and tried to kill him. Two of the three tugging lines had to be severed, and I was the only one holding a knife.

Chapter 32
Another Club

Clark Johnson once told me that leadership was like being beaten with a hundred clubs and trying to decide which of those clubs felt the best. His wisdom was far from conventional but rarely wrong, so I chose a club.

My first words were to Cory. "How far are you from the volunteer fire department?"

He sounded more confused than curious. "There ain't nobody at a volunteer fire department."

"Just answer my question."

He said, "Maybe five minutes if we hurry."

"In that case, hurry. There will be a black helicopter landing beside the station when you get there. Put the Cajun on the chopper."

"You've got a helicopter, too?"

"Goodbye, Cory."

Another glance upward into an empty sky left me calculating flight times, intersecting angles from every direction, and how many civilians we could stack aboard the *Lori Danielle*.

"Disco, I need you to put the team on the ground where Cecilia shot Gator and get to the volunteer fire station by Kenneth's former house, double-quick."

His one-word reply reminded me why my team was so efficient. Disco had a thousand questions, but dumping them on me in that moment would accomplish nothing more than adding clubs to my endless flagellation.

"Two guys are going to meet you at the station with Kenneth LePine. He's injured, but I don't know how badly. Triage him and make the call. Either deliver him to the ER in Houma, New Orleans, or back to the ship."

"Roger."

I shot a glance back at my newest prisoner, and the fear that had been in her eyes morphed into pain. "Gator lied to me."

As much as I wanted to dive headfirst into that mud puddle, it would have to wait. Finding Cecilia's liar had to come first.

The RHIB was slightly faster than the timber boat, so Kodiak was already on the beach when I ran Kenneth's boat aground in the mucky sand. The sound of the Huey's rotor blades in the distance told me Mongo and Singer were already on the ground and scouring the area for Gator.

My first call was to our sniper. "Sierra Six, Sierra One. Say position."

His voice came interwoven with gasping breaths. "I'm about a click south...of the beach...where we...last heard from Gator."

"Are you okay?" I asked.

"I'm waist-deep in...water that feels like goo... So, no...I'm not exactly okay."

I had little doubt that he'd claw his way out of the muck. "Any sign of Gator?"

He caught his breath. "I'm moving toward a plume of smoke to the south and dodging alligators."

"I'm on my way in the RHIB." I turned to our wounded SEAL. "Can you hang on for another half hour?" He nodded, so I said, "Stay here with the girl and figure this out. Just don't kill her."

If possible, Shawn eclipsed Disco's efficiency by merely nodding once again and press-checking his Glock.

I leapt from the timber boat and onto the deck of the RHIB. "Make your way south and look for smoke."

Kodiak spun the wheel hard over and powered away from the beach. Picking our way to the south was far easier said than done. The low-hanging trees, downed logs, and shallow water kept us moving at a snail's pace, and my impatience doubled with every new obstacle in our way.

"There's the smoke," Kodiak said with an outstretched finger.

"Get us there!"

He stuck the bow in the sand a hundred yards from the smoke, and we bounded over the tubes into ankle-deep muck as we trudged toward the tree line.

I cupped my hands around my mouth and yelled, "Gator!"

A trio of pistol shots sounded from somewhere near the smoke.

Singer rounded the bend to our left in a sprint, and Kodiak and I joined him.

To my indescribable relief, Gator came into sight, but my relief was short-lived. He was gasping as if he'd run a marathon, so I hit the sand beside him and immediately began my assessment. His pulse was racing, his face was bright red, and a bloody pressure bandage was wound around his left bicep. As bad as all of those signs were, most concerning was the tourniquet tied just below his knee.

"Talk to me," I said. "Where are you shot?"

He gasped. "Left arm. Not bad. Through and through."

As he tried to calm his breathing, he pointed toward his lower leg. "Snakebite. I don't know what kind, but I killed it. It's by the fire."

Singer grunted. "It's a water moccasin."

"Is it deadly?" Gator groaned.

"It can be," the sniper said. "But the tourniquet isn't going to help. Get that thing off."

Gator said, "I didn't know what to do. I thought it would keep the venom from getting to my heart."

Singer inspected the wound where the snake's fangs had pierced Gator's skin. "It's not good, but it probably won't kill you. You're in shock and pretty scared." He handed Gator a bottle of water from his cargo pants pocket. "Drink this, and try to stay calm. We'll get you out of here."

He took the bottle and downed half of it in one drink. "Did you find Cecilia?"

I said, "Shawn's babysitting her back on the boat."

"She's dangerous," he said.

I tried not to chuckle. "We figured that out."

Kodiak took a knee beside me. "Disco's ten minutes out."

The clubs resumed pounding me as I tried to create a reasonable scenario in which we could get everyone and the RHIB back to the ship as quickly as possible. Sorting out the quagmire in front of me wasn't something that could happen in the bowels of the bayou.

Mongo hefted Gator across his shoulder in a fireman's carry and headed for the beach.

Singer hooked a finger inside my elbow when I stood to follow Mongo. "Hang on a minute. Gator's in bad shape. He needs fluids and antivenin, now. He's obviously having a reaction beyond the effects of the venom."

That's exactly what I need... Another club.

"Sierra One, CIC."

I said, "Go for One."

Skipper said, "We've got a situation. Mrs. Barbour is missing."

"Missing? How? She's on a ship at anchor."

"We don't know yet, but the ship's on lockdown, and the crew is at general quarters."

I palmed my forehead. "There's nothing I can do from here, so handle it. Also, I need to know if Dr. Shadrack has antivenin for a water moccasin bite. We found Gator, and he's been bitten."

"Are you saying *venin* or *venom*?"

"Either is fine. Just find out if he has it."

She said, "Wait one." A few seconds later, she came back. "He's got it, and you were right. It's antivenin."

I said, "Tell him to prep for a severe reaction to the venom, a gunshot wound, and an alligator bite."

"My God, Chase! How is he still alive?"

"Gator has only two of the three conditions. The alligator got Shawn, but Shawn won."

The sound of the descending Huey caught my attention. "Gotta go. I'll see you on deck."

When I cleared the tree line, Disco was settling into a hover a few yards off the beach, and Mongo was wading through the shallow water. When the big man laid him on the deck of the chopper, Gator fell limply through the door, and my plan to sling load the RHIB vanished.

I pointed at Mongo and then into the chopper, and our giant stepped onto the starboard skid and propelled himself through the door as Disco pulled pitch and climbed away at full power.

As if I needed one more straw on my camel's back, my sat-phone rang.

"Go for Chase."

"Chase, it's Fred. I'm at some godforsaken airport in a place called Houma, Louisiana. Can you send somebody to pick me up?"

Until that moment, I had forgotten I'd summoned Dr. Fred Kennedy—the psychiatrist from The Ranch where I'd learned the craft of covert operation—to spend some time with Skipper to get her head straight.

"Your timing couldn't be worse, Doc. I've got snakebites, gunshot wounds, alligator attacks, a missing woman on my ship, an arsonist, a former Agency black operator in my brig, and I'm pretty sure my prosthetic just turned into a ten-pound block of melted electronics."

Fred said, "Oh, that must make this a Tuesday. I'll be here when you can send someone to get me. And one more thing...I think somebody just stole your Caravan after shooting out the windows."

"That's the only good news I've heard today. The thief is actually a mechanic ferrying it to Wichita for repairs. I'll send the chopper for you as soon as I can."

In Fred's typical, unpredictable style, he hung up without another word.

Kodiak, Singer, and I mounted the RHIB and headed back for the beach, where Shawn was entertaining Cecilia. Kodiak cut the engine as we drifted alongside the timber boat.

"How much fuel do you have in that thing?" I asked.

Shawn said, "The gauge says it's almost full."

I checked our prisoner. "Is the gauge reliable, and how far will that take us?"

She said, "The gauge is good. I filled it up this morning. It'll run for twelve hours on full tanks."

I replaced Kodiak at the helm of the RHIB. "Good. Follow me. We're running home to Mother."

Shawn said, "Hey, wait a minute. Did you find Gator?"

"We did. Disco's flying his body back to the ship, and your new best friend over there is going to spend the rest of her life in Angola Prison. Let's go."

I throttled up and couldn't hear what Shawn said to Cecilia, but nothing about the exchange looked pleasant.

We wound our way through the bayous as they switchbacked through the landscape until the muddy waters turned to emerald green in the Gulf of Mexico. I checked across my shoulder to make sure Shawn hadn't killed Cecilia yet, but she wasn't in the seat. That made me sidestep and chop the throttles. As Shawn pulled alongside, he pointed to the deck where the woman he believed had killed Gator lay on her side, still cuffed and squirming.

The run across the Gulf made Shawn's decision to put Cecilia on the deck make sense. The water was choppy enough to send the RHIB airborne more than once until we fell under the lee of our ship. It took three minutes for the deck crew to hoist both boats onto the LD, and those minutes felt like eons as we rose from the surface and over the rail.

My boots hit the deck before the crane operator let the RHIB settle into its cradle, and Singer landed right beside me.

I took the sniper's elbow in my hand. "Let Shawn know that Gator isn't dead. I just wanted Cecilia to believe he was."

Singer grabbed my shirt and locked eyes with me. "How do you know he's not dead?"

Chapter 33
Count the Boats

Two well-armed shooters from the ship's security team met me at the hatch leading from the weather deck to the interior.

One man said, "Where are you headed, sir?"

I reached for the hatch. "Step aside."

He laid a hand on my arm. "We're not trying to stop you, Mr. Fulton. We just need to know where you're going so we can tell the interior patrol."

"Wait a minute," I said. "Have you still not found the woman?"

"No, sir, but we will. The ship is only so big."

"Are you certain she's still on board?"

The two men glanced at each other and back at me. "Where would she go?"

I spun to my team behind me. "Put Cecilia in the brig beside Barbour. I suspect they have a lot to discuss, and I'd love to do a little eavesdropping. Then, clear the ship. They still haven't found the woman."

The first guard said, "We don't really need help. We've got it under control. We'll find her."

I gave him the most sarcastic smile I could produce. "How long has it been since you've been in a real gunfight?"

The guard checked his partner again, and I cut him off before he could come up with something to say. "*We'll* find her. It's kind of what we do."

The interior of the ship was silent except for the hum of machinery and my own boots striking the deck. The corridors and ladders were vacant and eerie.

Sick bay was a different story. Dr. Shadrack stood over Gator with an iPad in one hand and a syringe in the other.

I stepped beside him. "So?"

He said, "Do you want the doctor version or the knuckle-dragger version?"

"Let's go with knuckle-dragger if you don't mind."

He still didn't look up from his iPad, but he continued talking. "Snake venom is a complex mixture of proteins, amino acids, lipids, carbohydrates, metal ions, and a bunch of other trace material."

"This is the knuckle-dragger version?" I asked.

He ignored me and kept talking. "Antivenin is a mixture of proteins and hyperimmune globulins that comes from the serum of animals that have been immunized with snake venom. Gator is allergic to at least one of those proteins in the venom, so I'm treating him for anaphylactic shock. Do you know what that means?"

I stared down at my brother-in-arms, who had a pair of hoses protruding from his mouth and nose, and I listened to the ventilator breathing for him. "That means his body's immune system is trying to kill him, right?"

"Essentially, that's what's happening. I'm providing him a cocktail of drugs to suppress his immune system just enough to keep him alive while we try to help him fight off the venom."

"But you're giving him the antivenin, right?"

For the first time, Dr. Shadrack looked at me. "The antivenin carries many of the same proteins as the venom, so until I can isolate which protein he's allergic to, I could kill him if I start introducing antivenin. He would've been dead in a matter of minutes if you hadn't made the call to bring him to me instead of the ER."

"Minutes?"

He nodded. "Yes, minutes. Most ER doctors would've pumped

him full of antivenin within a few minutes of arriving, and that would've likely cost him his life. I've seen this only once before. It's extremely rare, but you absolutely saved his life when you sent him to me."

I parked myself on a stainless-steel rolling stool and let the events of the day wash over me. I made a billion decisions, and the one I battled with most was the one I got right. I guess that made one fewer club trying to pound me into the ground.

"Is he going to live?"

The doctor laid a hand on my shoulder as he walked from the room. "We'll see, but your Cajun friend is going to be fine after a few weeks."

"That's good news," I said, "but I'm afraid that's not the end of the casualty list. An alligator bit Shawn, but she spit him back out when he shot her in the head. He'll be down soon."

He shook his head. "Of course we've got an alligator bite. Why wouldn't we?"

Everything inside me wanted to stand beside Gator until he could walk from the room under his own power, but the need to find the rogue woman roaming my ship pulled me from the stool and propelled me into the CIC.

Skipper was monitoring the process and tracking sections of the ship that had been cleared. As my team swept each compartment, a guard from the ship's security contingent stood watch over the section, ensuring the woman wasn't moving behind my team.

"Brief me," I said.

She said, "Ship security swept the vessel with no luck, and our team has covered seventy percent without a hit."

"She's gone, isn't she?"

Skipper shrugged. "We'll know soon. Is Gator okay?"

"No, he's not, but the doctor's doing all he can."

She spun in her chair. "All he can? Seriously? That's what they say when the patient dies. 'We did all we could.'"

"That's not what's happening down there. He's in very good hands. Right now, let's focus on finding the woman."

She chewed her lip. "He's got to be okay, Chase. I can't lose another one."

I took her hands in mine. "Listen to me. Doctor Shadrack will take better care of Gator than anyone else on Earth. We're not losing another one. But I need you to focus. We'll have time to melt down when all of this is over. We're in it together, and we're going to come out of it together."

She spun back to her computer and marked another corridor and compartment as clear.

I lifted the radio and called Gun Bunny.

She answered quickly. "Go ahead, Chase."

"I need you to pick up Dr. Fred Kennedy at the Houma Airport."

"When?"

"As soon as possible."

"I'm on my way. Will you notify the captain?"

"Consider it done," I said.

Skipper said, "That's the shrink, right?"

"That's him."

She huffed. "I don't have time for therapy right now. We still have a lot of work to do." She motioned toward a panel in the console with a telephone handset plugged into it. "That reminds me. They put Cecilia beside Barbour...or McDuffy...whatever his name is. I've been recording every sound made in the brig since they locked her up. It should make for some interesting listening."

"That's brilliant. Nicely done. Can I plug in a headset instead of my grandmother's telephone receiver?"

She giggled. "Sure. Go for it. I'll let you know when the ship is clear."

I made the call to the bridge to get the captain's permission to launch the helo, and then I dived into the brig audio.

The first several minutes were Cecilia and McDuffy screaming at each other over whose fault it was that they were locked up on a ship. When the screaming match lost its vigor, the conversation turned to details not even Shawn could've extracted from our guests.

Cecilia said, "I think I killed a federal agent."

"You did *what*?"

"Yeah, I think these guys are feds. Chase has Secret Service credentials."

I could almost hear McDuffy's gears grinding. "No way. These guys can't be feds. They're cowboys. They didn't have a warrant when they hit my ranch."

"That's not a ranch, you pompous ass. It's an oversized subdivision lot."

He seemed to ignore the jab. "These guys are better than feds, but they don't seem to have any restraint. They hit hard and keep running like a tier-one team. Which one did you kill?"

"They call him Gator. I thought I had him sucked in, but you're right. They're good. He played me like a fiddle."

"What about the old man?" McDuffy asked.

She said, "I thought I had that handled, too. Before I torched his place, I left him out at Crooked Leg Cut. If there's anything left of him, it came out of the belly of a gator."

"So, the land and mineral rights will fall to you?"

"That was the plan, but I didn't count on whoever these guys are. Now it looks like we're both going to prison."

McDuffy howled. "Maybe *you're* going to prison. You're the one who killed two men and burned down one of their houses. I'm an in-nocent victim. I plan to sue everybody in sight when I get out of this."

She laughed. "I'm sure you will, but something tells me your law-suits won't go very far when they discover the audio recordings in my safe deposit box of you and me planning all of this."

"You little bitch. Virginia will find you, and when she does, you'll beg for a prison cell."

Cecilia continued laughing. "Your little make-believe wife is in this thing just as deep as you and I are. All three of us are going down,"

McDuffy said, "There's one big difference. You and I are still here, but she's gone."

I caught a glimpse of Skipper turning toward me, so I pulled off the headset to hear her echo McDuffy's claim. "She's gone, Chase. She's not on the ship."

I pointed toward the headset. "That's gold. I just heard the rest of the story, but we need to do a little digging into our missing woman. It would appear her name might be Virginia Barbour, but there's a pretty good chance that's an alias."

I made a call to the bridge. "We can secure from general quarters, Captain. The woman is gone."

"Gone? Where could she go? She's got to be on this ship somewhere."

I said, "My team and yours both cleared the ship, and she's not here."

"We need to count the boats."

I asked, "What?"

"The lifeboats... Somebody needs to count them."

We secured from general quarters and opened the ship. The boat count came back one short, and Captain Sprayberry exploded. "Nobody will *ever* go over the rail of my boat again without a camera watching it happen. I don't care how much it costs! Somebody better have a man-overboard alarm system up and running by the time the sun comes up tomorrow."

His tantrum, no matter how loud, couldn't make that happen in eighteen hours, but I had no doubt it would happen within hours of completing our mission.

The team convened in the CIC. Clark joined us via video call, and I briefed the transcripts of the conversation in our brig.

When I finished, I turned to the camera that would pipe my face directly onto my handler's screen. "Like the old saying goes, what me do now, Gurdy?"

He said, "I told you to stop calling me Gurdy, and *you* don't do anything now. I'll take it from here."

"What do you mean you'll take it from here? What are you going to do?"

"I'm gonna have a black helicopter land on your helipad and relieve you of your responsibility for the guests. What happens next is none of your concern."

"What about the woman McDuffy called Virginia?"

"You don't need to worry about her, either. Based on the fingerprints Skipper tried to run with no success, Ms. Virginia already has a relationship with the U.S. Marshals Service."

Skipper gasped. "She was in WITSEC?"

"Not that kind of relationship," Clark said. "It's more of a working relationship, you might say."

* * *

We spent another thirty-six hours hovering off the coast of Southern Louisiana until Kenneth LePine was healthy enough to fly back ashore. When we touched down five hundred yards away from where his house had been prior to the fire, there were two bulldozers leveling the tiny spit of land in preparation for the construction of the new house to come. Perched on the seat of the larger of the two dozers was my friend and Kenneth's son, Cajun Kenny LePine, with a giant cigar hanging from the corner of his mouth.

I shut down the Huey, and the rotors spun to a stop over our heads. Apparently, the few residents of the sparsely populated community had grown accustomed to hearing and seeing our chopper come and go because no one so much as looked up when we showed up.

"Do dat der be my boy, him?"

Somewhere along the way, a magical switch had flipped inside my head, and I could all of a sudden understand Kenneth. That both terrified and delighted me.

"Yes, sir. That's him. You know, I think you'd be proud of the man he is. I've never known a more sincerely kind, generous, and hardworking man...unless dat man be him's daddy, you."

The elder LePine rolled his eyes. "Don't do dat no more, Chase. You sounds like a fool, you."

"Come on, old man. Let's go have a cigar with your boy. I've got a feeling you two have a few decades of catching up to do."

"Dat boy don't wanna see me, no. Hims gots all dems peoples working under him and got dat fancy life off in da city. He done lef da bayou and never looked backs."

"Oh, he looks back, Kenneth. Trust me on that."

We climbed from the cockpit, and Kenny shut down his dozer.

Kenneth LePine stopped in his tracks as if he'd been frozen by some unseen force, and I stopped with him.

"Dem arms and dem legs out der in da bayou... Dat was da rougarou, wasn't him?"

The battle raged inside my head and heart as I struggled with the answer I'd give the old Cajun. Dr. Shadrack had posited a scientifically sound explanation of why the gators wouldn't eat the decaying bodies. He discovered traces of a chemical compound in the bone samples that would likely deter any animal from feasting on the flesh.

I came up with a simple way to explain the science to Kenneth. "Yes, sir. It was the rougarou."

Epilogue

Everybody needs a place to go where they can relax, be exactly who and what they are, and rest assured that no one will ridicule them, regardless of what craziness comes out of their mouth. For me, that place has long been my gazebo on the back lawn at Bonaventure, overlooking the North River. The Cuban Cohiba hooked beneath my right index finger dispensed a thin stream of beautifully aromatic white smoke while the seven cubes of ice slowly melted in the rich amber bourbon inside the tumbler resting on the arm of my Adirondack. For the moment, all was right with the world, and I knew there was nothing I'd enjoy more than that moment of luxurious silence...but I was wrong. One by one, the people who meant the most to me filtered into my peaceful realm and reminded me that being alone isn't the natural state of man.

Stone W. Hunter, a man I loved beyond words, stepped gently into the gazebo and settled into his preferred chair beside the war-torn cannon that was the centerpiece of the setting. "Good evening, Chase."

I raised my glass. "Evening. How are things?"

Ignoring the horrific wound that had been Hunter's shoulder and upper arm was impossible. The sniper's bullet should've killed him, but there was absolutely no question that the hand of God kept Hunter alive while the teams of surgeons did their best to rebuild the warrior's body. In return for the miracle, Hunter devoted himself to the Almighty and became a student of theology at one of the finest protestant seminaries in the country.

He found a comfortable position in his chair. "Things are good. I didn't like being left behind for the mission."

"I get it," I said, "but your orders are coming from a higher command these days."

He nodded. "Speaking of orders, I graduate in December and believe I'm supposed to join a mission in South America. They're building schools, providing medical care, and adding souls to the Kingdom."

"South America, huh? I guess you better bone up on your Spanish."

He laughed. "Spanish isn't the language these people speak. In fact, I don't think there's an English word for the language they speak."

I motioned toward the house. "The armory is open if you want to build a few kits to take with you."

He glanced skyward. "Thanks, but I'm carrying a different shield these days. I'll leave the bullets and bombs to you."

I admired and envied his faith while the memory of my parents and sister being slain in a Central American jungle two decades before thundered through my soul.

To my surprise, Skipper hobbled her way across the lawn and into the gazebo.

I stood. "What happened to you? Did you fall off a cliff?"

She gently nestled into a seat beside Hunter. "Anya happened to me. I think I've changed my mind about becoming an operator. Maybe I'll just stick to what I'm best at. You put her up to it, didn't you?"

I grimaced. "No, but I didn't stop her. This side of the wall is not where you belong. You're too important to our operation and far too smart to spend your life dodging bullets and spears. None of us can do what you do, but we could teach a monkey to pull a trigger and throw a punch." I motioned toward Hunter. "Case in point."

He pounded his chest like an old silverback and did his best gorilla impression.

Skipper shook her head. "Cute, boys. I get it."

Singer, our Southern Baptist sniper and the moral compass of the team, was next to plant himself in the gazebo. "Are we doing monkey impersonations now?"

"Just making a point," I said. "Anya helped Skipper decide she prefers life in front of a computer monitor over a life spent dragging her knuckles."

He said, "Lessons like that sting a little."

Skipper dabbed at her bruised cheek. "They sure do."

I gave her an opportunity to discuss another collection of lessons she may have been learning. "How's it going with Dr. Fred?"

She rolled her eyes. "I sent him packing after our third so-called session. I don't need his psychobabble garbage. I'm a big girl, and it's time for me to pull up my bloomers and live the life Tony would've wanted me to live."

I gave her a smile. "Bloomers?"

She returned the smile. "I know how sensitive you boys are, so I try to keep it classy."

Kodiak, the one of us who looked most like he belonged in the wild, with his unruly beard and equally uncontrollable mop, joined us and ran his hand across the barrel of the cannon. "Ah, the stories she could tell."

I raised my glass again. "We've got a few of our own."

"Indeed, we do, my friend. Indeed, we do. The difference is that nobody would believe 'em if we told 'em."

Our resident big-brained giant ambled aboard and plopped himself into his custom-built, oversized chair that would make any of the rest of us look like a child if we climbed onto the seat. "It sounds like I was missing quite the party."

I said, "You are the party, big man. We were just discussing how we're going to retire and leave the whole mess to you."

"Sounds like a great idea. Maybe I'll turn the rest of the team into wedding planners. Clark could do the flowers. I'm thinking Singer could be the...well, singer. And Shawn could learn to play 'The Wedding March' on guitar."

I gave the thumbs-up. "Sounds like a solid plan to me, but what about Anya?"

"She'll be our interpreter and physical security."

I laughed. "It sounds like you've got it all figured out, but on second thought, I think I'll postpone retirement another mission or two."

Mongo shrugged. "You're only putting off the inevitable, and you're crushing my dreams, so I hope you feel good about it."

"I'll get through it," I said. "Has anybody seen Disco?"

Kodiak said, "He's doing one of those Angel Flight missions, carrying a cancer patient to the Mayo Clinic."

"That's right," I said. "He mentioned that."

The award for most unexpected entrance went to Shawn, our SEAL. He appeared like the creature from the black lagoon, slithering out of the North River. He pulled the freshwater hose from the reel and thoroughly rinsed his still-wounded leg.

I called toward the dock. "Communing with the reptiles again?"

Shawn recoiled the hose and sloshed his way to the gazebo as he produced something from his pocket. He held up the treasure, and it became instantly clear that his token was an alligator tooth. He said, "I was just showing the locals what I did to the Louisiana gator who tried to kill me. I think we've come to an understanding."

Mongo said, "There's quite a bit wrong with you. You know that, right?"

Shawn took a seat. "Anybody can be normal. It takes somebody special to be this screwed up."

I pointed toward the house. "You're welcome to grab a towel and some dry clothes."

He shook the brackish water from his hair. "I'm a SEAL. Wet and dirty is where I'm most at home."

I took a sip and asked, "Hey, Skipper. Did you leave Anya in a bloody heap somewhere?"

The analyst said, "Not hardly. She showered at the gym and said she had plans with someone special. To be honest, I thought she was talking about you."

I threw up both hands. "Whoa! Don't start rumors like that."

I wasn't proud of the tinge of jealousy I felt at the thought of Anya meeting someone special, so I changed the subject. "What's the latest on the Cecilia/McDuffy criminal suit?"

Skipper said, "Funny you should ask. I did some digging this afternoon, and they've turned on each other like feuding dragons. Apparently, they're both trying to make a deal before the other, and the DA has tacked on eleven counts of murder, mutilation of a corpse—which I didn't know was a thing—and a bunch of other really nasty-sounding stuff I can't remember. It looks like both of them are going away for a long time."

The thought of Anya jetting off to meet the object of her affection stung again, but my conscience reclaimed its rightful place when Penny came down the stairs from the back gallery. "Look! The gang's all here."

"Not the whole gang," I said. A bitter taste rose from the pit of my stomach as I thought about the trauma my protégé had endured in the Louisiana bayou. "Gator's not here."

The same sadness that I felt was mirrored in the faces of my team and family all around the gazebo. Even Shawn winced at the thought of Gator's ordeal.

Penny watched the memory wash over us, and then she laughed. "No, of course he's not here. He's in the kitchen drinking your good bourbon in what he calls the reptile-free zone."

We turned to see the youngest member of our merry band of misfits waving from the gallery like Forrest Gump. "Hey, guys! Snakes are the devil. It's in the Bible. Look it up."

Author's Note

Here we are again at one of my favorite parts of the process—my author's note. This story was chock-full of tidbits I want to talk about, but I must begin with a note of sadness and celebration.

On August 26, 2024, just as I began writing this manuscript, my dear friend, Captain Barry Sprayberry, lost his battle with cancer but won his reward of spending eternity with the God he loved and served. I ask that you remember Barry's family in your prayers, and I promise to keep his memory alive and well on the navigation bridge of the RV *Lori Danielle.*

Let's talk about the rougarou now. You may have never heard of the terrifying creature, but it would be impossible to find a true Cajun who doesn't believe in it. In Creole and Cajun legends, the gruesome creature, with the body of a human and the head of a werewolf, is said to prowl the bayous of Southern Louisiana. I encourage you to do a little research of your own, and I highly recommend the restaurant bearing the name of the bayou's greatest legend.

Now, it's time for a confession. When I wrote the character of Cecilia Lachaussee, I immediately loved her, and I thought she might captivate Gator for the remainder of the series. Until I wrote the picnic scene, I didn't realize she was the villain. As you probably know by now, I never have a plan for these stories. I just write whatever falls out of my head, and I must admit that she was the biggest surprise for me in this story. Honestly, I'm a little sad for Gator that she turned out to be on the dark side, but it would appear that Skipper may have her eye on him. So, we'll have to see where that one goes.

While we're discussing Cecilia, I'd like to share an embarrassing story from my past. During his log-diving lessons, the Cajun queen told Gator, "Don't worry, Pretty Boy. Sooner or later, you'll do something to impress me."

Here's the origin story of that wonderful phrase: Many years ago— long before I met my wonderful wife—I invited a young lady to dinner one evening, and to my surprise, she said "Yes." After planning an unforgettable date, I picked her up and drove to the local airport, where I proceeded to open the door of my ugly old airplane for her. She willingly climbed aboard and buckled up. As young men will sometimes do, I thought I might impress her with my knowledge and skill at the controls of the flying machine. She did her part and appeared to be thoroughly fascinated with every detail. We landed safely at our intended destination and had a very nice dinner. On the flight home, as we began our descent into the airport, she took the control yoke in her hands and said, "I want to try to land. I think I can do it."

I chuckled to myself and said, "You can hold the controls as I make the approach and landing, but it takes a while to learn those skills."

She protested. "No, I really think I can do it. I watched you before, and I'm feeling pretty confident. Just let me try, and you can take the controls if I do anything dangerous."

I relented and surrendered the controls to her, believing that I would quickly take them back when the complexity and workload overwhelmed her. Much to my dismay, she promptly laid one hand on the throttle and held the yoke lightly in the other. She flew the most beautiful approach and landing I'd ever seen. Once we taxied clear of the runway, she patted my leg with a delicate hand and said, "Don't worry. Sooner or later, you'll do something to impress me."

What she had failed to mention was that she was a commercial pilot who flew freight in a Cessna 208 Caravan while building flight time to become an airline pilot. I never recovered adequately to ask her out again, so somewhere there's an airline pilot—probably a captain by now—who's telling the same story from an entirely different perspective. Who knows? Maybe she'll read this story and laugh.

As always, I admit when I make things up. Even though I write fiction, most of the scenes I create are at least possible, even if they aren't plausible. Landing the Caravan in the canal beside the hospital is the exception. I doubt that it's possible, but even if some super pilot—like my dinner date—could pull it off, the authorities would make certain it never took off from that narrow body of downtown water again. Such a daring maneuver would most likely be the end of any pilot's flying days and would result in some jail time.

One of my favorite parts of this whole journey is getting to write the phrases that Clark screws up so badly. I've even begun receiving email from readers with suggestions on new ones. I'm pretty picky, but I'll probably include a few of those in coming installments in this series. My favorite of this story was, "They're like loose cannons in a china shop, freezing the balls off a brass monkey."

The loose cannons in a china shop part is self-explanatory, but the brass monkey might need a little explanation. In days of old, when cannonballs were stored on the decks of warships under sail, a brass rail was constructed to hold the stacked cannonballs and keep them from rolling around the deck. These rails became known as brass monkeys. Legend has it that on particularly cold days, the brass monkeys would contract to the point that they could no longer hold the cannonballs. Sailors were supposedly heard saying, "It's cold enough to freeze the balls off a brass monkey." So, there it is.

I have one final confession before leaving you to move on to your next read. Since I write by the seat of my pants, with no plan of any kind, details often pop up that I can't explain. That happened in this story with Virginia Barbour. I don't know why I had Chase and the team take her into custody. Once she was on board the *Lori Danielle*, I was like the dog who finally caught the UPS truck. I had no idea what to do with her. When she disappeared, I panicked a little, but good ol'

Clark pulled me out of the fire. I'm still not certain what deal she had with the U.S. Marshals, but in the end, I liked having that little mystery hanging out there in the wind. I think it added a touch of intrigue to the story, and that's always a good thing.

Once again, I must thank you for your amazing support of my work. I'm truly in love with the magnificent career you've given me, and there's no end in sight. I vow to continue to tell the best stories I can, making each a little better than the last, because that's exactly what you deserve from your personal storyteller. And your personal storyteller is exactly what I want to be.

—Cap

About the Author

Cap Daniels

Cap Daniels is a former sailing charter captain, scuba and sailing instructor, pilot, Air Force combat veteran, and civil servant of the U.S. Department of Defense. Raised far from the ocean in rural East Tennessee, his early infatuation with salt water was sparked by the fascinating, and sometimes true, sea stories told by his father, a retired Navy Chief Petty Officer. Those stories of adventure on the high seas sent Cap in search of adventure of his own, which eventually landed him on Florida's Gulf Coast where he spends as much time as possible on, in, and under the waters of the Emerald Coast.

With a headful of larger-than-life characters and their thrilling exploits, Cap pours his love of adventure and passion for the ocean onto the pages of the Chase Fulton Novels and the Avenging Angel - Seven Deadly Sins series.

Visit www.CapDaniels.com to join the mailing list to receive newsletter and release updates.

Connect with Cap Daniels:

Facebook: www.Facebook.com/WriterCapDaniels
Instagram: https://www.instagram.com/authorcapdaniels/
BookBub: https://www.bookbub.com/profile/cap-daniels

Also by Cap Daniels

The Avenging Angel – Seven Deadly Sins Series
Book One: *The Russian's Pride*
Book Two: *The Russian's Greed*
Book Three: *The Russian's Gluttony*
Book Four: *The Russian's Lust*
Book Five: *The Russian's Sloth*
Book Six: *The Russian's Envy*
Book Seven: *The Russian's Wrath* (2025)

Stand-Alone Novels
We Were Brave
Singer – Memoir of a Christian Sniper

Novellas
The Chase is On
I Am Gypsy

Made in United States
North Haven, CT
14 January 2025

64411126R00167